# OXYMORON

To Ali, my son, who continuously pecked me to complete the Project

The Story-Teller

Dr Waqar Raza

(MBBS, MD, PhD, FRCPath)

(Professor in Microbiology)

As a hospital doctor, a scientist and a university teacher, I have widely published on topics in the medical field. My recent work, however, focuses on a different theme, *consciousness*. 'Oxymoron' has been borne out of this work.

The story portrays a uniquely constructed protagonist who has gone through a drastic change in his person, but not so much in his personality. Through this character, the story identifies *self* in the person and that which *self* owns within the person, setting the self apart from the objects listed in his belongings. The story posits questions of the sorts never asked before, of ethical, psychological, social, legal and philosophical nature, arising from the exceptional circumstances the protagonist finds himself on his journey to self-actualization.

FICTION: 5

Oxymoron

By Waqar Raza

Copyright © 2022 Transnational Press London

First Published in 2022 by TRANSNATIONAL PRESS LONDON in the United Kingdom, 13 Stamford Place, Sale, M33 3BT, UK.

www.tplondon.com

Transnational Press London® and the logo and its affiliated brands are registered trademarks.

Requests for permission to reproduce material from this work should be sent to: sales@tplondon.com

ISBN: 978-1-80135-134-8 (Paperback)

ISBN: 978-1-80135-135-5 (Digital)

Cover Design: Nihal Yazgan
Cover photo by Anya Osintsova on unsplash.com

Transnational Press London Ltd. is a company registered in England and Wales No. 8771684.

# OXYMORON

Dr Waqar Raza

TRANSNATIONAL PRESS LONDON

2022

# TABLE OF CONTENTS

# A NOTE FROM THE STORYTELLER

A story can be a miscellany of thoughts and feelings, observation and realities, and imaginations and fantasies. In its surreal form, a plot can obviously be contrived freelance. Even when claiming reality, it does not have to be tightly woven, like in some famous stories about Hell.[1] Taking this as an example, from the general perception of the hell being a place of ultimate torture, such a story can be constructed with relative ease by working up from its foundation.

In the current case, it is different. This is a story whose narrative is, no doubt, still woven with imaginations, but only on its warp, for it is picked with truth on its weft. The truth is extracted from the knowledge obtained from the human medical sciences and other sources, which reigns the imagination and confers it relevance to facts.

Its protagonist is a miserable chap caught up in an impossible situation, 'impossible' being a lowkey word for his situation. He has a history of bumping into conflicts here and there, on and off. He takes on one, to come across the next, like onion scales. By this time, it was a really big one, which took his life, almost. It in fact had arisen from his own unique constitution. It may sound interesting, but it was hard for him, particularly, owing to his social preference. As the author of this story, I am not sure if I had realized beforehand that, in this character, we should find the need to-be-understood deployed so dominantly over the urge to-be-seen.

This is a story of an unrelenting debate on his personal identity, which the rest of the characters get involved, people in his workplace, courts, families, so much as if they have nothing else to do. But it really hurts him when someone really close refuses to own him. That's it! Patience ditches him, so does hope. But, as always happens in stories, instead of giving up, in search of peace, he embarks on a new journey.

He now finds himself alone but at least he is not threatened by anyone. But, soon, he would meet some characters larger than his own stature, all there to test his nerves, but somehow, he manages his way through them – happily, I would like to say. Except, near the very end of his journey, on one side, he gets the blow of his life, teaching him a lesson - some meanings, too. On the other side, he gets the gift of an epiphanic moment filling him with meanings. He does not find his identity, nor does he find peace, instead he finds meanings. Only then he comes to know that it wasn't about conflicts, or peace, from the

---

[1] Book Riot 2016. *7 of Fiction's most intriguing takes on Hell*, by Emily Wenstrom (2016).

start, it was about the meanings extracted from them. This poor guy, Oxymoron his name, I leave him in your hands.

# A NOTE FROM THE PROTAGONIST

They call me Oxymoron, which of course isn't my actual name. What does it matter what my actual name is? People hardly remember it anyway. Many don't even bother thinking about 'Oxymoron'. But for me, I cherish it, for I have actually earned it; earned through living with contradictions.

For example, I had read medieval history in the university; but the subject I actually love at present is modern civilisations; yet, I spend my working life on an armchair job trying to make sense of compiled data. People usually don't understand this jumble and say it too. I would reply: some things I learned, some I understood and some I merely practice, leaving the questioner dazed. But then I remember, in junior years I was not particularly interested in history and languages either; I would miss the homework most of the times and get rebuked for being inattentive in the class. I liked mathematics in which, in fact, I was ahead of my classmates by a year.

But this show of contradictions is of course nothing compared with some of the other things to come later in my life. The things that can mess up life, in this case, not only my own but also of those linked with me – and by 'messing up' here I mean properly ruining, though done in a neat, tidy way. There is a lot that I've gone through in my life, misfortunes, trials, catastrophes, you name it, but nothing of that is included in the story I am going to tell – and, please, don't get me started on this petty, frivolous stuff anyway. Or, wait a minute; in fact, why don't I give you a taster of what the past has been like, if you please?

I think I have done not too bad for my CV: a director in Public Engagement and an advisor to the Defence Ministry. In passing, let me tell you a little about my institution. I regularly hear its perception of acting as 'big brother' designed to have an eye on the public or being involved in some psycho-invasive research aimed at breaking into people's minds. Owing to the confidentiality clause in my contract, I cannot reveal what it does, but my contract does not stop me saying what it doesn't, and I am happy to say my institution doesn't do these funny petty intelligence stuff and I know this for sure because I am one of its pioneering bosses. Considering my stature, I am regularly invited to sit on a number of important national committees and, my experience, to deliver training programs in the institution. To add a little buzz to things, I lead a research group, too, and have widely published our work. I was always like this. What else can one do in one life?

Despite all this, how about if in my junior years I was struck off from job, not once but twice. Why? Contractual breech because I had not been productive enough. In reality, I failed on the modern tick-box symbolism. Each time, to reclaim my job, I had to fight a legal battle. Someone in the ranks, at the end, would trivially apologise for an overlook, retracting their decision.

My reaching this position in the institution had not come by any easier either. Once, I was listed in the result sheet of a departmental exam as a 'PASS with DISTINCTION'; nice, isn't it? It was big one and, to celebrate it, I had parties over the next few days and booked family holidays too; and, then, I received in the post the result card. And guess what? it showed a FAIL. In fact, they thought I'd failed so badly that they placed a restriction on my retaking the exam. So on and so forth. Despite these setbacks, somehow, I have managed to keep my spirit intact and humour alive. Anyway, these cookies I shall keep for baking at another time. The story I am going to tell you here wraps a pinnacle specimen of a conflict; a tale of a trial in kind never told before.

It begins with my life jump-starting at a point in time, but that is not where my life actually began, as you will see. Again, I saw an end to it, probably with a suicide, or maybe even with a murder, or with something I am not so sure. From this, you may be inclined to guess this tale as being some kind of note of admission or a suicide note. You expect to see in it the unfortunate me, telling or even glorifying the reasons why I wanted my life to end like this. Plus, of course, you expect to see in it the list of those responsible for this tragedy whom I would want you to detest, some of whom you would like to see me urging the police to apprehend, straightway. But this is not a tale of a coward, hating life or telling on people, but of someone with the nerves of steel, wanting to live, but again, I am not so sure about this either. It is a tale in which no one is to blame, yet it stumbles on my loved ones, literally pulling me apart, splitting me from within, carelessly; but, am I sure of this? No, sorry, I'm not, yet again.

What must be the reason for such a cast-iron uncertainty in me, you might wonder? How did it eventually resolve? Rather than dragging around here, why don't I just take you with me, Oxymoron, when I am getting ready to clash with everything around me, myself included.

# PART ONE: FROM ME TO US

# A MAN MADE, NOT BORN

THERE WAS NO SIGN of me in the mirror; instead, the image staring back at me was of a stranger - a youthful figure. The doctors had told me of this switch but I was still in a state of disbelief. Joining the drill, the face in the mirror also folded in confusion. Suspecting a spectre, a stuntman, or a trick of some kind, I scanned the room. No one was behind the mirror. The room had minimal teak furniture, white walls without any frames hung, just some electrical sockets and a few unusual connections, marked with Medical $O_2$. Everything here was white, the ceiling, the bedframe and even the bedsheets, brilliant white, all neat and fresh, and with a clinical scent in the air of alcohol and detergents. It was surely patient room in a hospital and there was nothing here to suggest I was the butt of a joke.

There was some paperwork lying on the side table, looked like a patient file. I tried to read some pages. I swear I could not read a word of it, the doctors' writing; however, my attempt at reading assured me I was not in a dream; neither was I feeling delusional, no chance – I was alert and appropriate and was able to appreciate the perspective.

My attention returned to the mirror. The incessant postures I made in front of the mirror increased my confusion exponentially and my disappointment, too, on a similar scale. I felt like scratching my head: I raised my arm to reach the head, but in the mirror, it was not my own hand that was raised, neither the head my own that was scratched. I was obviously compelled to do more actions; the person in the mirror replicated the trail of my commands. I tried everything to reclaim myself, making faces, even some laughing, although surely it was not the time to laugh. But nothing seemed to work; even the laughter was alien to me, sounding like an empty can lurking around the floor of a wagon, which made me laugh even more, filling the room with a startling roar, and my mind with trepidation, which ultimately muted into a dull creepy silence.

'Terrifying,' in the silent pause, I hushed. 'Who is this in the mirror? Where have I vanished?'. Again, it was not I who whispered, nor was it from my lips. Exhausted, I literally fell on my knees. The left knee hit the metal frame of the bed, raising a roar of pain in me. The right hand impulsively hurried to rub and cuddle the hurt knee. The pain was mine, but the body parts were obviously not. The nurses hearing the scream rushed in and eased me into bed. However, soon, I was back in front of the mirror. I was trying to confirm the switch, and admit it; but in reality, I could not digest any of it - far from it.

This was the first time I had faced myself in a mirror after the events no one could possibly have envisaged beforehand. What I remembered was the rush hour of the morning of Monday the 14th July, 2025, on the way to work in the city centre, when a lorry hit my car on the driver's side - that much I remembered for sure. I also remembered how it towed my car with it, and me in the car, while my body was getting hurt like a canister dragged on the road. The last image on my mind during the incident that I could recall was from an imagination of my daughter whose hand slipped from my hand while I walked her down the aisle on the day of her wedding.

The next thing I knew was a few moments ago when I found myself lying in a bed, staring at the ceiling. Much different from waking up from sleep, I felt like my consciousness flickering, wavering between in and out of focus. Then I stretched my body a little, the way I always do while waking up in the bed. There was a kind of unusual pain in all of the limbs, some sort of numbness in the limbs as if them fallen asleep after being in one position. But the pain literally melted away in the next few stretches. Then I detected movement in my hands and then in the rest of the body.

I noticed my feet did not reach as far down the bed as I expected. Unsure, I put my hand on the leg, and then on the other leg; they felt more muscular and stouter. 'Is something wrong with the hand?' I gave my hand in the other, rubbing and caressing them. They felt stronger but softer. I was aware of a supple body but unusually not through pains and aches that I was used to.

'No – enough of this; now, who is this lying with me in the bed?' 'No, in fact, who is it here instead of me?' Then, I started smelling things, not sure of what, and hearing noises. My systems were obviously waking up one by one, or was I hallucinating? 'Accident', 'hospital', 'family, 'job' all thoughts that came to mind showed I was appropriate. 'Oxymoron, you are in trouble, again, my friend', I thought. Then I saw on the clock on the table along the wall on my left side: 5.00 pm, 14th July. And then I saw the door opened and a team of doctors in blue gowns and caps, gloves and masks, entering the room.

They asked me questions about my state and examined me. I wanted them to explain to me how I had reached the current situation. They told me about a patient from a road traffic accident brought to A&E, barely alive with his whole body irreparably damaged but the face, the head and the brain inside it completely spared.

Their account further unfolded that the surgeons were operating the same day on another patient, a youth, with a brain cancer. That the cancer was massively large, they knew before hand, but that it was also widely spread, invading the surrounding tissues, thus inoperable, they only learnt once they opened the head. To make the matter worse, the operation field was flooded with blood that would not stop, leaking from a source they were unable to trace. The end was surely imminent for the operation and for the youth, the team reckoned at a moment of surrender. But, obviously, they did not give up on ideas. At the very moment, the chief surgeon conceived an idea. He opined for using the youth's healthy body laid on the operating table to house the brain from the battered person to replace the cancer-ridden brain.

"What? You switched the bodies?" I drifted into a deeper confusion, looking at my body again.

"Yes; that is exactly what was done; I was there in the theatre," one of the team boasted.

I was speechless. They handed over to me a packet, describing it as my belongings. They wrote up in the patient-notes some further instructions and investigations, encouraged me to move around in the room, and left.

No sooner had they left than I was up. The first thing I looked for in the room was a mirror, and there was one, man-size, stuck on the backside of the wardrobe door. I still remember vividly my first appearance to myself. That was it; jammed in front of the mirror, staring at myself, I was not able to tear off it or from the image. I blinked, had another look, and then another. I had had one thousand looks at the person in front of me and one thousand questions in my mind looking for answer.

"Who am I? What am I doing here? Where is me?" questions after questions, not in any particular order. Looking at the mirror I thought how far had I come during the last few days! It was only on the last weekend, when I was mowing the back-lawn of our house. In fact, my duty has been only to blow deciduous leaves and to weed the flower drills; mowing is not my job. Zeitoun, my wife, has appointed my son Ayaan, 20, for this. From this team job plan, you surely can guess from who wears the pants in this marriage. Ayaan hates garden work; he really does. "I would do it for you," I say; "but to make the deal a win-win, in return, I wouldn't mind accepting your offer of a shoulder massage." Plus, in the deal, he would do it at the first go; mowing would only follow. Shoulder massage is always on the table from my side a demand to barter with him for anything, although we always end up in having argument over the quality of the massage, that it was not deep enough or it has not lasted as long as we'd agreed. This time even before reaching the stage of the argument, Mum intervened, ordering his release from duty, not knowing he was in fact serving a contract. On this point, Ayaan winked his eye, wore a winning smile and walked away. I had to keep quiet.

I started the mowing. Not normally to anything literally, Zeitoun turned a blind eye to my doing the lawn instead of Ayaan. About halfway through the grass, I noticed the presence of Lehman in his garden, my left side neighbor. Lehman is roughly of my age, a high street solicitor, an interesting, pleasant tall guy, with no hair on the top-end, mostly permanently gone, others all-time erased at the roots. We have been good friends over the years, and both like to indulge in over-the fence gossip. It was funny that our first introduction after my family moved in this premises was over-the-fence too.

He was setting chairs in the garden. "Lehman", I said. "I suspect tomorrow is going to rain heavily".

"I know" he said. "But the grass can wait for the next weekend; today we have family friends visiting us. In fact, you might have seen this lady recently on the screens. She went missing for the whole evening during her mountain trip."

"Yeah, I have. Yes, the one a police search party found up there during the night, luckily unhurt," I verified. "Is that right that she is coming? It would be fun to see her in person and perhaps also say hello to her."

Just by then Lehman's wife brought the visitors in to the garden, a couple, with their pretty baby, in blue, cradled in her arms, in her hand hanging a brown paper bag sopping with oil, apparently from a take-away. He introduced me to them as a Director of Intelligence. Did he really have to mention my title? It sounded so funny, 'a director on-the-fence', I thought. I got attracted to the baby in her arms, facing right at me. The first attempt at peekaboo with the baby got him interested, further rounds met his smiles and then some with soft giggles, too. The baby must have been looking for a reason behind the sudden appearance of the face, or its disappearance at the same speed, and be amused with not finding one. Babies can afford such pleasures, achieving them so cheaply, without having to buy costly tickets for a posh comedy theatre. The tragedy though is that babies grow up pretty quickly when, as adult, you know, people become pretty expensive at laughing.

The mum waited till I finished playing with the baby. Nearing the end, we changed glances, her full of pride, mine of praise. Changing the topic, I said, "I particularly found your comment on the screen interesting that you felt painfully claustrophobic in the jungle. I always thought jungles were pretty open places." The thought of 'claustrophobia' right away shrunk me in the body in which I found myself now trapped. From the trance from the last weekend, I was torn by this feeling of claustrophobia.

The nurses came in to check things. Each time they came in the room, they found me standing in front of the mirror. My eyes at it, I will throw at them questions, but only to have one pet response, "keep the questions for the Chief Surgeon; he comes late in the evening, after the theatres." I thought of the packet they had handed over to me earlier; maybe it provided me some explanation. The packet contained a metal chain, a smart phone, a pair of blue jeans, a checkboard shirt and a pair of shoes, none of which belonged to me.

***

"Good evening. I'm Mr Ashkol, your neurosurgeon. How are the things?" He was a fairly strongman, with the grey appearing on the temples, looking studious and busy, surrounded by a bunch of doctors and nurses. They were all neatly dressed in blue plastic gowns, gloves, and surgical caps, an awesome sight. He conducted my physical examination, inspected the head wound, went through my notes, gave instructions and ordered some more tests. He nodded few times, looking at me, not trying to communicate but like when you look at a thing, and then he looked at his team, with his eyes scanning in the panoramic dimension, obviously feeling pride about his achievement and satisfaction with the progress. He returned to me one more time, "any questions?"

Depressed and awed, I said in a vanishing tone, "thank you doctor, but your team have just explained that you'd switched the bodies during the operation?"

"Yes, you can say that, although what we actually switched were just brains; only way for you to survive in conditions." I saw the smile on his radiant face vanishing, to be replaced with irritation from my questions.

"I'm really confused. You would not have gone ahead without discussions?" said I, ignoring his English, limping without articles.

"Parents wanted their patient saved at any cost - in any form - whatsoever." "Where is senior registrar? Could someone see consent is filed in notes?" he looked at his team.

"But what about the patients, were they consented at all?" I protested.

"You were under, on table, not much time, no any other chance - literally. Your donor, a director in some office - situation with him was impossible, but then he carried organ donation card on him – which made our life simple," he paused. "Any one knows for which department he worked, this director?" in a lighter mood he again looked at his team.

"In Public Intelligence," I replied instead. "Surely, you appreciate I am that Director," I protested.

He looked at me, his pupils dilated and chin dropped, visibly, as if I was a stunt who had caught him by surprise, then he sneakily looked at the name sticker in the notes "No, you are youth - that is what is recorded here too; that is what we had done in theatre – in operation – officially speaking, really."

"No, please don't do this to me. I am the Director; Oxymoron - that is my name."

They all laughed, he noisily, and others inaudibly. The name I uttered was as a matter of fact, having forgotten since long the word had meanings too. But that might not be the only reason that made them laugh. I bet they would have considered the youth in his twenties must have gone crazy to call himself director of some company. At this lighter note, the surgeon excused himself, "alright, can someone arrange for this patient a Psychology consult? Let us move on." And they moved on, literally like that.

As soon as they'd left, I checked the patient-notes. It read, Nahaar ..., and 25 March 2000 against date of birth. 'Here you go,' I whispered. I quickly realised that they wouldn't have many answers for me anyway. What else could have they done apart of saving life, of Nahaar, as they think? They couldn't not have taken the choice they had taken. Surgeons are not philosophers, not in the least; the intricacy of the subject of personal identity can be beyond even regular philosophers. The current situation was my own predicament, in which I found myself, which only I would solve, I knew for sure. This wasn't the first time I had been bogged down, though now I felt doomed, too. I needed support. "When can I see my family? Have they been here?" I asked the nurses.

"Waiting for greenlight from the Infection Control Team to the visitors. You were labelled as serious infection risks, you know," the nurse said. "It is OK now. Shall organise soon."

Off the bed again, I was back at the mirror. I was looking at the image again, and again, touching and feeling all around the body. Weighing up things, 'This guy in the mirror, I have never met before, have I?' I was hoping that any minute I would emerge from the wall, kick out this person, and recapture myself - just like that, like in magic films made for small kids. Approaching retirement, I was rather good for the 60 mark, tallish, with thinned frontal hair, and those on the temples turned mostly grey. An injury in early childhood left a scar over my right eyebrow. I would raise an eyebrow while trying to conceal the scar, which developed into a habit. I had crow's-feet prints, one on each side of my dark brown eyes. There were footprints of spectacles on the bridge of my nose, for which I always got nagged by my wife, but would never make to the optician. Talking about the nose, I had aged such that you would not overlook the boundary of my nose expanded from its original landmark in childhood. And then the ears that had grown out of proportion, too. More recently I'd worked upon my weight and fitness. Obviously, it was futile now, plus the ugly ears, the snooping nose, everything I loved, everything I was used to, all gone in a second, at the blow by the lorry at my car. All is merely a memory now, just history. They must have buried my remains, what else? I could literally have witnessed my own burial. The surgeon was right. Oxymoron had indeed died. I cried over my own death.

But, then, no one can ever cry over their own death, can they? Comforted with the thought that I was actually alive, I smiled amidst crying. If you saw me then, you would have thought I'd gone mad. There I was, still alive, now smiling too – in my 'second go', right there in the mirror. I stood gracefully, as a charming handsome man, of around 25, middle height, with a beard grown to short stubbles, and dense blackish brown hair on the scalp, cut short to near the roots, with a wound around the circumference of the head neatly clipped. I now had a perfectly equilateral pointed nose sitting between wide cheeks which were looking pale by a touch, with a hint of glow. The face was cut to fit the Golden Ratio, sitting on broad shoulders. This was an outlook any man would envy to have, whom any girl would dream to see as a partner.

With these findings rushed in me a gush of glee. Improper and strange though it was, it felt to me not just as a barren flashback typical of mature age but as a spark from a bad connection under power surge. 'What – I'm at the 60 mark; try to be decent,' I rebuked myself. Embarrassed, I thought of a defence, 'excuse me, it is not me, sorry – it must be the young man, soaked in hormones; not me, for sure.'

Enough of the mirror, at one point, I became fed up; but would I believe myself I would not be returning to it? I took a step aside; I kind of enjoyed it, no pain in the knees, no aching muscles. Another step, then another; I started strolling around, then literally running, aimlessly, as if floating on the air, making U-turns – smartly, acutely, dancing, trying everything. Amidst this busy traffic, the door opened and someone entered. I put a break on me, felt dragging on the floor like when Daisy Duck chasing Mickey Mouse spots a trap ahead. I pretended nothing was going on. The nurses were in light mood, too,

13

"O, by the way, your pictures gone viral, your news top trend. Many nice words for Oxymoron as well." They also thought I was Nahaar, but I thought arguing with them was of no use.

So is the story of my first day of life, life of one-day old new-born man. One last look in the mirror, lights off, and I was ready to go to bed. I had already broken my resolution about the mirror, which made me smile. With eyes closed, I saw the images of my family; Zeitoun and my adorable kids, Aliya, 23, and Ayaan, 20, as if they were stuck to the back of my eyelids, waiting for the screen to roll down. One by one, the images animated into characters.

Sitting in the lounge, I see Zeitoun entering the kitchen, then doing other chores in the house, like a busy bee. Our marriage, around 25 years ago, succeeded a love story, a story that continues till today, though she has copied the contents from the chapter of love to paste on to the chapter of care: kind heart, caring hands; although words she uses can be somewhat tough. Albeit, like anyone else, she has her share of peculiarities. She is either for all or for none; people for her are only good or only bad. The proverb 'one bad fish spoils the whole pond' can explain it, provided you allow me to twist it a little bit. For her, one bad fish in the pond means the whole shoal bad. At another level, a small fin broken at the corner should mean the whole fish gone repugnant, she would insist. It must be counted as a miracle when she let me off after being unfaithful, which I was once, in a small way, and I admitted it; and she let me off in a graceful way, never reminded me for the 20 odd years, since then, so far. With this, she indeed bought me in body, mind and soul, in all the three departments. With just one stroke of a hammer, she chiselled a slave out of me. But that is only in theory; in reality we have found a slave in her, for 24/7. Could I have a day without her? No. Could she have a day off in my life? No. My wife, my family, we all are gummed. In daily life, whether she is tough or polite, caring or pretending to be indifferent, it all depends, but when she's decided to call the house in order, it will only be after the event that we, the rest of us, will be able to utter any word, mainly of calling each other chickens. In a relationship, there are women more like a lover or there are those more like a beloved; again, there are women closer to being a wife or there are those more akin to being a mum of your kids. My lady is only a mum, a born mum, leaving no space for any other feeling.

These thoughts came like a swell against which I was surfing, and I fell off the board, the water shaking me like a rag doll. I shouted, 'Zeitoun, help?', but of course when I opened my eyes, there was no sign of her around or of the kids. Thinking of kids opened my eyes and awakened in me the question, "when can I see them?"

14

I went back and pulled down the screen over my eyes one more time. On it now appears the star of the family, reading a book in her rocking chair. Right from childhood, Aliya is daddy's daughter. Be it difficult homework, issues at school, wrangles with friends, or rows from mum, everything must be shared with dad, on daily basis. With the years passing, she has found a liking for historical fiction and paranormal, matching with my romance with these topics. I remember once we both reading from the same volume of Harris' *Imperium*, her page marker being a peacock feather and mine a tree leaf made of toughened paper. In this way, each of us could even spy on where the other was on the story, and tease each other on sluggish reading speed. She enjoys watching thematic films, again a taste pinched from me. I have kept my spirit feeling young and bouncing of her, I have to. She has grown into a kind of serious young lady under my influence - give and take. A perfect blessing in a daughter.

My family is small. Let us see who is left out: Ayaan. A mild gentleman, the younger of the two. He enters into the house and goes straight to the kitchen, looking for mum. Mummy knows more about him; monetary dealings, needs, problems, all with mum. Though, when I return home from abroad or from somewhere after a gap of days, he would parade his love for me, competing with Aliya. His company is sweet except he does not spare much of it for me – 'envy' comes to mind. Though when he enters an argument in philosophy, just beware that you do not want to miss anything from his logic. He is an outsider in the family. Strangely, Aliya listens to him, cares for his preferences and takes his advice. He then conducts himself as the older brother, head up, eyes at the ceiling, thinking and worrying, as if he has to lower his wings on Aliya to protect her. Except, of course, the times when they squabble over tiny things like a phone charger misplaced or earphones gone missing, when he gets the shout, invariably.

In these ruminations, I did not remember how long I remained imbued lying in the bed. I hoped to see them soon.

# NEW LEASE

ON THE DAY-TWO OF MY NEW LIFE, I got up feeling positive. "So, this is the new disguise with which I am going to play – happily, with a fresh start." Though, doubts quickly started creeping with my resolution leaking. I was not prepared to forget me, my face printed with crow's-feet around the eyes, my aching joints, my tired muscles. I wanted me back, right now. I wanted a release from this cage, this body of the youth. I tried to confront this thought, but my defence was weak. The more pleadings I did the more crushed I felt. Standing there in front of the mirror, the feeling of weirdness in this tangle filled my chest with pain that would not abate, with panic that would not wane. I began to tremble, then shook, then stiffened. I heard my heart thumping, felt my head throbbing. Cold perspiration showed on my forehead. My hands shuddered, chest tightened and gut was gripped. I smelled a dead body around me, the smell of my own body. I rushed to the bed and fell, with a darkness creeping over me, interrupted now and then, like light filtering from dark honeycomb clouds floating in front of sun. I heard nurses shouting, "Help; emergency."

"Breathing - OK; carotids - beating too," yelled a female voice from very close, with her soft cold fingers glued to the side of my neck. Her face must be next to mine, for I could even sense the scent she wore. Nice smell. From this closeness, a glimpse of an improper thought crossed my mind. Obviously, hormones – clashing with me. Was this a time for such things? I slowly regained command from this fragility, though was run down, more importantly, sad - deeply. The nurses said they were calling in the people from mental health to prevent this happening again.

Later in the day, a team of two, a man and a girl, identifying themselves from the Mental Health paid a visit. The older man did the talking while the younger girl took notes. He was rather flabby guy, filling the bedside chair. He came across as rather sloppy, dressed without much regard to colour choice, wearing a large black frame, rather too large for his face, and with his graduated-haircut showing shades of bold-ombre probably owing to wearing out hair dye, needing a redo. With his elbow on the side table, the index finger on the temple, with the rest of them folding on his cheek, he started to interview me, but I noticed he was more focused on me rather than what I had to say. It was one of the most disjointed conversation I recently had, with misdirected obscure questions, not really helped by my equally non-sensical feigning responses. I guessed he mainly wanted to know how I felt after the switch; my problem was who I was after the fusion, a question which did not concern him. He did not seem to have time to go deeper into my feelings, nor did I feel enough connection to share those feelings. He diagnosed that I suffered catoptrophobia, which can simply be called as the fear of mirrors. 'The mirror in the room must be removed,' he recommended. I protested, for my main attraction was about to smash. I hated his solution. However, for the healthcare, mental health box was now ticked - irony of modern healthcare system. Straight after their visit, two people came to board the mirror, masking it. They must have thought how childish had I behaved in front of the mirror so that the mirror must be removed. I was embarrassed, but they ignored me altogether.

Left with no mirror in the room and no other business to do, I went to the window looking out. My room was probably on the first floor looking out at a vast garden from its window. There were colourful floral parterres distributed within neatly kept lawns with evenly cut lush green grass-carpet. The garden was riddled with free-flowing curvy swirly pathways lines with green hedges, paved with ancient looking stone, with small patches of grass and ferns, probably forcing through the crevices of the concrete flooring. Quite a few ornaments and mushroom-shaped tables were arranged randomly in the garden. In the landscape were scattered several mounds of ancient dusty stones, mixed with craters of water, featuring noisy springs or quiet overflow pans. The one close to my window had bubbles randomly erupting from the peaceful surface, like popcorns from popcorn machine. The bubble game was catching, inviting me to guess the spot of the next bubble arising. The garden was populated with birch trees, and with birds trafficking between them, some resting on their branches. There was a thick forest at the far end of the park, beyond which was a vast desert wasteland with scanty planting.

There were a few people and some families hovering around the far side of the garden. Then, I saw a man entering my view from the left side of the garden, walking up the whole length of the middle pathways, faithfully walking along its curves, strolling leisurely, not marching freakily. I chased him till he disappeared into the woods. 'Surely, he would return; but, in real life, those who are lost in the woods, those of them who end up in the wasteland, they never return to the garden.' 'Except of course, I am the first drop of rain – thanks to medical advancements.' The man appeared again, near the far end and peacefully walked back along the swirly paths. 'You too have to tread along the paths paved for you, Oxymoron', I told myself. 'And serenely.' 'Alright, I have lost my body, and I am sad, but the panic attacks, I would not allow to come back.' This was the resolution I pledged at that moment to keep and I have been trying to keep it since.

Distracted from myself, in a state of calm, I looked around in the room. It was a fairly welcoming place, its furniture nicely set, a welcome bag lying on the TV cabinet, a water kettle and pleasantries on the side table. I went to the washroom, this time looked at more carefully. It was of nice size and clean, with a bag of toiletries and a toilet role in place. And there was mirror here, which they had forgotten to board as well. I washed my face to refresh myself, but ended with a patch of skin from my knuckle taken off by the edge of the tap, leaving a painful spot.

I realised I had to learn to use the wash basin. With plenty of time at hand, I wanted to practice it. 'OK, position your face in the corner above the basin as deep as you can. If you don't, the splash would miss the basin, wetting your clothes and spoiling the floor. Now, spread the pan of your hands under the tap to fill. Next, lower the pan slightly and then move it to one side away from the tap. Go past the tap and now raise it to deliver the water on your face. If you did not move the pan of your hands away from the tap, its sharp edge would catch the knuckle of you thumb.' And I looked at my knuckle. My feedback to the hospital was 'fire the architect of this bathroom'. I had idled around to find another mirror. Though, having a mirror around me was not the solution; to get life back to normal was objective, for which I must have my family around me.

# REUNION

ALL DAY I HAD been thinking about my family. I knew they also would be counting the minutes. There were so many things to talk about and go through. I had not been away from home for so long. 'But what would they think of the new me?'

'We should find out only when we see each other.' The evening approached the six-mark on the dial when the nurse came asking if I was ready to receive the special visitors. So, I fixed my eyes on the door, ready to see them.

There they were, two people, a couple – but not of my family. I could quickly size up the situation: they must be 'my parents'. Disappointed, confused and distracted, I forgot to welcome them aptly. Sitting on the bed, I just bobbed my head. They flooded the room; the mother tossed on the bed the gift-wrapped package she brought with her and rushed to cling with me, her arms around my face. The father was calmly standing facing me, with his eyes moist and his hand softly on my shoulder. Truly loving parents; though, their adoring and loving gestures embarrassed me to the core; their naïve mawkishness felt to me too intimate at which I just cringed. The experience was terribly strange, even inappropriate, for I might even be older than each of this couple. Though, at this stage, to me they did not appear to have taken a notice of my confusion.

Eventually, after the rush, they eased into drawing two easy chairs sitting along the wall close to the bed, on my left and on my right, and settled in them, holding my hands in their hands. The mother was a slim, fair-skinned lady, of passionate mannerism as if love was pouring out through the pores of her skin. She was sitting on the chair, but keeping herself on the seat seemed hard, for every so often she would get up to pat my back or kiss my forehead or put her hand around my shoulders. Her voice was very sweet and polite; I cannot do any better than explaining it as a sound to my ears like honey to the tongue. The father was a tall, large-framed man, very well dressed and posh in his manners. In appearance, we both, he and I, in my new format, seemed to have been cut from the same cloth, except, of course, I had a higher thread count with no barres or knots. He came across as a refined man but was a bit short on words, also putting inaudible stress on consonants. There was noticeable tautness in his demeanour, too, as of someone from a military background. He mostly spoke to his wife and, in most cases, just responded to her. He would, on and off, throw at me a strange baffling, searching look.

First of all, she tried a few names of whom one I guessed was 'my sister' who she said could not come for some reason, and the other 'my grandmother' who she said was waiting at home, counting down the hours to see me. I nodded in sheer oblivion. She skimmed over all kinds of questions, from 'how I was feeling' to those related with my future plans; though, uneasiness prevailed throughout, growing by the minute. She would ask a question, and finding me paused, thinking, the father would respond on my behalf. I was trying my best; I just did not have the answers.

Eventually, she said what detonated amidst my thoughts: "Would you like to move in with us. You may feel alone in your apartment while your wife is away." This said unplugged a shaken bottle of soda in my head. Soon the froth would perish, leaving me numb. But, dogged, I somehow continued to pull through each of these lurches.

"Now, besides Zeitoun, do I have another wife as well?" I hissed.

"Zeitoun – another wife?", the lady was staggered with my whisperings.

I wondered how on earth could I have answered that question and they would be satisfied. I was trying to carve a response when she said, "I am sorry; we knew about your wedding; we knew about it even before it happened. But I told your Dad we shouldn't interfere and let you go ahead." I noticed the husband looking the other way, nodding his head, probably getting nervous in *fremdshamen*. She said, "sorry, past is past; it is your life; we are very happy to go along with your plans, absolutely." This part had revealed that I had allegedly wedded this girl against the wishes of these parents. Each of their efforts of initiating conversation had met a yes or a no response at random delivered in a cold disconcerted way from my side but, now, on this 'wife' question, a complete silence.

I was overtaken by exhaustion from guilt and frustration, to which was now added the fluttering worry of meeting with this new character, 'my wife'. I just nodded meaninglessly, not being able to ask even a single question about her, even her name, where she was now and when she was going to return, I could ask none of them, fearing many more counter-questions coming my way. After all, I was supposed to know this information better than them.

It was indeed a uniquely disturbing scene of disconnection. At short notice, I could not decide when to inform them of my predicament and how. The husband conducted himself rather as a bystander in the room, the wife was not deterred by the arid communication. She tried several things to get me on, but with each failed attempt, they apparently drew closer to the horror that their son did not exist anymore. Then, suddenly, the father broke down. There was then this solo tear dropped on his cheek, which must have come from far for this refined man. And then I could see the light in mother's eyes dimmed, too. He held her hand and, between sobbing, uttered the truth that he knew their son was no longer there. He said he did not know how to break the news to her. Sitting beside someone who looked like no one else but their own son (is that what you were after?), they cried for his loss. And the person who looked like their son would not comfort them. Tears gathered in my eyes, too, but I did not wipe them. I just resigned to the irony of the situation.

And then they got up and walked to the door. Just before leaving the room, the father turned his face coyly asking if it was alright if I could return to them from among the belongings of their son the neck-chain as something to remind them of him. I wanted them to take the whole packet, but thought it was rude to say so. He thanked me for the chain and asked if it was alright with me occasionally to let them to see their son. Without waiting for an answer, they turned into the corridor. I wasn't sure if they would ever return but they might. They might return to see their son, but not to find him.

Alone in the room, reflecting on the visit, I felt unhinged. Had I been too indifferent, impervious, insensitive? Guilt overtook me, the guilt from having the youth snatched from his parents, merely to serve my purpose, in short, my life. To the guilt was now added the shame of being ungrateful to his parents. But they were not seeking gratitude; they were looking for their son whom no one could return to them.

'But there was a person in front of them, whom they recognised as their son?' I asked myself.

'The person is all about thoughts he holds. And, the thoughts had switched the bodies.'

They could not meet their son, but at least these nice parents had a chance to see him. But, then, what about my own family.'

'What about them; they will be visiting, wouldn't they?' I was alarmed with the tone of my question.

'They would - maybe; but they wouldn't even recognise me.'

The apprehension swept over me, 'but I will break through the barrier; I will share everything with them. I shall tell her the stories of her childhood - Aliya, my daughter - the stories of her when she was in my arms. I shall remind Zeitoun about how we walked together through difficult times, and walked together in the moon nights. I shall offer my shoulder to Ayaan to put his face on.'

Then I looked at my shoulders, at my hands and at everything, 'No, he would not accept my hand, none of them would.'

I cried, 'they must let me in, or else, without them, life would not be life.'

Between tears and fears, I gave the nurses the number to call Zeitoun, to let her know that things were alright now and I was waiting for their visit. The nurse returned asking who Zeitoun was, complaining that the lady on the phone was not very keen on the subject, though she promised to visit the next day with her children. Listening to this, I became numb, only to wake up to embrace a panic attack. A panic which was not of the daylight type of someone caught in cage or facing a peril, a kind that causes the limbs to shake and the heart to pound. It was rather of the brand veiled within the heart, a covert action that cracks one from within, the pieces crumbling. It was not a firework erupting and exploding but a play of bleak shadows sinking and collapsing. It was a panic of the ultimate type. It was the checkmate. But, no; what I had not yet realised was that even worse was to come my way. 'Oxymoron, get ready.' I patted myself.

Deeper within me was some hope, too. 'Things for me always work out, at the end, somehow,' I reassured myself. I felt at least for now I had some energy to keep the hope going, at least drag it till I see my family. Though, the hope in me was vexing and wanning every minute as if it was controlled by a rheostat or like a kite tumbling in the merciless wind. I couldn't dare playing the film on the screen of the back of my eyelids for tonight.

\*\*\*

I noted in my diary 17 July, 2025, the date I was hoping to receive my family the first time in my second life. The pressure of waiting can corrode your soul, but when it is mixed with misgivings, it can actually erode it. I would not take the pressure, sitting in the room. I asked the nurses if I could go for a wander around. First, I wanted to discover the main garden of the hospital. I wanted to do all its paths. The smell of flowers mixed with woody and earthy scents slackened my mind into tranquillity. The sunshine tickling the cool breeze set my body into motion. I recalled the scents I could smell now and the walking I could easily do now, the things of the farthest past which were lost in the oblivion of the old age. Eventually I got bored with the garden, with its breeze and the sunshine, and I smiled on this thought. Was I feeling like young people do, wanting to do something bouncier and more vigorous than doing garden-walks? I decided to leave. Though the fears on the back of my mind pulled me

22

back to the walking track, 'God knows what they think of me when we meet tonight. Would I return to my home? If not, where else would I go?' Frozen with fear, exhausted, I walked back towards the building. Though when I reached the entrance, I passed by it, turning the other way.

I came across a sign-plate reading 'Medical Assessment Unit'. Outside the unit was parked a van of Patient Transport Service with its hind doors wide open, carrying a wheelchair facing the other way. With time at hand, I paused at the scene. Of the pair of healthcare workers in attendance, the lady went up the van, uttered few words to the patient in the wheelchair and unlocked the chair from its station. She steered the chair backward and launched it over the tail-lift. The guy pulled the lever to bring the chair down. I could see the patient now, a frail lady, her body covered with blanket, her face bloodless, pale white, reduced to skin and bones. With her eyes focussed at void, she was unaware of what they were doing with her. I found myself wanting to stay there a little longer.

Once on ground, the man slid the chair out from its stand and steered it into the Unit. He parked it in the corridor at the backend of a queue of wheelchaired patients, just besides the vending machine. He casually took the paperwork to the reception, from where he acquired another file and wheeled another patient back to the van. I could see this patient as well, again a lady, who seemed unaware too, looking equally unwell, with her eyes closed. The other attendant matched the details on the papers with the wrist band on the patient. The team of the two loaded the wheelchair and embarked on another trip to elsewhere.

I believed the patient care in the modern times had perfected to fine details. The workers were obviously auditing hazards at each of the critical points of the patient movement. The patientcare no doubt was flawless now; what was missing though was care of patient, in fact, the patient, the person in flesh, now carried around as a thing. I wondered how, from this point, the society could turn the wheel back to its basic script, back to the tender and warm human values from its current legalistic, dry and formal readings, the standard operating procedures, the guidelines. But would anyone appreciate the distinction? I did not think they would. A person from the old, I would have to survive the current dispassionate time of indifference for the life now ahead of me. I returned to my room depressed.

***

For the rest of the afternoon, I waited in the room, sometimes with the eyes on the door, the other times with them closed. A touch after six, the door moved inward and with it my heart in my mouth, though it was just a nurse coming in. But, then, she told me they were there, waiting at the nursing station. I stood up from the bed, thinking only if I could run away from the situation. The door opened again. I first saw Aliya popping through it; she looked at me curiously. Then came Ayaan, followed by their mum - one by one. The bulb inside me lit, but my heart had a stand still.

They walked straight towards the chairs set for visitors, ignoring me standing near the bed. Where once, on my return home after a gap, Aliya would rush to the front door to embrace me, wrapping her arm around my back, clasping her hand on my shoulder, and with the other, tapping my face, delicately rubbing it. And, Ayaan would scrape her hands off to vacate a place for his face; and, where once, on my return, Zeitoun would wear smiles on her face beaming with delight, like wood-knots shimmering in fire – what I got now were just their distant suspicious searching stares. It hit me like a fist on the stomach. The bulb in me blurred. And there was the silence, the unending silence; as quiet as statues, that we all were. In that silence, I heard an empty thud – that of the circuit breaking.

They were sitting not far from me; mum was in the middle, her hand in Ayaan's hand. Aliya on the other side, mostly looking at her mum, and while casually scanning the room she would throw a passing glance at me as well. I couldn't miss the age lines on Zeitoun's face deepened over these few days of lamenting. There was a faint twitch in her eyelids, and she off and on was biting her lower lip too as if trying to hold back from crying. Her eyes were moist, which she dabbed few times, but they remained moist, despite. I was sure at this time she needed me around. 'Curse on me. Where have I gone?' 'Planets away; somewhere, but not here; remember, I have died.'

Zeitoun for once could not hold her sobs. Ayaan held her hand patting it lovingly, while she would not try to draw it back. He asked in the softest of voice, "Mum are you alright?" I waited for this moment for silence to break.

"Zeitoun, your husband is not dead," I dared saying.

The watershed moment had arrived. She looked at me as if looking in the void. Aliya intervened, "we are just coming from the mortuary in the basement. The body of my dad is waiting for burial."

"I know exactly what you are going through. I too am sad on my demise, but in fact for you I am not dead, for I know you, Aliya, from the day you were born; I know you, Ayaan, too, and of course, you, Zeitoun. Now only if you people gave me a chance to join back the family."

24

Zeitoun remained detached while Ayaan was listening these lines carefully, though Aliya repeated herself, "you certainly are not what you think you are. You are not my dad, please. His remains are waiting for burial." So, she had drawn a line under the things.

But it was not fair at all. I was broken like their mum was broken. I too had come through a lot. I wished if an Ayaan was there to hold my hand, too? If an Aliya was there to put her face on my shoulder and say 'Come on Daddy, it is going to be OK?' But what I was getting was a denial of my identity and a refusal to accepting me back in the family.

There was nothing left to be said. I wished they had gone sooner, leaving me to mourn in solitude the loss of the father of the house. And, they would leave soon, their silence said it all. She held her mum's hand on this side, and he the other; they helped her out of chair. Aliya said, "We have finalised the funeral arrangement, which is organised for the coming Tuesday." She then handed me a note, "Time and place of the funeral service if you wanted to attend." After this, they walked towards the door, out of the room, never to look back, except my daughter who gaze at me as if saying she would be back soon. I did not understand this gesture, but wished she had not left any hope behind.

I just remembered only the night before the incident when the two of us, Zeitoun and I, walked in the light of the full moon. Whenever we walked in the moonlight, she would be looking at the moon, I at her face, to find the golden hue from the moon glowing at her light tan, and we would find ourselves jammed at one place, our eyes locked on our objects. And now, how to rationalise this visit? Not much was uttered in this family meeting. Obviously, they were not looking for their dad in the first place; they had visited the mortuary to finalise his funeral. Having accepted the loss, they were in fact mourning on it. But Aliya! She argued against my reunion with the family, yet she stood in the door leaving behind a ray of hope for it.

# OVER MY DEAD BODY

SUDDENLY, MY THOUGHTS shifted at something else and locked on it. It dawned at me that the mortuary was just two floors down, and in the mortuary was lying me, dead. A hammer hit at my head and a fist at my stomach. I shivered with the horror of seeing my dead body. I dreaded the dead climbing the stairs, turning right on this floor, walking in the corridor and now entering the ward, the first room on the right and the knock on the door. I even could hear the footsteps of a limping man. Then, this person enters the room and I see me standing in front of me, asking why I have forsaken me. If this was mere hallucination, my taking the trip to the mortuary and meeting with my dead body was truly possible. 'Possible!' I hissed, 'it is merely a question of going or not going.' 'Shall I go?'

I did not exactly know how it would go, but how could I not go to see my dead body? 'Come what may, I must.' Thinking something vague, I put my cell phone in the pocket and sneaked out of the room to find my way to the basement. My turbulence found peace of some kind, or entered a lull, while I was walking in the long dark corridors of the basement looking everywhere for the sign for Mortuary. Calm and composed. I saluted the attendant on the reception and gave him the details of the corps. He walked me to a dark sad cold room. On the way, he asked me who I was to the dead person. How could I have answered that question, for God's sake? I just walked with him quietly.

He came up to a barrage of fridges, opened the far end one and slid out the middle of the three draws a little bit. He then lifted the white sheet from the corner to reveal the right foot, checked the details on the bracelet loosely tied around the ankle. My heart was now pumping, the moment of blatant truth approaching. He pulled the draws to the full, put his hand over my shoulder, drew me closer to the body and left. I was lying on a metal tray, covered with the white sheet.

I held both my hands over my heart, trying to hold it firm. I paused while collecting myself scattered. How much energy I needed just to lift the white sheet? 'No, I just cannot do it. Shall I return?' 'No; no going back from here. The chest on which you are folding your hands is not yours own; the heart which you are cuddling is not your own either. Your own chest, your own heart, your very own self is right here under the sheet – Lift the sheet – OK,' I said to myself.

Then, I freed one hand from the chest, and clutched it over the corner of the sheet. But I could not lift it. All I wished at this moment was if I did not

26

have to come to this moment, if this person under the sheet had not forsaken me. Only if I had died in one piece. Only if I was here with my body lying on the cold metal tray under the sheet. 'But, no, it is terribly cold here. The metal plate is covered with icy haze. For the one thing that Zeitoun was fed up of me was my all-time feeling cold and of my sneakily putting the heating on in the house.' And I smiled over the memory of the argument that regularly resulted, without a word of it ever changed. Absorbed in the past, I did not realise when and how I had lifted the sheet. And, there I was.

'Where have they brought me my face pale skin arid stretched tight around the cheek bones with thin veins visible lips blue eyes staring blank nose pinched stiff it is real cold here cold can hurt you know I am shivering please put the heating on don't you realise it can hurt' - I protested, paused, then I calmed down.

'Good Heavens, the eloquence, the dignity, the aura, the presence of the person all packed in this structure and stored in a drawer in this freezer waiting for disposal into the belly of earth listen don't hurt me OK get out of way leave me to me I shall take me under the earth gently and lay me down kindly'

I lifted up the face from the tray that I used to wash with my hands – the hands which were now broken, probably crushed, wrapped in white dressings with blood dried over them. I held the face. It felt very cold. I watched it for a while. I felt the facial hair as little stubbles. I dabbed its forehead the way I used to do often when nervous or anxious. I noticed a faint smile on its blue lips. From what I knew of myself, this smile was out of sarcasm. I knew I was kind of addicted to sarcasm, but was this a good time to display it? at the time of death, for God's sake, no. 'No occasion for criticism; just forgive - for once.'

I kissed the face a goodbye and gently replaced it on the tray. I took its pictures with my cell phone, although I thought I would immediately delete them. Then I noticed it slowly slumped slightly towards the right, showing the left temple. It was here at the temple that I used to tap with my fingers in deep thinking, in my right hand my favourite pen on the paper. I could not resist the urge to see the rest of the body. I carefully rolled the white sheet towards the feet, and, looking at my body, I was lost.

'See how brutally they have hurt me my body splintered dismembered all around look at me the lorry please no it is me don't nudge me this is not fair see there must be a lot of space on the other side wait please look what have you done look Aliya please look my skin is unstitched all around covered with islets of blood crusts look what have they done to me they have smashed my bones crushed my chest you know it can cause pain please what wrong did I do to you don't punish people like this Zeitoun this lorry has crushed me these people are cruel no Ayaan please pick me my blood gushing out could someone stop it please Aliya sorry my daughter really sorry I would not be there to walk you down the aisle on the day of your wedding.'

I drew the sheet back over my body. I could not bear to stay around any longer. It was a distinctly cold, dark and miserable place. I pushed the drawer back into its slot. In a trance, I walked listlessly out of the room.

With my sentiments thoroughly jumbled up, I left the place terrified, unsettled and baffled. My knowledge of the medieval practices of bodily mutilation and dismemberment as punishment or revenge found a parallel here. Mere graphics of Guy Fawkes and alike in a slide show, showing their bodies mutilated, quartered, even eviscerated, even all done in their conscious presence, seemed little compared with a conscious one actually meeting with their full body, covered with blood-soaked dressings, presented on a metal tray.

But I had left the scene without doing anything about it. It seemed as if I had left behind a close friend, bleeding to die or already dead. I held myself as selfish, unfaithful and ungrateful opportunist. I was angry on what had happened to me and to my body. In the new body, I felt nothing but caged. The experience was not the kind of another experience in one's life but the one of its kind. Then I saw the light. I could flip the coin. I felt victorious for endurance, tough for keeping the nerve and lucky for standing against the odds. I felt bold, but not scared or timid. I saw hope, but not gloom or apathy.

These mixed feelings took bestial forms, wildly running around, leaving crisscross tracks on the canvas of my sentiment screen. I did not exactly know what to feel and what not. And, there was yet more to it: among these animals were some doozies trotting around, for which there was not a name that I could use and you would understand.

I was not aware that I'd reached my room. Exhausted, I fell on the bed. The scene from the cold foggy metal tray would not leave me. I clicked on a picture of my dead face sleeping on the tray and then quickly unclicked it. I clicked it one more time but put the phone on the side table. Then I picked up the phone and looked at the picture. The figure taunted at my courting with this new body. I looked at it again and found no mercy; it derided me even harder. Deeply frustrated, I yelled at it, 'OK, I have left you to die so that I could live with someone else. Fine, I am not loyal to you. But for God's sake, I am not enjoying this life either. Hell has broken on me. Family, friends, past, future, all gone. You have taken a short-cut to the finish line, thank you; the longer route given to me to reach you is not even easy, just in case you thought otherwise.' At this point, I pumped a large bolus of air from the lungs into a sarcastic laugh, 'See you soon, but, in the meantime, please don't disturb me - please.' I promised I would not think of my dead body again. I selected the pictures and deleted them. But would I keep the promise to let the memory vanish from mind and the pictures from the trash bin? As water does not dwell on goose feather so would this pledge not be on my mind, I suspected – and hoped.

However, being in a flight of thoughts, I delved into yet another soliloquy, 'Zeitoun, what is this nonsense. You are suffering because I am not around you while the fact is that I am wasting my time here. You must be telling to the mourners about the terrible story of my accident, pasting it on the top of the cordial stories of our past. You must be having me visiting you in your dreams too, sometimes even smiling, other times looking miserable, maybe even covered with blood. Why all this hassle? I am right here, present myself to tell you - no dreams, but real, first hand, true story. I want to narrate the story of my fatal accident to you and cry on your shoulder. Be reasonable, would you please. Look, the kids are feeling wretched. At least, for their sake, let me in, my girl, please. I promise I would work double hard to keep you people happier.'

'Have you finished your sermon?' I interrupted myself. 'Do you realise they have a corpse down in the mortuary, waiting for a burial? How can they take you for the corpse? What should they do with it? Just desert it! And, by the way, who are you? A stranger, looking of the age of her son.'

I felt deflated, 'OK, alright, perhaps, Zeitoun, you shouldn't let this or any stranger enter my family.' This marked an end to the hope of reunion. Wanting to take the things off my chest, I cried - endlessly. Seeing me this way, the nurses came in and assured me they would not think any further social visiting for me was a good idea. That was the Day Three of my new life.

# EJECTED INTO THE WORLD

I LISTED MY ACHIEVEMENTS so far: one: Nahaar's parents – done: I let them down; two: my own family – done: they have given me up; three: my job – messed up: not sure how to get back on track. Am I forgetting something here? Yes, four: a wife inherited with this body – I don't even know her name. And, I would not think of anyone taking the place of Zeitoun, no, for God's sake, no. The anticipation of the horror of meeting with this character was a cross on my head crayoned for drilling. And, of course, the question that could make the heading was, where do I go from here? Properly caged I was.

Later, with the evening getting darker, doctors of every stripe, the heart doctors, the liver doctors, the kidney doctors, you name it, came to examine me, all to find the organs and systems in me akin to their specialism sound and finely working, giving me good news. But, was I really interested? The source of my despair was beyond this. Having failed to find a place back in the family, I started focusing again on my constituency. My mind was trapped in this body, and I was craving freedom from this shackle. But, where would I go if not in this body? And equally importantly, the youth would not survive without me either. I was his custodian, or was he mine? Two lives on stake – knowing me, I would not think of taking someone else's life for my sake. So, there I was – nowhere, and nowhere to go.

But they would not even wait for this all to sink in before discharging me from the hospital. The bed-pressure in hospitals in modern healthcare treat patients like things tossed on a conveyor belt. I noted in the diary, 'Morning, 20 July 2025. The nurses have indicated that I should be ready for discharge from the hospital.' In the round, the visiting surgeon was happy with my progress and gave me a plan to return to outpatient clinic for wound examination and medical reviews.

"And, where would I go from here?"

"To your home—should it not be that way?" he was a bit lost, first—his face showing a question mark.

Then, it suddenly eased, "Oh, I see. But I do not know the answer. Perhaps, the Social Service could do something about it. Have they been in? I shall make sure that they are involved before you leave. But, please get ready for discharge from hospital anyway."

The next day, on 21 July 2025, I was given the discharge papers, a list of instructions and a four-week sick-leave note. The nurses wanted to do the packing for me but I had nothing on me to pack. They brought me chocolates, had selfies with me and bade me farewell. But I wouldn't go without seeing my dead body in the mortuary. One step to exit, the other towards the basement. In this altercation, I ambled aimlessly in the corridors looking for the signposts for the mortuary but would keep on missing them, without making a turn. Finally, I had to accept that I should leave without seeing it but agreed with myself that I would attend my funeral.

With these trepidations, I was looking for No. 4D, Noor Crescent, the premises the Social Services had allotted to me. I had signed with them a temporary tenancy until I had sorted out my own place. It was a pretty modern estate with cottage flats sprinkled along the slopy wavy roads and paths, outdone by the green. It was a difficult place to find an address. With the map in hand, I was strolling on the wavy paths. Each time I had walked by an elevation, I could see the glimpses of the city. On this particular summit though, the skyline looked significant: a dome in the centre, with neighbouring taller structures and a clock-tower on the right. This was the City University building. The part of the road next to this cluster, visible from here, showed bustling traffic. Beside it was this building with a small central done, surrounded all around by the green, visible from here in the tangent. Was it my institution? It was - certainly. Under its dome was the lobby and the reception, my own office being not far from this landmark. It wasn't long ago when I was wandering around this area, presiding over meetings, attending training.

With my seniority, the department where one works for so long becomes a kind of second home; for me, now it was the only home. I moved from the scene but kept on reminiscing, thinking of my team in the department of some of the nicest people I knew. I remembered Aurora Bird, my second-in-command, the astute one, a slim built, average height lady, roughly of my age. She was my sidekick, counsel and support during the long years in the job. I felt excited to see my team, specially, Aurora.

These thoughts hitting the mind assured me that I was still capable of hoping, of looking forward. I was happy to find deep down I wanted to live. In the coming days, bracing this hope would be more important than anything else on my sundry to-do list. With these ponderings, I found myself standing on the door of 4D, trying on the lock. The instructions had it that I entered a passcode, quickly to be followed by the key turned, but I could not get the timings right. Eventually, I did what an elderly would be expected to do, which is to knock the door of the neighbour, seeking help.

A boy of around twenty came to the door. To avoid his suspicious looks, I hurriedly explained that I was the new tenant of the flat above them and my current predicament.

"My brother is the right person for this sort of job. He is technical." He said and disappeared. He soon returned, took the key from my hand and sorted the lock in a second. Then, looking at me, completely bamboozled, he smiled and said, "we are twins - identical twins. But I am the doer of the two of us and the guy whom you have spoken to is the thinker, exclusively. I hear that you are our new neighbour."

I nodded, still surprised.

He extended his hand, "I am Nash, and my philosopher brother is Logge. You can trust me for minor house chores. I have our room filled with tools."

I spread my hand towards him, "nice to meet you…I am Oxymoron; work in education. Thanks for your help - and the offer." I smiled back at him, "if you are twins, I am mosaic. Payback in surprise. Now if you want to find it out what it means, come along sometime. And, don't forget to bring your brother." He turned and went downstairs thinking and I gently close my door behind me.

'Now then, what have I got in this house?' A pretty spacious flat, it seemed well provided and fairly neat. I was worried about the type of cushioning in the bed mat and sofa seats. Zeitoun always got it right for me. It was for her to describe the salesperson my preference as neither like brick, for it can hurt, nor too bouncy, for it tires you quickly. I remembered her having hard talk with them, destroying their sales strategy, asking a cut on the price, followed by demanding yet another cut on commission, but particularly, getting the texture of the cushioning right. She was always like this, leading on all kinds of bargaining and in negotiation art. The bed was good but I would need to get few chairs soon, I concluded in my first round of inspection. But then I remembered I did not need to worry too much about back support. After all I was young now. I wanted to make a to-do list. The foremost item was to buy a mirror, a man-height mirror, but the most daunting job was on my calendar, the one of attending a funeral.

# MY FUNERAL

IN THE FUNERAL SERVICE, which was brief and to the point, they prayed for Oxymoron; I prayed for the long life of whatever remained of him. They had arranged for family, friends and colleagues a special service too, which was to take place in a side hall of the building. I went there to attend this part. I guessed none of my acquaintances would recognise me but still did not like being noticed. I quietly walked the side gangway in the hall and found the nearest vacant aisle seat. Coming from the sun, out in full bloom, I found the inside the hall not well-lit. To my vision adapting to the dark, slowly emerged a rostrum and, placed next to it, my coffin, covered with a wreath, made up with Marigold and Tagetes blossom, and a rickety metal bier, on which the coffin was fixed. Zeitoun had obviously remembered the flowers that I liked. Thinking of her and feeling her pain of the moment of separation that morning, I felt the warmth of a solitary tear slipped down my cheek, but obviously I could not go and sit beside her to comfort her.

By now, the things in the hall were becoming visible. It was quite a large place with a classroom seat-plan for about a hundred people. It was pretty basic and practical sort of place, a kind of purpose-made-boring artefact, which scratched my mind. Everything here, the furniture, the wall paintings, the lights, were imbued with sadness; even the air. I felt I was breathing in melancholy all the way and breathing out gloom. The faint murmur of people conversing was punctuated with the ticks from the wall clock. The fragrance from wreath seemed to have a special tinge to it, as if informing about the corps it was covering underneath. I felt increasingly uncomfortable here but resisted leaving, for, of course, I would not leave my own funeral, neither did I want to be noticed leaving earlier.

I looked around. Of the figures present, several I could recognise. It was ironic that in my life I could not get them all, and so many of them, under one roof at any one time.

In the front row was Ayaan sitting, looking like the man in control. He nicely fitted in the army fatigue jacket which I bought for him only last month. At one stage, he turned his face to the row behind him a work friend of mine, Dawn, a cheery figure, and eyed up on her, asking to take the rostrum. The lady introduced herself and picked some interesting items from my biography, quite nice things to the ear, though I would have liked the most important of its features, 'Oxymoron' mentioned as well. How come she forgot it. She might have thought calling a late person with this title was being rude.

Then came on the dice someone from my institution who piped up my professional achievements. With a titanium frame slid down right to his nose tip, this completely bald middle aged read out my praises from a paper as if he was presenting an audit report. Nice words, though I thought only if they could have been matched with equally highlighted support from this official and from his colleagues in HR for me when I was alive. There were those in the management, the skulduggers, who tried to kick me out of job, not once, but twice. Indeed, listening to this discourse made me feel bitter, making me forget there was a coffin in the room and my body in it.

This piece was followed by my profiling by someone from our neighbourhood, who happened to be none other than Lehman. He was sitting on the far end on the front row, with his wife and the lady who was lost in the jungle, with her baby. It was nice that they came, even this lady who barely knew me, apart from one meeting in passing.

He labelled me as a nice friend and a pious, righteous person. Nice friends we were, no doubt, although he forgot that I once had troubled the neighbours on the other side (luckily not him) with a trivial boundary issue. On the subject of my piety, I just had to laugh, for I knew he never thought of me like this in my life. For this overlook or a deliberate mistake, I could forgive him, but for me, I knew that I had been vicious to people, jealous, mean, you name it. I used to steal stationery from the office, though without ever being caught. I wore false modesty over my occult arrogance. When I was nice and generous to the people, I was so to fish for their compliments. The faces of those I had bullied with my eloquence snapped at my face one by one. No, the bottom line is that I wasn't pious at all; I could digest his discourse but just as an attempt at my post-mortem dry-cleaning.

For the next few moments, standing behind the dice, a friend of Zeitoun talked about how nice I had been with my wife's friends. Yes, my wife, I adored her, and yes, to most of her friends I was really nice, for they provided a jovial company to her. But some of her friends I detested, for they regularly tainted her mind with stories of how their husbands had flouted and, as a result, how they got snubbed by these ladies, something of a technique Zeitoun inevitably learned and tried on me, too, frequently.

My uncle, on his turn, acclaimed me as a thoroughly dedicated family man. For God's sake no, my dear Uncle, you know I'd cheated on my wife once; we had even discussed it. O' people, the person whom you try cajoling with these vain scripts cannot hear anything and those who hear them couldn't care less.

But these speeches taught me a lesson or two. I spoke I would rather loudly, 'in the past, you have been vile, Oxymoron. Why don't you try living a life at least now that people have in good faith described you'd lived.'

In the meantime, I saw Ayaan walking to the dice. I quickly took a snap of him walking past the coffin. But before he uttered a word, I'd left the scene. I would not bear his pain at the time of his father departing from him. I gave myself all kinds of excuses for leaving but deep inside, out of shock, I had lost awareness. I felt forlorn in that room. The clock was ticking on my burial. How could I witness it and remained sane? What if someone asked me to help lifting the coffin, or to help lowering it in the grave. Maybe I would start belly laughing my head off. Or else, I would behave in one of the other manners inappropriate for the occasion, causing disrespect to my own funeral and disgrace to myself. I also questioned myself what I was doing around, alive, during my own burial. I realised whether I'd witnessed the occasion or not, whether I had died or alive, the body in the coffin was mine. Soon, they would take the coffin to the cemetery, at which point, the chapter on my bodily living would ultimately close. From here would emerge a strange era of my non-bodily living. Obviously, this era had already started. I returned home, strangely feeling accomplished, as if, with the burial, I had achieved something heroic. As its mark, I had another look at the pictures of my dead body and pasted beside them the picture of my coffin.

# SERENE SOLILOQUYS

THERE WAS NOTHING much of the physical ailment from which to recover during the period of sick leave; however, there were riptides of thoughts sweeping me to the deep waters. Every so often, I attended to the guy-in-the-mirror to get used to him. Trying to negotiate peace with this guy, hoping resolution, I let the debates on the conflict to be had freely. Let me share some of these soliloquies and monologues giving insight of what went on.

I would start by asking me, 'so what is it that you have against the youth being with you?'

*'Nothing personal really; just why should I be forced to reside with anyone, let alone within someone. I am in a cockpit that I cannot leave during the plane in flight? This truly is life-imprisonment, isn't it? Which of the wrongs that I have done is this punishment for?'*

I would say, 'come on; it is not that bad. Not finding this new home, where would you be right now? with some rotting bones in the earth. This body, man! this is a gift. Living in cockpit is caging if the plane in parked; fly it and have fun. You are as free in it as other people are in their bodies, aren't you? In fact, you are even more privileged now than before.'

*'How?'*

'Now, you are handsome, young and strong. Come on; don't get me started on this one. For long, you did not play badminton with your old, paining knees. Pretty recently, you were gasping for air while going upstairs; now hike mountains - no problem."

*'Would I really be able to play badminton; really! I guess for this I would have to train this new person from the scratch,'* a spark twinkled inside me, though, it fizzled out as quickly, *'Has playing badminton now become the purpose of life? Do not be so silly.'*

'OK, if badminton does not charm you, how about freedom from the infirmaries of the elderly with which you were stricken, their list rocketing by the day.'

*'That sounds much better, though I don't like the foot size now, too big; and don't ask me about the legs.'*

'What about the legs', I started smiling.

*'As if this pair has been borrowed off from a Gypsy horse. I have not imagined this much fluff on human legs before, for God's sake, no.'*

37

'We can go on and on. You must realise there were limitations with your previous body, and there are some issues with this new one, too: it breaks even, does it not?' I had already realised the mistake in using the word 'limitation'.

*'Don't play with words. What I said was that I felt limited in this new body, not that I experienced limitations with it.'*

'OK, fine, you feel limited in the body of the youth. How about his body made a slave to you? Would that not be its limitation greater than yours?'

*'Yes; perhaps, it is – indeed; but, you see, the bodies don't think. You know it is only a problem of the minds.'*

'Since when has the power to think become a curse?' I hammered the iron feeling it was hot by now.

That said had caused a little shift in the prevailing views. There was a blissful flicker that passed through my heart. I had a moment of wordless thinking. In fact, I felt grateful for being a part of the arrangement with this new body.

\*\*\*

Yet another session went like this:

'Now, what is wrong with you?' I would start.

*'I miss my face, my body.'*

'Just for the sake of it?' I spoke.

*'That's being cruel. With the face, I have lost my identity, and you think it is something frivolous. Everyone likes their face, give or take a few. Without my face, I feel alienated from myself; I have been torn apart, literally.'*

I said, 'agreed; you have indeed been separated from your body; but, equally, you have been stapled with another one, possibly a better one. What about those who lose their limbs or the eyes or something of the sort, in wars and in accidents, but get nothing in return, or just a limb of wood, or an eye of stone. You lost all in an accident, yes; in return, you get all anew, live and real. And, you know that people can be asked to pay for these things, for a wooden limb, a face-lift and for a nose job. You have got it all for free and one of the best ones.'

*'It is pretty ironic, isn't it? You do not really understand what an identity crisis can be, do you? You think a body of someone else better than mine must be better for me.'*

The mood had grown hostile, so I kept quiet, fearing more to come.

*This crisis is not just about facial identity. The youth has invaded my character, too. I hope you appreciate how one in their mature years can be embarrassed of feeling juvenile, inappropriate, unpredictable. While I am expecting to take time getting up from chair, this new arrangement prompts me to run. Like a powerful Ferrari in the hands of a senior citizen – I simply don't know how to handle this machine?'*

I was irritated with the continuing contention here, 'What about when, in the past, you got up in the morning and would not see a thing until you found your specs, busying your one hand, and, with the other, you held the bed rail so that you could get on your feet. And, then, one day, you suddenly realised that you could in fact see without specs and sprint right from the bed without having to hold the rails. Ferrari or no Ferrari, that is what you've got now; just deal with it.'

*'I promise I will; but please see for yourself if any of these ideas make sense: a senior director, of 25 years of age; a son of the parents who are younger than him; a father of the age of his children. Bizarre, isn't it?'*

With these funny and weirdly wonderful comparisons, I just erupted into a laughter, at which point, quickly, I had to put my hand on my mouth to mute it, lest the startling noise of my laughter would go wild. On this lighter note, the interchange ended.  Then, there was yet another moment of wordless thinking.

***

In another session, a monologue would open with something like this:

'So, what is that which makes you sad?' I would ask.

*'My family has forsaken me.'*

'At least, you know they are healthy and busy with their lives. You appreciate children must exit their nests one day, sooner or later, only to return to their parents on occasions or on events. Or, they would now and then just send a greeting card. Then, there comes a time when you even look for a greeting card and don't see one, for months and then for years.'

*'Your account is depressing. Children leave nest, true; but, Zeitoun and I could have been together in waiting for chicks to return, to revisit.'*

The argument had entered impasse but I decided to change the tack, 'you never know things with your family might take a turn to you favour.'

*'How do you mean?'*

'That which appears as an end to the road may be a just a bend in it. Why don't you try something entirely different here? If returning to your family as the man of the house was not possible, how about returning to them as a family-friend?'

Another sparkle glittered in me. This was a big one, very bright. I suddenly remembered Aliya's last glimpse of her leaving the hospital room when she gave me a peculiar look and, with this, left hope with me. *Who knows?* I spoke.

*** 

Another of these sessions would go like this:

I asked, 'Now what is it this time?'

*Things scare me – the things ahead.*

I asked, 'so, what is it that scares you the most?'

*Doom; alienation from the society, depression, you name it.*

I responded, 'doom. Why?'

*I see total dark as to what the future holds. My previous body mellowed over the long years; with this new one I go astray surely. Will embarrass me one day, I bet. You know what happened in the hospital when the nurse came with her face close to my face while checking on my breathing.*

'Why is it a problem?' I smiled.

*Not just a problem, it is a big nuisance. You know the desires; the lowly desires of the youth, which can make you feel lecherous.*

I said, 'but, the trained minds should be able to hold a bull by its horns and a snake bare-handed. If anything, yours will be an exciting example of battles of mind with body.'

And, there was another pause for wordless thinking.

# LET IT GO

TIRED OF TUSSLES AND internal wrangles, that evening I decided to unwind. I let go the fears of the future and let in the pleasures of the past. My mum and dad were not alive now but the memory of my adolescence with them was a pleasure in solid. Our house was a standalone small edifice in a newer state in the periphery of the city, still developing with lot of masonry work around. I was a keen observer and used to slip away from home to watch them working. Once my father asked me what I wanted to be when grown up, I said, "a mason, that is what I want to be."

My mum hugged me; my father laughed, "you must be watching a lot of the building work these days?"

We used to have a piece of land, not far from the state, my father used for agricultural farming and its smaller part as an orchard. We even had a swath in it reserved for growing vegetables for our own use. There was a house in the middle of it and a barn besides it, but both were unused. My father once explained that we did not live here but in the city for my schooling.

My father would leave for the farm early in the morning and return by the time I would be getting ready for the school. When I grew up, especially during school vacations, my father would take me to the farm to ease him in small chores, helping in weeding, pruning, picking up loose fruit and like. He would say to my mum, "our son is tough like a natural farmer, but I prefer he went for higher education in science or something like that."

An assortment of the stories from that part of life zigzagged in my mind. My dad had a bike, which, when I grew up a bit, he got a child-saddle fixed on its top tube. I would step on the pedal, from where my dad would give me a hand in my launching on the saddle. If by any chance he had picked me up without my stepping on the pedal, I would be completely upset until he reversed the whole process and let me have it my way. What can you say: that was me? With my parents, I got things my way, I could afford that I got them my way.

My mum used to have a hand-run sewing machine which she would use to sew our clothes. I suppose then every household must have one, - that was kind of time on families – with not many readymade clothing available on the high street. She would sometimes let me run the wheel of the machine while she would focus on the finish seam of the cloth. I liked this job so much that I should happily add brooming the floors to barter for it. My mum was passionate for me, their only child, to get into life sooner. She would frequently talk about my future, particularly about my bride, an imaginary girl, tall, pretty and whatnot, arriving from Ferryland. Around the time I got my first job, a family, old friends of my parents, visited us for few days that summer, and she, their eldest daughter, Zeitoun her name, was with them. We had a chance for a brief conversation and that was it. We were engaged. Would I by any chance then know that this girl, who was about to enter my life, I would leave, in a manner unheard, leaving behind just poignant memoirs?

From the memory of that bright summer morning when I had the first word with Zeitoun, my imagination, skipping all in between spanning around 25 years, reached the date 14 July 2025, reached another summer morning. It was a morning blushed with shy sunshine mottled with thin debris of high clouds, when I departed from Zeitoun the last time. As usual standing in our terrace, she bid me farewell for the day, and that was it; she bid me farewell for the life. I left home to meet the moment; the moment when my life switched paths, with a lorry out of the blue hitting my car. All that endured by me in this briefest of the moments indeed would need an epoch to relive.

# THE CAGEY SELF

S UDDENLY I ROUSED FROM the nostalgic past, realising the supermarket would be closing early for the Sunday and my kitchen supplies had bottomed out. On the way, I ran into the twins. I must say they were exceptionally well-groomed chaps. The one with the blue shirt reminded about me the word 'mosaic'.

"You must be Logge, is that right?" I thought he was the philosopher one, surmising on the term that I had told Nash. I noticed he was wearing a blue shirt, while his brother Nash was a white shirt.

'Yes, I am interested in your story, though I shall bring Nash with me, if that is OK. Nash, you told me about this. Would you like to come? We usually like to be together."

"Of course, come anytime; we shall have fun."

On the way back, my both hands were laden with four bagfuls of grocery and I was thinking walking home would be tough. I saw them again. They offered to offload me. Reaching home, I asked them to stay for cold drinks. Sitting side by side, they amazed me with the exact match between them, between their voices, even their gestures. "I guess you have to agree to a dress code on daily basis to tell who is who."

"True – though we are lucky; my brother is not bothered about colours, which give me free hand in choosing a colour that I like," said Logge in an indifferent tone.

Nash raised his hand, "No; I just accept your choice, out of respect." He then turned his face towards me, "I have told this joke a thousand times before. Logge is older than me by a minute or so, that is on the witness of our mum, which means unfortunately I have to show some respect to him."

They spent the next few seconds in scanning the place, "wasteful amount of packing they use for deliveries these days," said Logge, the guy with the blue shirt, looking at the half-open package from what was delivered this morning.

"Yes, but they pack computers perhaps more carefully. I like this brand for working on graphics… I prepare presentation and stuff like that on it. I used to have a similar one but left it in my previous place. For other work… and for surfing, I use laptop - faster and handy."

"O, seems like some serious work you do. What do you do?" asked Nash.

"I'm into kind of research."

I was waiting to reveal but felt I should wait; the ice between us had not yet melted enough. I asked them to make themselves comfortable. I pulled the package near to me and started unpacking. I knew their stories of confusions they must have caused around to be in high demand, yet I asked, making it something asked in passing, "guys, the two of you must have muddled the minds of many; have you ever confused your parents, too."

Nash laughed, "yes the parents as well. Logge has a skin birthmark, which I don't. In our early speechless years, it was with this mark, our parents used to make out who's who." His laughter gained volume, "though there was a problem here – a big problem. The mark was in his nappy area. Imagine how many times they would have pulled our nappies down just to find out who's who. That might be fine in private, but then, mum once needed to do this manoeuvre in public, on which she apparently apologises when she mentions the incident."

Not wanting to petrify them with my strange maniacal laughter, I controlled it with difficulty. In said, "a far… car, a real … farce."

He quickly came in, "it is not finished yet. She keeps on reminding us about this event now and then. It does not stop here. She shares this tale with our friends and cousins." He looked at Logge, "tell him what happened when Maria heard this from mum the other day?" Nash looked at me, "Maria is Logge's friend." Logge hid his face behind his palms. Nash finished the saga, "Mum told the story to Maria in our presence."

"So, how did Maria react?" I became impatient.

"She was first embarrassed, then she cheekily screeched a laugh, then she burst into a belly laughter, eventually ended in choking."

"O, my God, this tale is real comedy gold. What a lively mum you have. I tell you what, this must be your payback for the troubles the two of you must have caused your mum."

"Lucky; half of them she even does not know," Logge said.

Atmosphere had softened by now.

Logge said, "you don't mind asking a question!"

I was attentive.

"The way you talk is different, kind of … you know … like old people talk. Sorry, but the whole thing is peculiar, you see. I mean you… you are of our age

44

- Ok, plus or minus a few years - but you are different, I mean, in your behaviour. For goodness's sake I don't know what I am saying - you know what I mean!"

Nash added, "why don't you say it frankly, Logge. Oxymoron, you look young but sound like dad; look at the words like comedy gold, payback, etcetera. In fact, let me admit, we have talked this on your back – dying to find out why."

"Well done guys, you are not far from the truth. I look young and, yes, I behave old, yes again. So then, you have got the first glimpse of the mosaic person," I enjoyed my story released little by little.

"Yes, but that is the question - exactly. How come?"

"In fact, I am 58 - past 58-mark last month," I handed them coke in glasses, "would you like some ice cubes?"

They both slowly tossed their head in unison to say no.

"Is it a no to ice or to my age?"

They kept looking at me.

"You might have heard of an Oxymoron?" I asked.

"So, then!"

"If you haven't, Oxymoron is a director in Public Intelligence."

"So!"

"But that's not why he is famous."

From this point, I rehearsed to them some salient bits from my story, while they kept staring at me, weighing my words against my appearance. I showed them from my phone-gallery the pictures of my dead body, also some Google images of older version of Oxymoron. It was Nash, the chap with white shirt – that's how I remembered who's who - who asked the next question, "how they managed to join two people into one so neatly?"

Logge outshined this question with one of his own, "why do you think you are Oxymoron and not the youth?"

"Because if I had said I were the youth, I would have to go to college to start again." We all laughed. I continued, "No – in fact, ownership by category happens to be a thought; its claimant has to be the thinker, and thinker lodges in the brain where thinking takes place. Bodies cannot think; they only belong."

I noticed they were deep in thinking, so I continued, "the example I am going to quote here may not completely fit but, you know, it is the jockey who gets the prize for the toil of the thoroughbred …"

Logge did not let me complete, "so – wait a minute – are you saying that you are the 58-year-old brain to which I am talking. Is that right? Against what I know, that is, I am talking to a young-looking man… An incredible situation, really."

I said, "if you ask me, similarly I am also talking to the brains, the two young brains."

"I have never thought that way," said Logge. Nash nodded in agreement.

I said, "you both look the same, of course – that is being identical twins. So, when I talk to you, Logge, if I were to talk to your face, which is the same as Nash's face, I might as well be talking to Nash. This must be an absurd situation, and, to avoid it, it must be accepted that when I talk to you, I must talk to your brain, through your face and through the paraphernalia arranged on it but not to your face. Remember your brain is unique to you but not your face, quite apparently."

Nash said, "I differ… no… The brain is a part of the body. In twins, like their bodies, their brains must also be the same. Remember, the physicality is solely dictated by the gene bank, something I and my brother share between the two of us. Remember, we are identical twins."

I smiled, "well- that is true. Is Biology your major, Nash?"

Logge raised his hand, "in fact, Nash will soon be finishing a degree in Genetics; he is brilliant at it – given - it suits to his mechanical instinct. But the question in front of us is of Philosophy, which is my realm, and I must tell you I am rather good at it."

The boys looked at each other with adoration, imitating envy. I enjoyed the moment.

I continued, "beautiful; perhaps if together you could work up this question."

Nash schooled us with an account of human development. He ended up by saying: "you can see how a human person is simply a piece of engineering art. It starts with genes, first laying the foundation, then adorning it with organs."

He continued, "by way of example, first, genes construct rudiment of the skull; in the second go, they fabricate a rudimentary brain in it, etcetera."

"In the brain, like in a metropolis, genes lay a rail-road network, populate it with stations, rest-houses, lodges and towns plus also build a city as its capital. In this network run the thoughts, managed and hoarded in the populated areas."

Logge intervened, "if that is the case, this they must do even without the prior knowledge of who will be the residents in this metropolis or how they will be using it."

Logge had made a stunning statement. Its value was clear, but for now I wanted them to pursue a different course. I intervened, "identical gene map between the two of you – identical brain structure, essentially comprising identical blueprint of the tracks and circuits. – everything is identical between you. If the main function of the brain is to think, the two of you must think in the same way - I mean, exactly the same, all the times." I looked at them intensely, waiting for a response.

Nash said, "no, surely, we don't think in the same way all the time."

I said, "is it not then the case that the genes don't poke their nose in the business of thinking."

Logge responded, "you have got it right. That is what I have nearly said earlier. On one side, the architect doesn't know the future resident of the building it has laid out, genes being the architect, thoughts the resident. On the other side, the resident arrives at its allotted places in the building without prior knowledge of the building-layout. The two are of different genres, belonging to two different worlds."

Nash said, "I disagree. I disagree that thoughts arrive in the brain. What if thoughts did not have to arrive? What if they were in fact mere upshots of the physicality itself – as simple as that?"

"To assign conscious thought to genes is simply ridiculous, impossible to test and disprove," Logge said.

Nash raised the question, "not the genes but the physical structure that they lay, which props up thoughts. That is what I have said. Is it not the case that brain damage affects thinking and consciousness? Let us not forget the genetic predispositions for different psychological conditions, for example depression, bipolar states, etcetera."

Logge replied, "don't draw me to a slippery slope, Nash. An association does not have to be cause-and-effect. Roads have not caused the cars that run on the road, nor the cars have caused the roads. In the same coin, physicality and thought are two different species. A physical structure giving rise to thoughts is as unlikely as thought giving rise to structure. Thoughts are metaphysical quantities."

I intervened, "OK, let us concede the minimum that the metaphysical run on the physical road-rail network in the brain."

They kept quiet, looking at me in a peculiar way. I realized I had just managed to repeat the obvious. Goodness me, these boys were so unforgiving. Anyway, I thought this was good point to progress. I said, "thus you match between the two of you in physical appearance and in the brain structure, both attributed to your identical gene map. From here, in the metaphysical department, you depart from each other, hence one aspiring philosophy, the other genetics. Yet, the two of you are more likely to match in your thoughts than two genetically unrelated people can match between their thoughts. Can you examine this problem?"

There was a bit of distraction, which bothered me. Logge made a ring of his thumb and index finger of right hand and rotated it over the other wrist, pushing his wristwatch upward. He rubbed the skin where its metallic buckle was and said, "I think I have nickel allergy. Nash, would you like to try this watch? In fact, this allergy, you would have as well, for sure. For God's sake, it is horrible."

"Don't you remember that blue dial-watch, Logge? I already have the allergy. Mum said she would find me a nickel-free one."

I intervened, "you see this is another match here, although of physical nature. The similarities in your thoughts or behaviour may be countless, though there are some stark differences as well."

Logge laughed, "clearly there has to be therefore more to the story than what identical genes can dictate."

Nash ignored the rib, "this proves my point that thought don't arrive in the brain but prop up locally. We have agreed that the genetic instructions go as far as laying the road-rail tracks. Perhaps these tracks are set such that they provide a multi-purpose competence that can be trained to use in different intellectual operations, mathematics, logic, poetry, etcetera.[1] in other words, genes only lay the hardware; and hardware creates the software …."

---

[1] Yulia Kovas and Robert Plomin. Learning Abilities and Disabilities. *Current Directions in Psychological Science*. Vol 16:5. 2007

I said, "that is good explanation. But … then… of course, quite clearly, you, the two of you, must be pretty close on several things, habits, likings, temperament."

Logge said, "we share the hardware – we also share home, mum and dad, cousins, school, teachers, for God's sake so much we share. We were brought-up in a particular environment. Equal in age, capacity, in many things, we perhaps have been groomed in parallel, hence we share more features than siblings of different age would do; yet we differ because we have different inclinations."

Boxing his hand on Logge's knee, giggling, Nash looked at me, "please ignore for-God's-sake in his speech. Another of his bad habits."

"And you don't have to parrot out *et-cet-ra* every so often." Logge reciprocated, this time banging Nash's knee with a thump.

With tapping of my pen, I gaveled the two to order, "boys, I am trying to focus."

Logge said, "do you mind if we could have top-up coke, this time with ice?"

I staggered to the kitchenette to fetch some ice.

Logge sipped his coke and crushed a cube between his teeth. Suddenly, he took off in a different mode, "it is a situation of half-glass-full or half-glass empty. It is clear that we have identical genes, also our brain structures being identical. You may like to bag everything else with this lot, the personality and the behaviour, the likes and the dislikes, intelligence, the experiences and thoughts, the cognisance - for God's sake, put everything you can think about the person in this closet. But, does that sharing – the ultimate sharing - of all the thinkable personal properties make you and me as one entity… as one individual?"

"That is not possible," Nash said.

"What is not possible: reaching the perfect match or becoming one individual?" Logge asked.

Nash replied, "neither. The one depends on the other. My reaching a perfect match with you in the business of thoughts is impossible which makes me a distinct self."

Logge asserted, "no; we are two separate individuals whether we have different thoughts or we don't. The self is the ultimate, unshared artefact in an individual."

The lines had clearly been drawn. The moot point had been reached. I waited. There was more to come.

Logge continued, "we are separate individuals because we demand justice done between us. Because my hunger satiated would not automatically kill yours. We are two irreplaceable selves, and to remain thus, whatsoever." He ran his fingers in his thick hair, "the notion of 'two' applied to things simply tells them apart – people no different."

He paused here, sipped the coke with dying fizz, making a face.

Nash was silent. I said, "so despite any number of similarities, you remain as two individuals, meaning individuality is an independent feature of the person – As simple as that - awesome." I looked at them.

I continued, "can we then elucidate the origin of the self if it has nothing to do with genes, even with the learnings."

Nash ignored my question, "I disagree. I see my own self based on what I think and how I conduct thinking. Logge, you must know the fallacy in your arguments. Why two people seek justice between them is because they want to settle a difference in their thoughts. Your argument that hunger being subjective posits the notion of an independent self, to which I can agree, but it does not decipher the nature of self."

He continued, "I repeat that the distinction of a self relies on the distinction of the thoughts it holds. If it is all about thoughts, then the self is nothing but a conglomerate of thoughts running in a unit, in a person. A separate existence of a SELF is thus superfluous. Why do you have to invent this entity separate from thoughts?"

Logge said, "what if that is the case."

Nash got irritated, "the place (he nodded at his brain) has nerve cells laid by genes, a valid scientific phenomenon. Then, under duress, we have admitted a metaphysical commodity in it, that of thoughts. Now you are pleading also for another one, a SELF, to join the club. It would swamp the place and ruin its simplicity."

Logge replied, "after finishing the physical, the genes are called off from the duty. Then they should not be concerned with the metaphysical. Materialism does not concern the metaphysical."

Nash said, "no, that is not true; you can use electronic means to spy on the thoughts running in the road-rail network in the brain. Even there are gadgets available to locate stations and towns in the brain where certain types of thoughts are cooked and where they are hoarded."

Logge said, "true, but these clever gadgets only inform about the electrical activity, a side effect that thoughts generate in the network in the brain. To comprehend these signals as thoughts in the form that humans understand, you need humans, conscious human, to understand; nothing else would work."

Nash rolled his eyes, "Logge, Logge, your enthusiasm is unsurpassable."

Logge said, "you mean I should try condensing my enthusiasm. Here it is: may I assert that consciousness is an attribute of the self, not of thoughts."

He continued, "thoughts may indeed be nothing more than electric signals until they are comprehended by consciousness, like soundwaves are silent until they find an ear or photons dark until they find an eye."

Nash kept quiet.

Logge sipped from his coke, which was by now dead, and said, "the story goes beyond. The sound is silent even beyond the ear and light dark beyond the eye until they find the consciousness."

The twins were unstoppable; they had so far clashed fiercely on the nature of the SELF.

Nash said, "can I go step by step?"

Logge said, "you always take the longest route! It annoys the hell out of me."

Nash got annoyed, "because it is good for your health." But then he smiled, "but perhaps it is hard on your brain… sorry."

We all laughed.

Nash continued, "OK, then, take the example of artificial intelligence. The entity called self is not separately installed in its design nor it is found in it. In fact, you cannot even construct this entity. Yet artificial intelligence works fantastically."

Logge said, "artificial intelligence is about intelligence, not about consciousness. Albeit, its input values are consciously prepared, output values consciously comprehended."

There was a long quiet pause. They were probably deciding who was the winner, and who would be licking the wound.

Logge asserted, "by all means, consciousness is different from the thoughts it is supposed to comprehend.

"OK, so where do you see this self sitting, this conscious being of yours?" Nash provoked.

Logge said, "I see a special lodge in the metropolis in the brain layout, reserved for the self with a blank plaque gummed on its face wall. The title of the self neatly clacks on the plaque into the slot sculpted for it, the clack which starts the life. Intellectual faculties taking their turns in arriving at their corresponding stations in the metropolis. From the small years of life, these faculties smoulder, learning to hurl thoughts along the rail-road network, ready to get cracking at the time approaching maturity, or else this process, getting to the speed, in fact precipitates maturity."

There was an awesome silence. I broke it, "Nash, you have laid the foundation of this discussion, and Logge, you have finished it - with graceful simplicity.".

My intrusion did not seem to break the silence.

In the meantime, the doorbell rang. I attended at the door to receive a nice-looking mature lady, who boldly pronounced a hello. And, there was this snubbing look that she showered at me as if to say, 'o' you, get out of my way'. Nash yelled from inside, "yes Mum, what's up?"

She swiftly extended her hand to grasp my hand from the fingers, straightened it palm-up and tossed a cell phone on my palm, "a call for Nash the caller says is urgent."

"You mean, for the guy with the birthmark on his nappy area?"

Surprised, she allowed herself a slight smile. Nash came to the door, took the phone from my hand and put it to his ear, at the same time spreading his hand towards his mum asking her to wait. He quickly finished the call and introduced me, "Mum, this is Oxymoron; Oxymoron, this is my mum."

"Oxymoron!!! Is that your real name!" she ridiculed me.

"Yes," Nash intervened. "A Director at notorious Public Intelligence. He is 58."

She rolled her eyes, tossed her head, turned about and walked away. We returned to our seats. I laughed, "Nash, I bet you wouldn't try on my intro again."

Once settled, I tried to restore the discussion with a question, "clearly the SELF has the duty to comprehend electrical signals as thoughts. Surely, it must have other duties assigned in its job plan."

Logge said, "the self receives thoughts for which it relies on road-rail networks, and, to integrate them, it employs stations, lodges and towns. For itself, it is housed somewhere in the city, at the final destination of all intellectual processes. It conducts these roles purely for its own purpose, the intellectual purpose."

He continued, "the intellectual purpose is served with selection of certain thoughts over others. It is the self that selects, thereby commands the intellectual operations of gaining knowledge, acquiring learnings, collecting experiences, holding beliefs, feeling emotions, maintaining memory, recognising faces, telling truths from lies and the rest."

"The self, the metaphysical, for this purpose uses the physicality of the brain," he spread his hands, as if, at this point, he rested his case.

Nash quickly picked the last point, "it has to be the case. What else if not physicality on which the self relies? After all, we have come back to the same point that the self is nothing outside the physicality it depends, haven't we?"

Logge laughed, "we have just agreed earlier that the genes lay the structure, wash their hands off and go home."

"Yes. But, along with the rest of environmental factors. they can complete the whole person, including thoughts and your new buddy, the self," Nash was clearly sarcastic.

Logge said, "Nash, what is your main anxiety about the self as an independent entity?"

Nash said, "by dropping the possibility of the self manufactured in situ, we have to accept that the self is installed on the brain. From this point, you would argue for existence of an independent source for the self. From there, I guess, your job would be easy. You have already alluded to such a source when talking about genes setting up the physicality. Then you said the genes lay a structure without the knowledge of how this structure is going to be used, and by whom. I guess, from here, I am sure, you would argue that the one who has installed the self must have conceived it first, and then must have instructed the genes to engineer an edifice to receive this self and the family of its intellectual aides – you can add moral faculties in the list as well. This argument is simply a case bordering at the realm of religion."

Logge clasped his hands together to make a fist, on which to rest his face, bowed a little and looked up at his brother with a smile, "fantastic – so that is your worry."

He looked at me, ignoring Nash, "I sometime wonder how people used to think before Darwin, or perhaps, as Darwinists strongly believe, people before them did not think at all?"

He asked his brother, "if you are a Darwinist, you are absolutely limited: you have to put all your eggs in the Darwinism-basket whether it has enough space for them or not."

He gazed at me, "if we must as well put these eggs in that basket, let us ask Nash for help as I have not studied Evolution examining the self. Nash, what is the position of Darwinism on the existence of the self."

Nash replied, "no, not the self, I have not studied it in any serious way."

Logge said, "no blame for arguing for Evolution, with which one deciphers biology, because it is so much in fashion. But you see, everybody assumes its truth in a every case even before knowing it is the case. I worry this mode potentially debilitating my ability to reflect if I am in place of Nash."

Nash changed the tack, "for a start, people have even doubted the self itself as an illusion. I can quote some authorities here."

Logge said, "not sure of this, but I know for sure that there isn't an entity in biology not attended by Evolution and the one not attended is outrightly discarded. I fear the state of the self is an example of the unfortunate ones."

Nash rolled his eyes, "then, let us have your thoughts on the self?"

I smiled with joy in anticipation.

Logge said, "please bear with me for a minute or two to explain. You know the famous maxim by Descartes 'I think therefore I am'. Since intending is an operation of thinking, would you agree its corollary as 'I intend therefore I am' is justified? Thoughts have intimate relation with the self and its existence. They can be reared by the self or are portrayed on it. Subtly differently, intending is a function of the self. The self exists because it intends. And, intention exists because it can be frustrated or advanced. My plan to work late at night can succumb to my irresistible sleep. The other way around, I can resist the thought of food even when the data in my brain hold me as hungry, food is available and I love it. I must therefore exist as a self to guide, resist and choose thoughts and actions via my intentions."

He had a sip of coke and continued, "but to respond to your question more directly, I shall take the example of stroke patients with paretic limbs. These patients can be helped with physical rehabilitation. The success of any such intervention requires the patient to have the force of intention behind the plan, which is the will to move the limb. Interestingly, the intention when present can be recorded by detectors."

Nash got particularly interested, "how do you know this, Logge?"

"From a physiotherapy Instructor. Remember my summer internship this year in the rehabilitation center near the superstore."

Logge returned to the topic, "if you were looking for further evidence for the self, here it is. During rehabilitation, some of these patients get frustrated and angry with the slow progress. What does this indicate? You get disappointed when you cannot achieve that which you want to achieve. This – want – is in fact an intention-not-met. It is therefore clear that intention must exist separately from thought, indicating to existence of a self as the agent intending."

"Intention separately from thought!" I asked.

"Yes, thought of food is different from the intention of taking it. Thoughts are for the self to manage; intentions are from the self."

Nash first kept quiet, then he nodded his head sideways, "you have built a sand castle, Logge. You have very cleverly evaded my objection."

"Which objection?"

"Why are some psychiatric illnesses associated with genes defects if it were not because of genes that we do thinking and the rest of intellectual stuff?"

Logge said, "it is not because of the edifice that the genes lay that we do thinking; it is rather with it that we do this function."

He continued, "bad genes lay faulty network and shoddy stations. Such distorted layout impedes thought process. What do you do if the front door of your house is not big enough to let pass the big piece of furniture you have bought? You try various things to get this piece in. You can turn the package sideways, use the larger backyard door, buy a smaller size piece, get the door resized or you live with the old piece. Likewise, how does the self manage a damaged network? It learns to squeeze its way through it; it uses an alternative circuit; it changes its mode of thinking; or it succumb to the defective mode. To avoid the last option, people can use medicines to alter the circuit itself."

"It sounds nice - but as you just said, medicines work on the network. How do recreational drugs work if the brain is one thing and thought another? They work on the brain, yet create new mental states, happy thoughts," Nash pushed the point a little further.

"They do, of course. But their bad impact on thought is through meddling with the chemistry of the circuits that these drugs cause. They meddle with the doors and channelise their thoughts through different ways. We should not forget that door in the story is a facilitating factor as well as a limiting factor," Logge said.

Nash tossed his head, "if thought can only be as precise as the health of the brain allows it to be, what is the need to postulate the thought being independent of genes, and self independent of thought?"

Logge looked at his brother with a smile, "you are back at questioning the existence of self." His face was glowing with passion, his eyes focused, "if you really are stuck there, we should not forget that the two of us have identical gene-set and brain structure, yet are at odds with each other – right now. After all, why?"

Nash was quiet.

"Nash, let me put my case in a different way."

Nash remained quiet but interested.

"You know our mum and dad love us dearly, more than anything else. If physicality is the whole story, we must assume that this special love must have travelled with the genes transferred from parents to kids."

"Yes, I agree."

I had been noticing Socratic dialectic method that Logge had been using, showing his grooming.

"But, then, the question we want to resolve is how come parents love their kids. They have only donated their genes to the kids rather than acquiring the genes from them."

He continued, "you have to accept that gene have not dictated this special love, an emotion which only orchestrates itself in situ on the mind. I know people have attempted to explain this under the guise of 'selfish genes, but in this construction, the word 'genes' is superfluous, leaving the self to act."

"OK-ish," Nash nodded his head.

I was almost certain that Nash had wanted to pursue the argument further, perhaps using the point of evolutionary advantage of parental love but he was little exhausted. Indeed, by now we all must be worn out. They both got up at once, these twins. I thanked them for their time.

Nash looked at his brother, "Logge, thank God, time is over on your elaborate explanations, etcetera. I was nearly fossilised."

Logge replied, "thank God that you moved step by step, albeit at a tardy pace, for God's sake…"

Nash sniffed, "do you smell something burning…? in the kitchen. Oxymoron, what have you done there?"

"Oh, disaster, chips in the oven… for you guys. No timer on. Sorry." I rushed to the kitchen to switch off the oven. The chips had carburised.

I praised the young men again, but on my lip was lurking a question, with my eyes on Logge.

Logge took the praise with a smile but winked to the question, "I know what you are thinking. If you were thinking to find out who I think the self actually is, I am out."

I sighed, "I know. Anyway thanks." The question of nature of the self thus remained for me the most elusive one ever since - but it would remain my quest.

Near the door, Logge paused, "you know why I don't know the self? Because I am not a witness to its synthesis; I only begin with it. I am not aware of its installation on the brain, the installation of this utterly unshared, outrightly grand artefact of the individually individual self."

Nash looked at me, nodding at his brother with a tender but impish smile, "I am proud of this bloke. Sometimes, he even amazes me." He then blinked his eyes a couple of times and rolled them by half a circle. I was sure they would have continued wrangling between them even after they had left.

# OXYMORON AT WORK

SESSION AFTER SESSION, day after day, cycles of wordless thinking alleviated my identity crises and emboldened me to face the challenge. And, then, the questions of the self amply pursued by the two young people made me feel important in the mosaic, rekindling my urge to live. By and large, my inner turmoil resolved such that nearing my return to work, I was almost ready with my usual demeanour with robust mind and jolly heart. But, the one issue I did not dare to touch was of my imminent meeting with my 'wife', which the parents of the youth had mentioned. I did not have the language with which to reflect on this subject, nor could I predict with any clarity her expectations from me or her reaction to this new situation. I left this boat floating on the waters.

It was the morning of Monday the 15th September, 2025, when I was getting ready for the job. I spent some good time in front of the mirror trying to adopt afresh the guy-in-the-mirror and to adapt myself to him. One minute of buoyancy and the other of ifs and buts, in these pulls and pushes, I was baffled. Only if I knew what to expect, as most of that on the way was of the unknown. Though, one name repeatedly came to mind, Aurora, the team leader of the research group working with me, the cultured Aurora Bird. She had been with me all along my career - in fact, we both started in the department on the same day. With posh mannerisms, she had throughout been my soul mate.

I arrived at the reception around 10.00 am. Jill, our reception clerk, greeted with her usual formal greetings. Rustling through papers in front of her, she asked if she could help. I simply asked for Aroura, not ready yet to open my Pandora box. Without raising her head, she asked if Aurora was expecting me and, without waiting my answer, she asked me to wait, nodding to the chairs along the wall. A moment later, I saw Aurora gracefully emerging from the darker side of the corridor. Just as the sunflower wakes up with the sun, I was cheered up by looking at her and moved my eyes with her.

She saw me from distance and leapt for few steps, swaying on the sides, showing how perked up she was at sighting me. A familiar breezy smile on her face told me she had known all about me, perhaps also seen my pictures in the news cuttings. She even tried to hug me, something that came to me as a complete surprise. My forceful hesitation shocked her. Clearly, something was not right between the two confused people. We settled on the chairs along the wall. She looked away from me, not speaking, with her hands busy in tics. I could not bear the silence any more. I slid side-way on the chair to face her, "you know Oxymoron?"

She looked at me but kept quiet.

I just said, "Aroo, this is me, Oxymoron,"

I was the only one in the team who used to call her this way. A familiar sound from a stranger hit her. With her hand on her chest, her eyes wide-open, her gaze fixed at me, she stood up and took a step backward. She cupped her hands over her cheeks and halted like a movie reel jammed at a frame. In the next frame, her hands would be freed, her lips shaped like a ring, and the eyes squinted. And, then, she loosened up, visibly, like a pneumatic tube seeping from its valve. A resilient soul that she was, Aroura recoiled to her normal. Holding my hand, she walked me to my office.

She asked me to take my chair and herself sat on the other side of the table, staring at me. I could guess the state of her mind, probably busy in perceiving my earlier face phased out, while the current one phased in. In the stillness prevailing in the room, she was doing her journey, fast and smartly. Eventually, satiated, she broke the silence, "I knew you were returning to work today, of course - I was waiting – did some homework too, some thinking in anticipation of your arrival. But, no, nothing could have worked - too much to take in. You realise, don't you?"

I just smiled. I looked around in the office. Everything was the same as I had left, the draft I was working on lying in the middle of the table, copies of journals, some opened on the table, others lying around in stacks, a ball point stuck in cleft of a book, the dusty lamp shade, the phone with its cable overspun, the stapler behind the computer screen and jar full of pens on its side. It looked like just as another day, as if I could get back to work as a matter of course. Although, there were also a couple of things different: someone had washed my tea mug and placed it back on the shelf behind me and, of course, the waste bin had a new liner.

I shared with Aurora my story in full but was not sure, still in flurry, if she was able to absorb it. I suggested we go out to meet with the rest of the team. We bumped into few in the corridor. For me, obviously, they were like as usual, except no one paid any heed to my presence. Aurora asked the secretary to get everyone in the seminar room for a quick lunchtime chat. For the next full hour we had at hand, we talked. This time I took her through my emotional journey and my predicaments. I talked to her everything, even those of my unexpressed fears which even I was keeping from myself. The only thing that I did not tell her was about my new wife whom I dreaded to meet.

From across the table, she leaned forward in her chair, put her hand over mine and said, "I need some time to get used to your new façade, but I can see you through the things very clearly. You have changed; no - my God, you are another person, obviously, but I am sure that I can still reach you, Oxymoron." And, then, she exclaimed with a smile, "Indeed, you have lived by the word."

"Which word? oh, you mean, Oxymoron," I smiled in reciprocation.

By now, it was time to go to the seminar room. They already had gathered there, about a dozen of them, my research team.

Aurora announced: "Definitely, our visitor does not need introduction, except he does look like who he is. He is no one other than our Director, Oxymoron."

They were glaring at me. In disbelief, some of the faces were void, others in a trance, and yet more looking in shock. Of course, to me they were all familiar faces. Ignoring their hissing, she reminded them, "we have gone through his story as it happened."

I understood it very well that any level of anticipation and preparation would fall short of pacifying them completely. Then, she turned her face to me, "welcome Oxymoron, you are welcome back at work."

She gave me a moment to look around, get familiar with the atmosphere and a chance to say a word or two. There was David, the savvy research lead, ever-ready with panoramic information, a mentor to the upstarts in the team. I was always proud of him. "Hi David, a brief on the grant applications that we were working out the last time is due. Shall we meet this afternoon." Everyone laughed while he nodded his head in disbelief. And Naila, the Team PRO, – she would usually be deeply focused at your face while talking to you, almost mollycoddling, but today her eyes were rather deeply fixed on my face, like teeth in cheddar. With my eyes searching, I found her in the corner. Then I announced, "where is our Pretty Asha?" Asha was the quality lead. Elegantly suave with delicate manners and fragile intonation, she was the favourite of all. I would often address her this way, and she would take pride in it. But today, it was different - she just slipped out of the room quietly, perhaps of shyness. Apparently, they had enjoyed on my return; for me though, my return was more than that – much more. By knowing them all as before, I recovered my confidence, as if each of them putting their approval stamp on the lease of my new life.

Aurora also gave the staff an opportunity to say something for the occasion but quickly sensed that the staff did not know much what to say. With her usual social skills, she took over the initiative, gave me an update on the current things, and dismissed the meeting. Life started. The show had to go on, as they say. And, it went on in my case, well, with the usual twists and turns of life; but for me, I was about to pick up on the way some from the acute variety.

***

I bumped into the first batch of twists straightway. It was the second day of my return. I had just finished the departmental review meeting on projects and grant applications when Aurora returned with a worried face. She normally had a calming effect on everything happening in the department but at this moment she was different.

She closed the door behind her, sat down on the chair across the table in front me, and asked, "who do you think the staff should recognise you as?" She did not let me answer this. "But, hold on. This question can wait. Much more importantly, HR has just called, which I expected was about your return-from-sickness form. No, it was a call of a rather more serious nature." She paused here. I could guess something big was coming my way. "They have put the same question as our staff can ask, but in a different way. They think you did not survive the accident, thus do not exist in their payroll, and that you are not the one they are expecting to return to work here."

She paused again, "In fact, they have instructed me to ask you to leave the premises -immediately."

It was a shock of epic proportions, the most troubling aspect of which was the threat to my allegiance to this place of my solace. Where would I go? What would I do? How would I live. The anguish from depleting me of the source of income was killing me. Only this morning I was calculating the days before I would be receiving my salary. The house that I had inherited from my parents I had already sold, with its proceeds to buy one for my family. My father had left me a farm but its rent was not enough even for a week's worth of kitchen.

Calmly watching me, Aurora said that she understood the point the HR had made. She said that it was not a personal but a legal issue, the issue of identity. Then, she left her chair, walked around the table to come to my side, placed her hand on my shoulder and said, "I will stand by you and we will do this difficult walk together." The days to come would testify that she stood by her words.

# COURT UNDER TRIAL

WE WERE ASKED TO WAIT in the office of Mr Gus, a renowned barrister in the city. A few moments later, a man of tallish height and muscular build entered the room. I thought he must be spending some good hours in the gym on daily basis. Though his face gave a different impression. It was riddled with thinking lines. Properly worn out, it was of a typically dull person, if I may say so. His hair had receded irregularly, leaving no definite front line, while he wore a faint moustache, and a beard with its upper border running along the jawline, sharply curving upward to gang with the opposite side, under the lower lip. Looking at the contrast between his face and body, an impish thought flashed through my mind: 'Did he also have a below-neck body job done to him. I was not sure how he would manage to impress a judge or a jury, but, surely, he was a highly rated in his professional circle; that's what I had heard, exactly.

After the exchange of pleasantries and case introduction, he sounded mildly excited. He immediately showed his agreement to take the case. It was followed with a long discussion, and, to my astonishment, Aurora led on the discussion with a guile of a person trained in legal matters.

Mr Gus concluded the session with his summary indicating that there was one primary question to consider: what in a person represents the agent 'I'? Is 'I' about the personality and the character resident in the person, the one who thinks, learns, reacts, recognises and remembers? Or, is it the physical part, with an appearance, with a face with which people recognise 'I', with unique fingerprints and a 'retinographic' map stored somewhere in population biometric data? In other words, what is it in the 'I' that represents the unity of the person? I remembered all the dialogue that I had with Logge and Nash, the young men living in my neighbourhood. But I also realised that the material we spoke then was about biology and philosophy, what we were about to hear was law. Soon I would learn the distractions with Mr Gus' mediocre appearance outdone with his wisdom and his eloquence and style in the court.

Aurora conceived some notional questions from this primary shoot: how does the agent 'I' associate with, and relate to, self, and with other agents and things; and, what might be the contents of that association and relationship? With this, she really impressed me. We all seemed to agree that these questions were relevant to the case, encompassing the meanings of person and identity. At a slower pace, Gus asked, as if making an announcement if I was happy for him to present my case in the court. With my yes, he rotated a file towards me, with his finger on the dotted line for me to sign.

***

I returned home feeling relieved, a feeling that you have after your worry are lynched on someone else's hook, in this case, of Mr. Gus and Aurora. 'Hope this guy could take the case through,' I whispered. Aurora was confident about this and about the case discussion having gone well. What a person and a friend Aurora was, clear in head, methodical? She reminded me Hypatia, a polymath of Alexandria in the medieval time, a friend and counsel to the Governor Oreste; except, the finish point of Hypatia's life was tragic - profoundly: she was murdered for political reasons by a mob motivated by madness.

I wanted to please myself with buying a gift for Aurora. 'How about Hypatia's face molded on a coin, made into a necklace.' I just ordered one on online, a gold-plated piece. The agent on the chatline asked me if I liked it choker type or pendent. I imagined Aurora and described the slim elegant neck, and the agent endorsed a pendent type.

The next day, we heard from Mr. Gus's secretary that he had filed on my behalf a civil case in the High Court in which he solicited for an equitable legal injunction issued against the defendants, the management of the Public Engagement, requesting the court to prevent them from banning the plaintiff, me, from working for them. He further sought on my behalf a declaratory judgment on my civil rights and on my numerical identity as stood in the statute in the context of my physical make-up recently transformed.

There were some pre-trial negotiations between the two sides; but, as I was told, considering the significance and unique nature of the case, it was agreed for the sake of legal clarity to seek a decision from the court. In the meantime, we heard that a lawyer on behalf of Zeitoun filed a brief, indicating that she had a take in the case, holding beneficiary interests. The court also indicated that it required representatives or input from Law, Finance and Culture Ministries to attend the case.

***

It was the morning of 25th September, when I entered the courtroom with a heavy heart and flimsy hopes. I was alone. Aurora decided not to sit beside me lest the Employer management might take a bleak view of her scheming with me. I found myself in a huge court room, its walls lined with wood panels of walnut effect, its high ceiling decorated with chandeliers filtering dim light, struggling to illuminate the sturdy, over-polished, slightly worn-out walnut furniture. There were swathes of chairs for the audience, mostly occupied, facing a room-length, curved dice, on its other side a row of carefully spaced, high-backed chairs with red velvet-cushioned backs - all still empty. The aristocratic cadence in this room would take you far in another world.

However, the theme was broken by those present, all kinds of people, some formally dressed, others in modern informal outfits, an array of cool colours mixed with hot ones. Most eyes were glued at me: some might be searching the line of fusion of the two people gathered in me, I wondered. But they were all quiet. The reverent hush was broken now and then by a hesitant cough or a brief hiss, making the silence heard. I had in the past delivered lectures in hundreds around in various auditoriums and halls but, in this room, it was different. Wrapped in nervousness, everyone was as still as furniture, infusing the courtroom with a ghostly vaporous air. Even the court clerk, the only moving object in the whole scene, seemed to be a part of the ghost.

Looking at the clerk reminded me to ask her before the Judge had arrived if I could take notes of the proceedings which she approved. I thought I would be needing these notes in telling you my account of these proceedings. Though I could not possibly be irking you with legal references or precedents, nor would there be many quoted for their scarce relevance to this premier case, I thought. I hated taking notes as always.

Everything in order, the judge arrived in the room, and, in deference, everybody rose from their seats until she had taken the middle chair on the dice. She was a middle-aged lady, looking elegant in her court dress. Her methodical mannerisms reflected someone well-versed in the discipline of the court. I noticed in the ceiling over her chair a grill, lashed with it a ribbon fluttering with conditioned filtered air. My heart fluttered, too, with trepidations. She glanced around at the assembly and then reached me sitting next to my attorney in the front row, looking at me for a fraction of a second longer than one might expect, something she would continue to do now and then during the proceedings.

Mr. Gus was invited to introduce the case. He rose from his seat and slightly bowed to the court, "May it please the court, my name is Donald Gus." He then introduced me, the plaintiff, also swanking my achievements, of which I did not particularly see the relevance; then he listed the facts of the case, perhaps already well known by everyone present, for the publicity my person had attracted during my time in the hospital. At one juncture, he raised his arm to pinpoint me in the audience, highlighting me as the first case of brain-transplant in medical history. It was indeed an unnerving moment for me.

He said that among the questions arising from the case, the one on which the court had to deliberate was the meaning of 'person', and, associated with it, the question of 'personal identity'. "The court may please deliberate then which of the definitions of 'person' is pertinent to the issue of the continuation of job the plaintiff has with the current employers, the defendants in the case," he continued in the legal jargon.

Mr. Gus pronounced that the case comprised several aspects with philosophical, social, personal and, of course, legal implications, as well as some practical ones. He said, "unfortunately, the court cannot lean on the philosophical meanings of the person or of the personal identity, for the philosophers over the centuries themselves could not have reached a consensus on this subject."

I thought, 'surely my philosophical reflections on the meanings of person are done with.'

He continued with his argument, "it has to be acknowledged that the two families of the plaintiff, one of each of his parts, the brain and the body, both have abandoned him. But the management, while barring the plaintiff from work, has taken yet another view of him on grounds which have nothing to do with those of respective families."

"The first set of his relatives, his wife and the children," he continued, "identified by the plaintiff as his family, left him because they did not recognize him as one of them, but not because he did not recognize them as his family. That is based on what we could call as social aspect of personal identity, meaning how the society recognizes a person: which is with personal appearance," he concluded this point.

He continued, "then, we take the case of the parents of the young man, whose body was restored in the operation, the one now you can see sitting in this room – as far as the function of seeing is concerned." He paused for a second, and looked in my direction; in unison, everyone, including the Judge, now had a chance to look at me properly. He returned to his argument, "the parents were initially thrilled to see their son still alive on the face of his certain death from a brain tumor. However, they could not reconcile with the mental record of the plaintiff and, despite seeing their son in this person, actually did not find their son in him. This is where the crunch of the case lies. This is where lies the answer to our question. 'All that glitters is not gold', for maybe it is or maybe it is not; in the current case, something that glittered like gold was in fact found not to be gold."

He continued, "for the defendants to see this point, we have to read the dictum in its negative sense, which is: 'all that does not glitter does not mean it is not gold'. The management made a mistake here. They did not see the director in this person and assumed he was not. They took their decision just on the face value of the situation without trying to uncover the reality and hence did not pursue the right course."

He was now in real flow, "had the right course been pursued, it would have been even simpler for the management to pursue than it was for the parents of the youth. The right course demanded from them to establish just one fact: whether the plaintiff still possessed the knowledge and skills necessary to perform the duties he conducted before the incident. This is what they need to do now instead of what they have done. This is what I will class as the 'practical aspect' of the case, the pragmatic approach. It would be the practical aspect of the case, my Lady, not even the legal aspect, on which the decision has to base."

He further highlighted the need in this case for the preference of a practical approach. "There has not been a precedent recorded in legal case books of a personal identity changed after organ transplants, even involving the heart or the face. The fact is, there is no claim ever filed in the legal history that an organ transplant has changed the identity of the person receiving the transplant. In the current case, many organs, the heart and the lungs and the rest, in fact the whole body of a person has been transplanted to sit with a brain of the recipient. A whole-body transplantation differs from single organ transplantation only in magnitude but not in nature. The resultant patient's hospital record indicates that the surgeons on the case had referred the issue his identity to the Social Services. The service experts, rather than saying that the resultant person had automatically acquired the identity of the youth, opined that common sense should prevail in this matter, a vague but fairly indicative opinion."

He cleverly picked up the phrase, "common sense holds that the title of a bank account as such does not change after receiving funds from another account, be it a penny or a million. The employers had taken an exceptional course in this case: they hold that the title of the account must change if the amount of the funds received is above a certain limit. Why do they think so? Because they have confused the magnitude with the nature. The distinction they have made in this case is thus superfluous. If the honorable court finds this the case, it is requested to give the plaintiff a relief."

He then concluded his discourse, "at one level it is a simple case of determining the professional capability of the plaintiff to see if it was impaired because of the medical interference. At another level, the case seems very complex, with so many facets and aspects to consider in answering the question of personal identity, including the legal aspect. I have deliberately avoided expanding on this aspect for two reasons: the legal definition of the person depends upon his numerical identity, which, rather than it being a part of answer, in fact is a part of the submission to the court on which to seek clarity. Secondly, if we had decided to pursue the legal aspect of his identity, then the debate would have to be held at a constitutional level, beyond the jurisdiction of this current court setting. However, referral of this case to constitutional court without consideration of a *prima facie* relief to my client would mean an unfair and indefinite wait to be imposed on him before he could possibly rejoin his job."

He placed before the Judge his option analysis for the relief, "with this, I submit, my Lady, that, provided the plaintiff satisfied the management that he did not lack in any way in his knowledge and skills compared with his previous standing, the court has two options: the court may please take the first option by accepting the plea of the plaintiff, issuing an injunction for reinstatement of the plaintiff, that is, if the court finds it appropriate. With the second option, I plead for a *prima facie* case for his reinstatement while waiting for the deliberation in the court to finalize the process."

With these submissions, he gracefully returned to his seat. With his forceful oration, I was released from my nervousness as if breaking from a shell. It reaffirmed within me the one whom I believed I was.

The opposing council rose and bowed to the court. She was an attractive lady, showing in her manners no ignorance of the value of this factor. Her words were as distinctly delivered as marbles dropped on a concrete floor, even amidst the roar of a sold-out football arena. She said she was first an officer of the court before she was a council to a client. She expressed her awareness of the sensitivity of issue and of its legal implications. She assured the court that she would keep an open mind considering this case as an exclusive one and a learning experience.

She continued, "my clients, the Public Intelligence, has taken the action that they have taken based on the understanding that their employee in question actually had died from the injuries from the accident, albeit his brain was used in an organ transplant."

"It is not unusual of people leaving in their wills provisions for their organs to be used in transplantation or for research purpose. When one such organ has been successfully transplanted in a new person, it cannot be said of the donor that he or she is alive, or has returned to life as the recipient of the transplant. In fact, this person must be about to die, or they have already died, prior to their organs being taken out and transplanted to someone else. This principle when applied to the current case, renders the plaintiff, against what he claims, no longer alive, let alone an employee of the Public wanting to be reinstated. I repeat, he was about to die before the transplantation; after the transplantation was completed, he didn't exist anymore."

She continued, "my plea might sound ridiculous, while someone sitting in this room right now claiming to be that dead person, but people do sometimes adopt mistaken identities, wittingly or inadvertently." At this point the Defense rested.

The force in her argument shook my own confidence in my identity; I indeed thought if my family were actually right in disowning me. Maybe I was not the person who I believed I was. The judge too was shaking her head while looking at me, appearing to me saying, 'no, you are not the man whom you think you are; you are just making up a story.'

Feeling like a person on a sinking ship, I looked on my right towards Mr. Gus for help. He smiled, looking back at me and rose from his seat, seeking permission from the judge to speak, which was granted. He said, "I fully agree with the general principle of organ transplantation as narrated by the council; however, there are some stark differences to be noted in the current case." I thought only a barrister of some class would dare oppose the defendant's attorney on the points she had made.

He said, "it might sound surprising but a brain-transplant can practically be the same as a total body-transplant, for the two processes differ only in linguistic terms: it is the same in the end if a brain were to be joined with a new body, or a body clipped with a new brain." He continued, "similar to the usual situations in such cases, the potential recipient must receive the organ lest they would die, while the donor is already dead or about to die. In current case, both the recipient and donor were on the verge of death." Looking towards me, he said, "True, the youth, the person you can see sitting here in this room, would have lived only if he had received the brain; but it is true as well that the director, the person in this room who actually believes he is, would have lived only, too, if he had received the body to sustain it."

He took a sip of water and continued, "with this fusion, at the end a person has emerged whose particulars this court has been asked to attest. Just to summarize the positions: about this person, the person himself says he is the one with the brain. His own family rejects that proposition, regarding him with his face; his parents find him as the estranged son, who looks to them appropriate but with mental contents inexplicable to them. Now we hear that the employers consider him dead, even though we have a person sitting here, a real, live person. This person thus belongs to no one, not is he found in a database, but is seeking an identity. He has essentially to be one of the above, most likely the one he says he is."

He paused here to have a sip of water and said, "the question of which one of these persons he is brings us to the starting point of my pleading, my Lady, where I highlighted that the case had philosophical, social and legal aspects, but it must be the pragmatic approach with which a *prima facie* case for the reinstatement of the plaintiff can be established."

He said, "the question of mistaken identity from the defense council is a far-fetched idea, I feel sorry to say. However, in any such dispute, identity checks can be applied, like testing the person for the ability to retrieve the past information and to confirm personal data. It is not much different from asking a lost child who she is or who her parents are, etc. Since we are looking here for the lost director (a big laughter in the hall; I also enjoyed the joke), I suggest we take the route of assessing the professional knowledge and level of skills this person, I mean in the most rigorous way."

With these remarks, he came back to his chair. 'What a precise and elegant way to turn the table,' I thought. His speech won my confidence back in me.

At this point, the Judge summoned the lawyer representing Zeitoun. I looked around if Zeitoun was actually in the courtroom. I spotted Aliya at the aisle seat of the parterre on my left. We looked at each other. In that briefest of the encounters, I noticed the faint waving of her hand.

The lawyer came to the roaster, introduced herself and started, "the pain of someone which follows a personal loss is obvious, but the agony my client family have to go through is exceptional and yet the current debate has only prolonged it – the debate whether the father of the family is alive or dead. This has continued even after his demise, release of his body by the hospital and his formal burial few weeks ago."

She continued, "my client family visited the person in question in the hospital but did not find her husband being present there – as simple as that. It has been their considered view that they do not at all have anything to do with this person, a complete stranger to the family."

She said, "earlier, I heard the council saying in his pleading that he was not sure who lived in the process, youth or the director. The family is sure it was the director, the father of the house, who died; if he did not die, whose remains the family have recently buried? With the grief that they have gone through, the family wishes the matter be rested by the court by delivering a verdict declaring the director dead, finally and ultimately. Besides, obviously, there are some outstanding financial liabilities and benefits linked with the verdict."

It was a hard bolus to chew and acrid to swallow. Her arguments, although damming me and to me, had an incontestable emotional tinge. 'Here you go; I lost my case, and with it, my job.' I looked at Mr Gus again. Mr Gus went straight up to roaster and was straightway granted the permission to speak.

He raised his voice by a hint as if he was irritated, "the earlier comparison presented to the court aimed at assisting the court with offering the two ways open for it take: call him the youth or call him the director, but we must take one of them to assign to the person sitting in this room waiting for a name and an identity. In the argument, we then talked about who actually survived the medical intervention. From what I hear from the council now, it seems we need to focus more on the question who actually died on the day, which is an equally fair way of looking at the situation."

When this time he came this way, looking for water, I was actually annoyed with him. I thought, rather than being distracted by a fake desire of water, he should try finishing the argument, just in case he'd lost its string before concluding it. To my satisfaction, he quickly returned and continued, "to know who of the two actually died on that day, we need to consider the ultimate test of death. They…the medical professionals… declare a person dead, definite dead, when they know for sure the brain is dead, for which they deploy special tests. People can live through the period when their heart or lungs or kidney have stopped working. With proper support, the person can live after these organs are dysfunctional and dead, but when it comes to a brain-death, life-support is switched off, including the prospects of life and hope for it."

He walked close to the judges' dice and rose his voice, "with this clarity achieved, the question that needs asking now is whose brain of the two characters died on that day or perceived as dead? And, of course, whose brain is still alive and working?"

He retrieved by a step and said, "I rest my case."

After having been catapulted, I felt I had now landed on a soft ground - in one piece. I dabbed my forehead with the back of my sleeve and assured myself that I, Oxymoron, was in fact alive. I liked to believe, by concluding this cycle of arguments, Gus had ultimately won me my life. I felt all the avenues to show me dead had by now been forborne. What else could one say now, I whispered with triumph. I wondered what started as arguments for or against keeping me on the job had extended in the hands of these clever lawyers into debating who I was, eventually entering the ironic part of informing if I should be called as alive or dead. I regretted filing this case. I thought I should have instead disappeared into oblivion. I could have gone to my farm to work there. Luckily, it was over now, though my heart was not completely at peace with these lawyers. From the periphery of my vision, I stole a glance on the front row to know if they were itching to come up with another trap. And I was indeed not disappointed.

The council from the employers stood up and asked for permission to speak. She had been subtle, her manners captivating, her arguments mild but blunt in impact. She said, "I hear the council from the family that the family have been handed over the corpse of Oxymoron, which they have buried. I would not expect from the hospital to certify the identity of the corps before its release and from the family not to mistake the corpse of someone else for Oxymoron. And then comes the compelling point from the prosecution council that the youth in question was brain dead, hence assuredly dead. Inevitably, beside these two certainties must exist yet another possibility in order to explain the situation. It is our joint task to uncover that possibility."

She walked back towards her desk but, before reaching there, she turned and addressed the court, "if he, the person sitting here waiting to hear the verdict, is neither the youth, the brain-dead, nor Oxymoron, buried under tons of mud, then he must be another person, a new person, a third person."

She walked few strides forward and from closeness she addressed the court, "and you know, my lady, a new person cannot take the job of an old deceased employee without having gone through a proper recruitment procedure. I rest my case."

She had managed to avoid elaborate arguments about the case but, in a short-cut way, just focused on questioning my capacity to take the job. This was an ultimate blow. I was catapulted one more time. Who could rescue me from this? None, I was sure, was my fear.

Gus whispered in my ear asking what I had been doing on the day of my returning at work. Jaded with the question, I said, "just the routines, Gus - meetings, replied some emails and some usual paperwork." Though, I could not see the point of his asking this question.

He got up one more time and asked for permission to speak. I thought only if he did not have to waste time in showing courtesy but to hurry in annulling the impact lately asserted, lest I should lose my case. He looked at the employer's attorney and asked, "I am sure my friend has been given access to the contract this particular employer uses in recruiting people. If she had read it carefully, there is clause in it binding the employee to maintain the confidentiality of official information in all circumstance. Quite clearly, the Public Intelligence, with a fairly important façade, remaining constantly a focus of media and parliamentary debates and involved in very important occupation of national security would be expected to have a lot of information to keep confidential. Hence the clause on confidentiality must be meant seriously rather than taken frivolously as a check-box clause."

The judge nodded with a faint smile. I also got the point. Gus continued, "if the plaintiff is none of the two but a third person, having no business with the Public Intelligence, we should make sure he did not have anything of the confidential from the job place on him or else we risk national security. However, the fact is that he has around 40 years of record, of which uncountable items of classified nature, needing to remain confidential, all in his mind. He cannot divulge any of this in public in front of the court, for he feels bound by the contract, but the court can order an arrangement in which he can share some of the information with an appropriate person representing the employers to achieve their agreement that he has that information; in that way, also their satisfaction that he is truly their employee." As he walked back towards his chair, the hall was momentarily filled with the noise from the public, obviously showing reaction.

Gus returned to his chair and, just before taking it, said, "I rest my case."

At this point, the Judge restored the order, but was smiling. She adjourned the court and summoned the two main councils and the representatives of the government ministries into her chamber for a conference. The audience in her absence redeemed life, filling the room with whispers and murmurs. I looked for Aliya; she seemed to have left. At one point, the court clerk asked the attorney representing Zeitoun to join the conference as well. After a short while, the councils returned to the room, followed by the judge, at which point the atmosphere in the court regained the quiet air.

Opining on the nature of the case, the judge went an extra length, "every judge comes across cases uniquely difficult to analyze, and, over the period, I too had my share. But, this case …" She paused and tapped her palm across her forehead, "this case has been impossible- it has left the law, and me with it, riven in all sorts of directions. No legislation, no precedents to help it. Try the legislators, I suspect they would pull their hair, too. I would not be surprised if they also met an impasse, putting a ban on this type transplant for the future."

She then smiled and looked at me, "I hear that you are known as Oxymoron."

"Yes, Madam, that is my name." The room was rammed with a roar of giggle. Had I replied too quickly? But, then, I remembered, words had meaning too; they laughed at the word. 'Who cares?' Anxious, I just wanted to hear the judgment.

The Judge smiled, "you indeed merit this title."

The judge summarized the points made from the three councils. She paraphrased the main question in front of the court, "what is it in the person to which is assigned the identity of that person? Does the authority of identifying belong to that who identifies or to that who is identified?" Conventionally, identity checks have been objective but, in this case, we have departed from that convention." Her voice gained volume, "I have reached the conclusion that the court has no valid means available to it to identify this person. I am about to issue a court order agreeing with the notion that right of identity must in this case thus belong to the one who is to be identified, which is the director."

I let the tautness in my body slacken.

She continued with the verdict, "with the agreement of the councils, the plaintiff is given a *prima facie* relief to rejoin his job in the Public Intelligence, provided he satisfied a panel of experts appointed by their management that he had maintained the skills and knowledge he possessed before the medical intervention." She continued, "this could be achieved in one or more of several ways, for example, the plaintiff defending before the panel his recent research and publications."

I felt as if I had got my life back, in big gulps, a real experience.

The judge said the court and the councils were sympathetic to the family of the director for the difficulty they had to go through but could not as such accept their pray to declare the director outrightly dead. She said, "whether the family should accept the director back in the family or they don't is out of the jurisdiction of the court. However, since the director in his previous phase of life was about to retire from the job, the court instructs the employers to release the end-of-service remunerations, retroactively accrued in this case, to the benefit of the family of the director." She continued, "for the director's marriage, it could be considered annulled if any of the two sides wanted to take it that way. The director himself, given he'd passed the test of fitness for the job, must start his career afresh, accruing new pension but with pay-protection at his current scale."

Indeed, with this relief, I saw in me my emotions first storming and then, at the same speed, calming. They were like pupils at loggerheads in a classroom settling, all back to their seats, at the first sight of the difficult teacher. The pink ribbon fluttering on the ceiling grill above the judge's head stole my attention one more time; but this time it was my soul whose wings blissfully flapped with it.

I heard the judge going on further. She admitted the presence of contradictions in the judgement which she said were inevitable at this stage, needing further legal workup. She thanked my council for his suggestion of taking a practical approach, rather than a legal or any other approach, in reaching the decision. She said this decision should be taken in that light. To reach a final verdict addressing all the pertinent questions, including its legal and statutory implications, she referred the case to the constitutional court for further hearing.

With this proclamation, the court proceedings ended. Sorting her paperwork, the judge was getting ready to leave. I was imagining how excited Aurora would be, sitting in the back row. I bet she would wait for me in her seat and pretend not to notice my coming until I reached her. That was her, whom I knew, a lady with graceful manners. The court clerk announced everyone to rise from their seats. The judge left the courtroom for her chamber; people also started leaving, but many of them gathered around me, having a look at me, asking questions. But I was in my own rush.

I hurried to meet Aroura which I did on the double. Guess what? She was looking at her phone, ignoring me coming. I called her from close; she stood up from her seat, turned around, her chair between us, we looked into each other's eyes. Unaware of the surrounding, face to face, we were frozen in that stance, staring. Soon, she would fire up with a smile, with a reciprocal one from me. Across the chair, she extended her hand for a shake. We had had the warmest of a handshake, with a couple of extra shakings. We didn't talk, just walked to Mr. Gus. He was busy organizing his briefcase. We thanked him. He tossed his head slightly, acknowledging, while he undid his bands which he placed on the top of the pile in his briefcase and unbuttoned his collar. He looked cool, "Director Oxymoron, it was nice working on your case. Happy for you." Then he turned his gaze at Aurora, "Mrs. Bird, nice working with you.

Thanks, especially for your idea of taking a pragmatic approach. A torch in the dark."

So it was Aurora who had the idea of pragmatic approach, I just found out.

I said to Gus, "I had not shown you the contract! How did you know the confidentiality clause in it?"

"O, yes, that one. It was a difficult moment. It was a bluff but a safe to make. I just wonder I should have used this line of argument from the start; we wouldn't have to go through all the rest. It just occurred to me at the end."

Gus was obviously an amazing attorney, able to think on the spot, hence his fame.

He said, "let us set a time to discuss the decision and further plans." He then changed the topic, "you may like to know I coordinate a monthly Thinkers Forum in the city. It is open to everyone. You can Google it for details, in case you were interested." He took his briefcase and left.

Standing there, we were looking at him going, "a lawyer with some nerves; his confidence stunning, and look at his insight," I said.

Aurora laughed, "honestly speaking, I lost my hope at one point. I did not think much of the council representing your family, but when he came up with the argument as to who was dead, I was finished. He made me believe both you and your case fell dead."

I said, "my heart sank at that moment as well. But if you ask me, the worst moment was of her returning with the idea of the third person. It was when Mr. Gus was at his best. it was at this point, he actually fought back. Simply elegant." I smiled.

Aurora said, "Yes, of course, that one too, stunning effectively rebuttal."

I said, "but you never told me it was you who conceived the idea of pragmatic approach. But am I surprised on this? No, not really."

"It is his greatness to acknowledge this little thought from me," she said.

I said, "I might come back to the court to listen to this orator, fascinating to watch pleading."

She replied, "you would not be the only one; I bet a lot of people came today just for him, though others for the publicity of the case."

I glanced at Aurora, and we walked toward the door. I was thinking this was one of those few lucky moments when I got both what I needed as well as what

I wanted. And, for my family, I thought, never mind if they did not accept me back; at least, now they had some moneys coming in. Some of the deepening lines on Zeitoun's face might ease now, I hoped. I looked round for Aliya but she wasn't there.

"What next?" Aroura was in celebration mood, "how about a meal-out." We deserved this and planned it for the next day.

# CEASE-FIRE

IN THE EVENING, I BUMPED into the twins again. We agreed for a cup of tea together in a nearby café. Both the brothers were cheeky, but Nash was a special brand. He opened up, "I have a fantastic question needing booted?"

I smiled.

"Oxymoron!" Nash fumbled on this word a little. "How do you find yourself in your mosaic? I assume you are a fully operational person, are you not? Are you happy?"

"You must have heard the outcome of the court case on my identity earlier today. Hence this question." A sip from the very hot tea tasted nice, though heat on the lips needed an urgent lapping from the tongue. "To answer your question, no, I'm not. Though in this body I look young, and feel bouncing and peppy, no doubt, but still, I crave the old body, that of my own. I wish my body returned to me - by all mean – or, in fact, I returned to my body. I want to have my own ring-fingers, my wedding ring around one of them, even my own fingerprints."

He shifted his gaze fixed in the far corner of the ceiling with a twitch and voiced the next question, "not even your high social demand has made you any happier!!! I suppose the whole world would be dying to meet a mosaic, wanting to have a word. You are a special person - indeed."

I said, "true, but which person? My family have forsaken this person. The parents of the youth, whose body this person is riding around, were dead with disappointment at seeing him. How should have I felt at the site of my own dead body? Remember the pictures on my cell phone! Would I ever be able to share these feelings with anyone, unless, of course, with a mosaic like me sitting next to their corpse, like I had to sit."

I sipped from my cup but this time the tea tasted bitter, "I miss my face... my body…. I am very upset in this arrangement - a cage."

Nash turned his face to Logge, "you were wrong for once, Logge. A complete person is not a person somehow completed. Original body coupled with mind, from cradle to grave, that is the journey of a complete person."

Logge said, "but did we not reach the conclusion that notional things like thought and self use the physicality as a tool. Does it matter then which particular tool they use as long as it works?

I said, "with this new body, I expect to have less pains and more pleasures - would you agree? I hope I am right in this, but I might be too ambitious."

"I can see that you are right," Nash said without much hesitation.

I said, "therefore it is clear that my new body has opened the way to new experiences, something I would not imagine I would be getting with the old one?"

"Yes," Logge said, which Nash confirmed with a nod.

"Would that make me a different person?"

"I would imagine so, different person, for sure," Logge said, which again Nash confirmed with a nod.

"Then, if a switch in the bodies can create a different person, it is clear that the body is not just a machine, Guys. It listens to the brain, and to the self, the one sitting in the brain - yes. But it also impacts experiences of the self, and via this route, possibly the personality, the character and the behaviour."

"Yes, that seems acceptable," Both concurred with this conclusion.

Logge said, "but, then, as I have said, this conclusion conflicts with the earlier one where we found the self wholly residing in the brain, the body being merely a machine."

He continued, "I just remember the example of Steve Hawkins. As you know his body was severely less able, but his intellectual brilliance was possible despite because of his bodily functions were one by one taken over by computers and gadgets. This clearly means that the body is a machine."

I said, "both conclusions can be married together; they are flipsides of the same coin. Mind work through the body, but also with it. The person desires continuity in personal experiences. Do you know which is the core personal experience? The one that results from the self-image, a merger of the virtual image of the self with the body-image. In fact, the two are inseparable. Together these images comprise personal identity, a unique identity code."

They were still with me, "I suspect even Hawkins would not be happy with his brain carried around in a new body. But for that he himself would have made a choice – too late for the question."

"Now guys, the upsum here should be that you seem comfortable with the insight of the Mosaic? Don't you think that, in curiosity and novelty, the mosaic contests the twins?"

On this light note, they departed, happy, promising to return. For me, after the court decision, I felt even better as these insights justified my anxieties, in a way appeased them as well.

From here, I went to my home. In my mind was a debt I needed to payback. I wanted to meet with my buddy, this body, to negotiate a new deal between the two of us, a pledge of peace. It was a milestone in the journey of my settlement with the youth. I helloed him, the guy-in-the-mirror, 'we are friends, and not foe anymore. Let us have a fresh start. Neither you nor me – disjointed - anymore; all is one now.'

The guy-in-the-mirror smiled, 'you selfish – trying to encroach on me.'

I joined the smile, 'wish I had done it earlier. No fuss. I encroach on you, you on me, us serving each other.' I continued, 'I owe you for everything; I owe you the care, love, you name it. It is because of you I am alive - and young. Promise from now on, I shall feel for you – be with you – walk in your shoes, everything. It is my pledge – test me.'

The guy-in-the-mirror said, 'OK, three – two – go.'

For me, this resolution was not less important than winning the case. After longtime, I was happy to set me free from my past, and had a deep sleep. With the morning breathing on my face, I got up refreshed. I walked around in the house like a sleepwalker in trance, lighter, delighted and liberated.

# MATRIMONIAL STUFF

ON THE WAY TO THE RESTAURANT, I thought about my comrade Aurora, about the meeting with her. Some unknown tacit feelings were running in my head. She had stood the test of time for me, upright, unwavering, wise. From the closeness that we had recently achieved, she came across in her demeanour as non-invasive but not too distanced. She would be a soft presence but the one that had to be felt. She affixed passion to her sincerity, illustrious talent to our sporadic intellectual altercations. Her demure etiquettes of the earlier times now felt as composing into a mellowed character.

There were not many cars in the restaurant parking. I chose the far corner. I slowly walked to the building. I was thinking. 'Now when much of the dust on my way has settled, the tacit feelings must acquire substance' I thought. I was not sure if she had thought it that way as well. Only recently had I exited a tie, although not of my doing. 'She knows I'll miss Zeitoun. Shall I propose her now, and how? I now look younger, of my son's age. How will she take it? Acceptable! Agreed!! Is that what she is going to say?' And then something caught up my heart - I had a clandestine wife, currently at large, coming to meet with me anytime, the one about whom Nahaar's parents had given the news. First, I must survive that encounter before thinking of another avenue. In the meantime, I should sit tight, I decided.

There was not much hustle bustle in the restaurant, which I thought was a good thing; we needed uninterrupted atmosphere for perpetual celebration for our crisp success. Aurora arrived few minutes later. In a mood of talking, she too preferred a quiet corner. We eventually settled around a table of our choice. Showing an elegant sartorial taste, she wore for the evening a Gingham dress of the color of the sunset horizon and wine check-lines. With it, she had chosen emerald green minimalistic jewelry, which I thought rather stood out both from her face and from her dress as if the three were set in a concordant triangle. Her hair was done stylishly messy with some layering, which suited her face. I could sense a very subtle flowery perfume too. A proper party ambiance. Her charming showcasing was a pleasant surprise for me after I had seen her for years in flat dull outfits of varying shades, all from the family of grey colors. I praised her dress and her choice.

She said, "I wouldn't choose this color had it been only for my eyes."

I said, "Interesting - same with me. My wardrobe was jumbled with shirts with colours which looked good to my eyes but never on me. But ah, that is now all in the past."

She waited for me to say more. "Now, I have a new challenge. I have to start thinking juvenile choices. Question is who is going to teach me young stuff?"

I could see her face dimmed. I at once knew I had taken a wrong turn. I made her think she was not young, at least, not as I now looked. That meant to her our paths had parted.

Not knowing exactly how to undo this, I placed on the table the gift box that I brought with me. Again, it was a hasty impulsive action. I guessed she would be thinking that naïveté and haste of the youth must have oozed into my person, but she smiled, meaning she had ignored this mess. Or, maybe I was just being self-critical. No doubt, I was nervous.

"Now let us see what Oxymoron has brought for us." She took the packet and removed its packing – a golden coin tagged to a golden chain. Unsure, she stared at me from the corners of her eyes.

"Oh, yes, the face on the coin: it is of Hypatia. A polymath in Alexandria around 15th Century. She was the wise counsel to the governor of the city. For advising the unpopular governor, she was attacked by a mob gone mad at the governor. They were so mad that they killed her just for helping him. On the contrary, with your wisdom, you have saved a person who once has died," I laughed.

She wouldn't take that credit easily, "after all, you have managed to add a medieval touch in our story, from your learning in medieval history!" Tapping on the coin, with a spark in her eyes, she said, "I am indeed flattered with your giving me this likeness with Hypatia … but only if you had trawled a little further, to reach 12th Century, you would have noticed Heloise, the queen of love epistolary prose. I would be even happier with my likeness taken to her, albeit trivial, although she was proud of her love for Abelard and was not shy of expressing it, while I am - terrible!! And I am not a poet."

I looked at her but did not reply, nor did I dispirit her, unlike what Abelard did to Heloise. She waited for few seconds, then folded the chain around her index and little fingers, held the coin against her palm, faced her palm at me, keeping it next to her face, and asked, "How would it look on me?"

"You look pretty even without it." She blushed slightly. By now, I had recovered, slightly, from the earlier confusion.

Then she blinked her eyes, "now, who should we ask to get the pendent around my neck?" I was nervous a little. I went around the table. I rushed back to my seat, shrinking from the people around. What if they misconstrued me as a son trying to help his mother with her jewellery? Yet, again, I had thought like a young person rather than the old official. She seemed to have noticed this as well. But she was so happy anyway. The pendent mingled nicely with her emerald necklace but hardly added much to her beauty. She waited at me as if to embolden a young child to utter the first word. In return, I threw a rather boring comment, "it really looks nice on you." Once settled in the chair, I said, "Aroo, can I ask you something?"

She became intensely attentive as if it were her eyes with which to hear. Again, I was annoyed with my choice of words, possibly giving her a wrong hint. Finding hard to resist proposing her, I reminded myself what I had planned - to keep the marital ambit for a later occasion. 'Wait for the fog to clear,' I rebuked myself in my heart.

I pursued with my question, "tell me Aurora, what magic have you got up in your sleeve? A person that you have known for ever disappears in a blink, only to resurface yet in another blink but in a completely new format. And, you can see through this new format to spot in it the old person you have known- – without much hassle. How come, you did it that easily?"

Her intense face relaxed into a courteous smile, "I knew this question was coming." She reached her bag and took out a gift box, "unwrap your answer." Came to light from the box a globe of clear crystal glass. I carefully placed it on the table. It gleamed in the room light, glinting beams of shattering colours, scattering in all directions. However, my attention was at once drawn to a platform within the globe on which was lying a beautiful solitary red rose, sleeping like a baby and as fresh.

I said, "the flower is indeed incredibly pretty."

"It will stay like this for long, I hope: a fresh frozen rose," she said. "What if the globe is smashed?"

I got the point. A minute ago, I had compared Aurora with Hypatia. Now, how gracefully had she compared my person resident in the body with the rose sleeping in the globe? I was simply impressed. I conceded, "an ultimate comparison, Aurora. Against this one, the parallel with the Hypatia stands only second, by far."

I raised my volume, "as the rose can survive in a globe which if smashed can be replaced, so can the person endure in a body which if shattered can be switched."

She was still silent in waiting more to come,

I silently gazed at her face, hoping she would relieve me from the duties of guessing harder. She nodded faintly, but her eyes waited for more to come. I broke the silence one more time, "how easily did I manage to ignore the globe to attend the flower?" said I. "That explains how you could spot me in the new body."

"Yet more …," I said.

"What more," she asked.

"Nothing really - just some loud thinking," I replied hesitantly. Knowing her, I knew with this choice of gift she had also indicated, for going into the marriage, she would not care how I looked. I looked at the rose and then stared at her without blinking. I wondered how wonderful life would be with this friend, a nimble mind.

I praised her thinking behind her choice. But, yet again, she would not take credit for thinking out this allegory. She said, "don't look at me. It all is taken from the drama that you have created." She continued, "If you ask me, I was in fact shocked when I heard 'Aroo' from your lips in the corridor."

I kept on looking at her. She said, "if I were that clever that you think I am, I should have spotted you in that new body at the very moment you uttered the word Aroo. Instead, I was shocked at hearing my pet name from a stranger."

She continued, "but I recovered from the shock quickly, and there was a reason behind my quick recovery. I quickly recognised the person whom I loved. I loved the person."

She paused here, perhaps for the expectation that I should accompany her for a dive into the stream of her purest thoughts. Alas! I could not do it. At this point, she softly giggled, "I mean, for me, it is always the person inside, who matters, not the look." Visibly disappointed, she had changed the tack.

Helping the change in the tack, I also hassled her to switch the lights on in the memory lane, "I was happy to find my team and yourself, all there as in my memory."

"Well," she said, "if you talk of memory, I must tell you something from a recent story. Some time ago, out of sheer coincidence, I spotted a familiar voice on my car-radio. It sounded from a mate of mine from the school years whom I never met since."

She paused for a second, "Don't take me wrong - by familiarity of the voice, I don't mean of the same pitch or the tone. The girl that arose in my imagination from the voice in the radio actually used to sing in a melodic hum. Though, the voice I was hearing now was croaky, of rather deep, low pitch, manly. Also, the posh rounding of words of her adolescent years had now mingled with a hint of choppy style."

"A contradiction in terms, Aurora. With these differences, you wouldn't possibly recognize her merely listening on the radio" I said.

"Only if you think that just these features in speech determine familiarity. For me, familiarity must depend on something more, possibly something of the vernacular one employs, or of the mood of the person expressed in voice and in its tone – something unique to the person, perhaps as unique as finger prints," she was trying to overcome the vagueness in her statement.

"Did you eventually meet with her?"

"I gave my number to the radio station to pass on to her to call me back, which she did, thank you. On the phone, it became even clearer to me who she was. In fact, it was only after few exchanges on the phone when I called her with her nickname, Stick – the name was mined from her slender physique in school years. Although, when I met her a couple of days later in the coffee shop on the High Street, it was she who first spotted me, and even called me with my pet name, Globule. That is how they used to call me for my shape during our school years."

I giggled, "Aroura, do you understand that the information you just have volunteered can be used against you?"

She put her hand over her mouth and, looking at herself, said, "I have changed ever since, haven't I?"

I said, "interesting. The difference between the two of you in what you look in people - you listen to her to know who she was, and for her more important was the inscriptions in your look."

"Exactly," rolling her eyes, she nodded in sarcasm, for I had managed to repeat just the obvious.

This was an interesting story but I wanted her to talk about herself. I knew she was widowed several years ago with no children and did not marry again. But this was the subject she never had liked to bring up. But, again, I should not have wanted her to touch on this subject lest we indulged into marital planning. Why did I want that discussion, I really had no idea? But for tonight, my job was mainly making mistakes, one after the other.

From that point on, our conversation lost the flow. My repeated assaults on the conversation had derailed it. From now on, we would often meet unpleasant pauses – kind of pauses when something difficult needed said but not said. At this point, she would feign a laugh. I was sure she knew that I had been making silly mistakes, which I hoped would be forgiven as owing to panicking. She was therefore in the offing to help more directly. One time, she looked at me intensely, faked clearing her throat and said, "with me, you look like a toy-boy; don't you think so?"

At this point, I was left with only two choices: admit the gap between a lady in 50s and a man in 20s, or dismiss it as frivolous or irrelevant. With the former, I risked parting from her for good; with the latter, hoped fastening with her permanently, something not going to take off. A proper dilemma, but she could not appreciate the reason of my hesitation, nor did I want her to know about this.

So, for tonight, there was a triangle lurking around us, the one made of me, Aurora and my unknown wife waiting to drop in any time. Staggering with it was yet another triangle made up of me as Oxymoron, me as Nahaar and Aurora. The situation needed a proper combing. At this moment, I felt we had met an impasse; on this, nothing more needed said. The night was getting deeper and heavier; we got up confused and disturbed, and parted disheartened and frustrated.

On the way to home, feeling the distaste, I tried several times at recapping our conversation in different ways but only with one result that I had caused Aurora a hurt. Would I be able to offset this hurt? I felt intense love for her. The more drenched did I feel myself with love for her, the more I was crushed under the guilt of denying it. I reached home and carefully placed her gift of the sleeping rose on the mantelpiece in the living room lest it would break and I would upset her further.

# MORE MATRIMONIAL STUFF

THE NEXT DAY WAS A BIG day for me. I was back at my job. Peace in life returned, with it a routine. How blissful are the days classed as routine! Over time, just like the word Oxymoron had lost its meanings, the contradiction in my constitution lost its appeal, too. No one cared, including me, any more. Aroura and I got into routine as well. The thoughts of my family would keep my mind busy but only on the background, as if these memories had created a new department there, but I would not let them interfere with my routines. My family did not contact me, nor did I hope they would, except Aliya, who might call me one day. I recalled the message that I saw in her eyes when we came across the last time.

And, on that morning, she did contact. In a brief message, Aliya wrote that she would want to meet me soon. She wrote that she was waiting for the mourning in the house to wear down. Strangely, she did not mention Zeitoun or Ayaan in her message. With a teeny excitement and in anticipation, I shelved in my memory the hope of my meeting with her.

For now, I got peace which I had been seeking since long. But, not for long it stayed. Later that morning, Aurora came in the office to ask if I could by any chance spare an opportunity to meet with a girl, named Comely, insisting to see me, though she would not tell Aurora why.

A modestly tall girl of around 25 entered the office. I offered her a chair across the table in front me while I found her eyes transfixed on my face. In a silk flared dress, laced at the bottom, with pale green flowers on a thundery grey context, she was looking gorgeous. She had a chiseled face, her hair of tumbling spirals neatly dropping on her shoulders from a center parting as straight as a wheel spoke. A tussock of hair from her left temple was loosely drawn backward, clipped at the rear with a hairpin, bejeweled with a jasmine bud. An unruly tussock from the right temple was left to pat her cheek with every movement of her head, which she would off and on 'frustratingly' finger towards the back of the ear, each time failing. Framed with dense eyelashes, even more beautiful were her grey eyes, tearful, seemingly with joy, gratitude or relief, anything, but, for sure, not with pain, fear or grief.

The next thing was her introduction and the purpose of her coming. Although I regularly saw people in my office, my heart was pumping at the top speed with one kind of anticipation, with the other kind, my face was blank that she must have noticed.

"I am your wife" in reciprocation, she sounded poised and confused at the same time.

'Here we go!' a voice vented in my head. Suddenly, the feelings blitzed, the inappropriate feelings of young age, but the grip of the elderly overpowered all emotions. In rather a meek voice, I said, "you mean the wife of the young man." Then I gathered more power, "you must have realized that the things have moved on for you and for your husband; and that seems now the water under the bridge."

She ignored the gravity in what I had to say, "I know that you have received a new brain."

"I am sorry but I am not your husband, for I do not know you for a start, let alone to know you as my wife."

She right away turned pale, her forehead drenched with perspiration, her hands trembled, her bottom lip quivered, as if bearing the weight of the seized words. She could not gather herself. Then, she broke with sobbing. Her water-logged eye welled up, with tears trickling on the cheeks. Her grief had in fact seemed to be lifting the last leaf of the veil from her innocence and simplicity, and, of course, her appeal. I could just glance at her, fearing I would melt down instantly. At this fragile moment, inadvertently, I let her read hope in my eyes, hope of redeeming the relation - a fake hope, I prayed.

She kept quiet but, with trembling hands, she took out from her handbag a magazine to show me. It was a college publication with a lot of pictures, one of which that she showed me was of two young people, her and me, standing in front of a tuck shop, hand in hand, stylishly posing to the camera. Quite obviously, these two handsome people posed to the camera for the publicity of the tuck-shop, but the pose did show the two people being too intimate. Then, she showed me some more pictures of the two, disclosing close relationship between them, but at the same time, she was murmuring her protest why she had to come to a point to proving a matrimonial relationship in this manner.

I wanted to ask her more about who she was and where she had been in the meantime when her husband was struggling for life. But you don't normally ask from your own wife who she is, do you? She did not attempt answering those question either. Did she not feel the need of some explanations, or was she just obfuscating, I could not make up my mind? Or perhaps, she was just being under the spell of emotions from seeing her husband alive, or of the testing situation of meeting her husband who was refusing to recognize her.

She closed the magazine over her fingers on the page and rested her hand on the table. Her gaze in the void away from me, she blinked on her tears which rolled over her cheeks. In a croaky voice, she repeated, "why me – I don't know, I don't know!!"

It was now my turn to freak out and sweat. I left the room in search of Aroura for help; I had to call her in. With her iconic talent, Aroura swiftly sensed the situation. After a rather drawn-out pause, she opened in a croaky mawkish voice, "To me you are her husband; who else are you?"

I kept quiet. Comely had calmed down.

She continued, "to me you are her husband by all means. Minds can change, and personal identities switch; people lose memories, and they acquire new; the young age, and the elderly die – but, with any such change, will they cease to be what they have been in a relationship grid?" After another pause filled with a kind of despair, she herself answered, "no, not at all."

Astounded, I looked at Aroura. I sensed a strong appeal in her words, but there were tears in her eyes, too. I offered my soft rebuttal, "I do not even recognize this girl."

Then I addressed the girl, "did you say Comely your name? I have never met you before. I can accept that you can be the wife of the youth, now part of my person but I was not the one whom you wedded."

Aurora said, "at least, she is the wife of the person who is now your part, whom you have acquired. You cannot part her from you now. You have acquired her husband; you must acquire his past, too."

From the intensity in Aroura's argument, I knew from the word go that I was Comely's husband, come what may. I was dreaming to marry Aurora, but also dreading to meet this wife of mine. Now, Aurora herself facilitating this relationship put an end to my dream. This irony hitting me felt like my bare shin hitting an edge of a table. To make it double painful were the feelings that Aurora must have got her shin hurt, too. Thus, on the fine morning of Sunday 2nd August, Comely moved in with me in the flat at Noor Crescent. Aroura helped in organizing her shifting to my place.

# BACK TO THE SELF

THE LIFE OSSIFIED into a routine and the routine ran on its track, although, I would avail every opportunity of introspection. I often thought about the trialogue between Nash, Logge and me. I felt my next stop had to be an Evolutionist. I found a guy in the Department of Humanities in the City University, called Jamie, known in the university circles for his insights of Darwinism and for his eloquence and counted among the university chivalry. A common friend told me that Jamie was brash and brazen, all time prepared to pick a bone with anyone daring to differ with him. I still fixed a lunch with him.

The university café was packed with students, filled with a hybrid buzz of high and low pitch voices, intruded here and there with clattering from the crockery. The place was ornate with photomosaic of young scholars' outfits, some garish, others mild. The familiar smell of coffee mixed with the aroma of mashed potatoes and fried chips enriched the air. Holding my lunch tray carefully in front of me, touring around the café, chasing Jamie, I remembered my own good old days in the university. We settled across a small table, at an arm's length from each other, in a quiet corner in the hall. Funny, I could not resist thinking which way to flee if the debate between us got heated and Jamie started throwing crockery. Though, from across the table, he appeared cool, smiling, "Oxymoron, you look younger than many of my students - I know your story."

"Yah, a long one. How is work going?"

He dismissed my attempt at waffling, "tell me how you bear with yourself… in this format."

"Troubled. Things once welded together in me have all the way been seeking dehiscence. Set-me-free is the outcry."

"Don't try ducking the question" he raised his voice by a few decibels.

I said, "no, I am serious. Been struggling with the conflict in my arrangement."

He giggled, "come on Oxymoron, just enjoy your new span. Look around the youth; it is exuding, you its part".

Unimpressed, I kept quiet. I had already gone through all these debates. I murmured in mind that I was here to discuss some other serious stuff.

He stared at me, trying to read my face. "You wanted to know my views on the self. Your self is just a hologram, merely an illusion, spawned with your thoughts superimposed over each other," he showed a glimpse of his eloquence.

"Thoughts superimposed!! seems an interesting idea," I said. "However, to me, the self keeps itself at a distance from the thoughts it holds. The self to thoughts in a person is like a hinge to a door, the controller and organizer."

"This must be your personal view."

"It has to be. So is yours. The self seeks to look at non-self; the two are different."

"Interesting, but fluffy. Come with some solid stuff," he rebutted.

I said, "fluffy, yes, because neither of the selves of the two of us witnessed its own making."

"Absence from a scene does not stop you describing it."

I hoped he'd known better than this sophistry, but did not say it. I pursued, "if you know how to describe of nature of the *self*, its chemistry, I am seeking this knowledge."

He said, "what I know on this subject is that the intelligence and the rest of human intellectual excellence come mounted on the genes. Nothing of life exists outside them."

"You might have come across twins; I recently have met two identical twin young men who held that they were separate individuals despite the several parallels between them. Clearly, there must be something other than genes in their making."

He said, "differences among people can also subscribe to the differences in the experiences that they have in life. Obviously, experiences add to the person or to the thing that you call the self."

I said, "I did not ask their mum but wouldn't be surprised if she'd described them as two different personalities, developing from the start, much before any conscious experience that they could have. If that is the case, the self is a genre independent from the start, as such diferent from the genre of experiences it gains over time. In the example of twins, my reference is to the unique, unshared utterly private individuality of the person – the self, (I took this phrase from Logge), not to an experience added to it later."

I suspected Jamie would at this point use associations of certain genes with specific diseases. For example, the associations of specific genes with personality traits like neuroticism[1] and extraversion.[2] Indeed, that's the path he eventually took. He said, "faulty genes run in families, imparting disease, including mental disorders, but only to the members of the family carrying these genes."

He was in a flow, "further, IQ values between races are consistently detected as asymmetrical, the individuals in some races showing better performance that those in the other races. Further, efficiencies and capabilities within a community can be promoted by cross-breeding of good genes within it - Evolution confirms this fact. What does this all tell you? Genes are all that you have for everything, including the intellect. What else do you want to know?"

Feeling disgusted by his bringing in the eugenics, yet I did not argue against the biases of IQ test, nor did I tangle with his view on the composition of the self, of it being composite or indivisible. I just repeated the question which I had asked from the twins, "do you think the genes just build the house, the brain, into which its resident, the self, is smuggled, or, do you hold the genes constructing both the house and its resident?"

If I'd put his response in a summary, it would go like this: the genes lay the brain structure, in which they set tracks in a particular order, allowing messages running along them in certain orders. This should generate thoughts, which result in intellectual competency; and, many such competencies placed, one over the top of the other, create comprehension,[3] famously called as the self or the consciousness.

I said, "your story of the self seems to be the one depicting its assembly rather than its distinction, unless, of course, if you particularly meant to profess it that way."

He intervened, "no ..."

I hastened, "let me finish, Jamie. If you have posited this story as a scientific theory, it fails on several accounts, the most serious one being of the layering of the competencies in order to create comprehension. There is no test available, or conceivable, to falsify this theory and there is no other example of this phenomenon occurring in nature."

---

[1] One of the five personality traits in which the person experiences the world as distressing and unsafe
[2] Describes a social and outgoing person
[3] Daniel Dennet, 1991, Consciousness Explained, Ed Little Brown and Co. Penguin Science.

"Then to find out about the thing called the self, why don't you go and meet with this entity yourself, if it ever existed by any chance, when you can ask it about its own version of the story," he ridiculed me. Without waiting for my answer, he abruptly rose from his chair, with the extending of his knees pushing the chair backward a bit too far, causing it to screech on the concrete floor and to knock into the back of the chair behind his, which resulted in the face in the chair turning to us, with one eye closed because of the screech, and the angle on the same side of his mouth drawn to the eye, because of the knock. Jamie said sorry to the guy.

I left my seat, too, "I do hope one day I'll bump into the self. Anyway, thank you for your time."

I thought we had almost reached the moot point but, unfortunately, the discussion was aborted. Albeit a futile dialogue but it did confirm my belief that the question of the self did not belong to the domains of Eugenics or Biology. It must belong to a domain not yet clear to me.

Aurora laughed at my report from this meeting. She said I had asked the right questions but from a wrong person, "you must find a Sufi master to reveal the self to you. They are the ones who specialize in the self." I noted the point for the future.

# ANOTHER PERSON IN THE MARRIAGE

COMELY WANTED TO GO FOR a bigger house. The one she eventually liked was a modern three bedroom semidetached on the Rose Gardens. Two of the bedrooms were on the ground floor, one on each side of the arching hallway, and one in the attic, all featured with glasswork, oversized windows and glass cabinets. Looking over a nicely done rear garden was a sun-room, used as dining. Mirrors were hung on the walls all around the house. The one in the attic was really special - baroque, garnished with red floral carving on the borders and floral print in the center. The kitchen, too, had a big glass wall looking at the rear garden. The house, in short, was bathed in light, designed by someone having romance with glass and mirrors. I liked moving in this house also because of my affinity with mirrors. I suggested we called it the Comely House.

Comely wanted to use the attic as her main bedroom. I was also happy with that choice, because that was the most interesting room in the house, with its gable windows, colorful décor and extensive floor space, but, more importantly, because it was her choice. But, then, she quickly changed her mind, fed up with going up and down the staircase several times a day. So, we moved to the bedroom downstairs on the right of the hallway. She said she preferred this one over the one on the left, for she felt more inclined turning to the right from the hallway rather than to the left when coming from outside. Again, I always took it that homes are for the ladies - you must live there the way they like – even though, in this case, the left bedroom was bigger by a whiff and brighter by a hint.

Comely was not much into cooking, except on special days. Opening a can or ordering a pizza was to be preferred over preparing a dinner, and fizzy drinks over tap water. If not this, we will go out for eating. I was not particularly bothered with these obsessions; however, I missed the aroma from a busy kitchen. I missed Zeitoun having small talks while working around the cooker and I unnoticeably clearing the sink and doing other menial chores. At various stages of cooking, she would pass samples from the cookery to me to test, invariably saying, "my taste buds are a graveyard." I would laugh on this gesture, and loved it. The problem in this design was that by the time food was finally ready, I would already be well fed through the samples. But that was now all in the past.

Comely was sweet. On special days, like on long weekends, she would cook nice meal in big quantities to linger for few days. I would be around in the kitchen to help her. She would say, 'could you do this; could you do that,' and finish the job herself. It was our first time in the kitchen when she asked me if I could chop potatoes into tiny slices. Then she insisted in showing me how to do it and, in showing, she finished them off. And then she said, "in the kitchen, you don't seem to know even simple things."

Off and on, she would drift into talking about her university years. I wasn't sure if she'd realized that I wasn't actually privy to her such experiences. The experiences of my years in university were older by several decades than her age, now lost in oblivion. I would remain silent in these sessions, of which there were many, recurring regularly. She would suddenly notice my silence and change the topic, sometimes also showing distaste. Gradually, she became quieter and quieter. I thought she was doing her journey with my not being the person whom she had married.

Whereas I believed this marriage was the binder for all of the colours of the canvas of my life, its one particular color bled into the rest, muddling the painting. Comely was almost crazy in spending time with me, yet did not show much interest in sharing my thoughts. In fact, we did not make much conversation at all. She preferred the name Nahaar for me, which was most definitely reasonable, for it was for Nahaar that she married me. However, she did not particularly like the word Comely coming from me. She liked to see me smiling but no sooner did I speak a word than she would turn her face the other way. I thought it was not something to worry about, considering our odd marriage needing some initial adjustments. However, it soon unfolded that she was actually frustrated with my, Oxymoron's, omnipresence between her and her lover. I turned a blind eye to these signals, not prepared to give up on the marriage easily. I would try sharing with her the stories from the day and buying her gifts, always seek her preferences, so forth. She liked bohemian jewellery; soon her jewellery box got filled with a classy collection. She preferred Boho-Chic dresses in fiery colors; soon she got her wardrobe satiated with of flaring finery. She regularly wanted eat-outs; we had come to know all the nice eating places in the city and what they cooked best on which day. She was offended with screens used in her presence; I would not dare touching my smart phone when she was around. She did not like blue color in darker shades; the color was thus barred from our house and from my life. If you saw me with her, you would find a man properly cowed. You would think why? You might presume it was Oxymoron, the old man in me, overtly trying to gratify a young wife. No doubt, some of my taming had come from Zeitoun in my earlier life. But, now, mostly, I wanted to swaddle Comely with love to buy her love for Oxymoron in return. It slowly became clear that I would not possibly be able to best these of my labors in feting her or win her over. And, then, there came a time when she hoped I did not talk to her, or even talk at all.

Though, to be fair on her, the picture was not that monotonous. Like lenticular printing, our bond would reveal different contents from different angles. From another angle, she would show as a truly caring, concerned partner. She would be making sure food was made available on time and my clothes sorted. The house was kept in a superb order and kitchen store run systematically, no mess, no wastage, no shortages. At a personal level, even a papercut or a light headache that inflicted on me could put her into a panic mode. What else could one want from a partner in running of a smooth marriage?

I became used to this contradiction in her mannerism and to the cold-war between us. However, it imperceptibly started ripping me from inside - ripping me once again after the union on that night - the night of pledge - the pledge of peace between me, Oxymoron, and me, Nahaar. However, what literally defeated my patience was the argument, precipitously bloated out of proportion which took place on that dark Friday night. It started with her telling me she was thinking to go for a holiday.

"Of course, Comely, where do you reckon us going and when?"

A pause followed. Was she thinking how to leave me out from her holiday plan? She set me on an annoyance mode. But it was not for the annoyance that I made the next move. On the spur of the moment, I asked her this question that I always had in my mind but did not dare asking. "Comely, you were missing from the scene around the time of Nahaar's operation. Why?"

Of course, this was a genuine question, for she had taken many weeks before she returned, missing out the whole drama of the demise of Nahaar.

I believed she would offer an explanation on the lines that she had gone for holidays or the college history trip while she was not contactable. She would say, for her disgust for the phone screens, she did not take the phone with her, hence the communication blackout. However, what she gave me as an answer actually shocked me. She squinted her eyes in disdain, "it has nothing to do with you; it is something between me and my love."

"I am sorry but I am your husband."

"Yes, but not the way you think it is." She ended the discussion then and there, and left.

I had no idea how to cope with this niminy-piminy girl, who was now beyond me. Dejected heart-broken, I yearned to have a private word with Nahaar. I confronted him in the mirror. I found the young man standing there confused and worried. I hated him – hated him like never before. I discovered how hatred mixed with jealousy could truly be so venomous and hurtful. "So, it is the body she loves - not me - your body. You have gone- thanks – though leaving behind a problem for me, a big problem - your body."

I thought he was embarrassed, but he kept quiet. He could have asked how I could dare to marry his beloved, but he just kept quiet.

It was an impasse. I made a decision. I returned to Comely. I told her about my decision for a divorce. But with my just uttering the word 'divorce', she lost the control and cried, that broke my heart, setting me into panic. Anyone listening to this would assume domestic violence is taking place.

# SURPRISE GIFT

"SO, WHAT SHOULD I do now, Aurora, you think?" The next morning, I phoned her for a council. I apologized for the call over the weekend, "Comely will be happy as long as I could keep Oxymoron out of business; but what should I do for the poor guy? Where can I send him and how?"

"Render to Caesar the things that are Caesar's and to God the things that are God's," I heard her saying on the phone.

There was a long pause. I said, "shall we get together for another evening in the same restaurant - the two of us."

"Tonight," she said.

We met in the restaurant car park. Casually dressed, she was wearing the necklace with the coin printed with Hypatia's monogram. I also had quietly brought in my rucksack the globe with the sleeping rose. Inching towards the restaurant, we were so absorbed in talking that we found ourselves halted on the way. Not wanting to move, we ended up finding a bench nearby in the car park. "So, where were we?" settled on the bench, I said.

She looked at my face and I at hers, though I could not sustain my gaze at her, soon gliding my eyes at the things around. And, then, I returned, fleetingly spying at her eyes for the signal that I was looking to read. I had another visual round of the car park but this time I blanked her out. Though, if you asked me what I had seen in the park, I would say I would not have noticed even if there were an elephant walking around – an 'irrelephant'. Pretending flippancy, I had another visual round of the place but now, at catching her eyes, I infiltrated her mind. The very next moment, my heart in my mouth, I skated from the bench and, on my knees, turned to her, held her hand and proposed her. I proposed Ms. Aurora Bird to marry me - as well. At this moment, I did not care where we were sitting, who was looking at us and what they would think of a young man crouching on the floor in front of a lady of an older age.

Her response was unexpected as she actually started sobbing, "I was hoping to hear this word from you decades ago. I wanted to hear this when you came to tell me that you were marrying Zeitoun. Later, my own marriage failed because I could not get you out of my mind. Even after you had taken the cocoon of this new body, I thought we were made for each other, but could not say it loud. Indeed, I was waiting for you to say this word the evening when we were here last time. Then, budding from somewhere in the horizon, came Comely, to snatch you from me." She laughed, "so more or less, all these years, I remained a wife-in-waiting."

She took a deep breath full of regret, "and, now I hear this word when it is already too late Oxymoron, is it not?"

I felt her pain anew, even though I had already known most of the story. I said, "do you remember when you urged me to accept Comely as my wife? Did you know your broken voice and tearful eyes wrenched my core? I wanted to propose you that night when we were here the last time, but I couldn't, for I had the pending fear of this girl coming our way – Comely, whose name even I did not know at the time."

"I felt it too, but now, is it not too late?"

"Why late, Aurora?" I asked, "for God's sake, please do not tell me you are already engaged somewhere else."

She said, "for sure, the law of the country would not allow a second marriage."

Relieved, I laughed with joy. I was thrilled with the thought of my life spent with her. Her not declining my proposal was like my foot in the door. From here, together we would untie the knots on the way. Our first challenge of course would be to persuade Comely, secondly, the law. But, also, in my heart, I was struck with my fear of failing in this sophisticated polygamous relationship. Vacantly staring at the ground, I thought of the prospect of a successful marriage with Aurora being only a distant dream. The more I thought about it the farther it seemed – like a kite cut from its cord keeps tossing further away, randomly, at the whim of the wind.

Aroura, seeing resignation on my face, said, "you are not thinking to axe the idea, are you?"

"Just getting anxious about it, more so about its outcome."

She was not someone to give up. She smiled and I with her. I said, "for once, the insoluble obstinate triangle between Oxymoron, the youth and Comely can transform into a balanced rectangle - fair and square. I get what I want; the youth get what he needs."

She smiled again at the simplicity of my take, but then affirmed my view, "in one way, the case is indeed simple. You see, two people in you – two types of wants, likings, luvs. Then two of everything, even wives."

I became excited, "yes, there can be two of each in the list. The older suits the one person in me, so be it to the other; the contemporary suits the other person in me, come what may for the former. The one likes honey on the toast, the other needs high-energy drinks. The one prefers early to bed and early to rise; the other is thrilled to run where other people just walk. The one likes to rest leisurely with his partner, chatting around the things at length as if there is no tomorrow; the other rushes around the world showing his wife the Great Pyramids of Gisa and the Famous Berlin Wall, all in one go, as if there is no tomorrow." I stopped here, feeling a bit swayed with my own argument.

"OK, now, well! what next?" she changed the line with a hint of sarcasm.

"Aurora, you have been on good terms with Comely. You were the one who kick-started this marriage. Comely knows that you are aware of the tussle between me and her. Would you talk to her?"

Aurora said, "Comely would want sureties – needing securities, that only you could provide. You know a second wife is like a wolf to the first. Best it comes from you, Oxymoron."

I felt weak, "tell me how do you see the conversation going?

"She would like to know this marriage must happen for her sake. She is not happy in the current setting. I am happy for her being the first lady, the lady of the house, the status she would retain. Me only as a help, help in everything, including relations – hope she would appreciate this."

***

But, no, Comely would not concur. As for the argument and its merits, she quickly got the point. However, to share her husband with another wife remained a non-starter. Almost seemingly lost, I tried to sum up the discussion, "don't you agree that in your husband is a part which you want to ignore or even hate?"

Fearing a trap, she stared at me quietly. I felt for her but had to remind myself the need to pursue the course lest my marriage with Comely risked breaking.

"It is for that part in me for whom we, the two of us, you and I, must find some busyness, some kind of roll, a job. This way, you hope to feel less interference from that person, that is if he is engaged elsewhere, engaged with Aurora. And you know Aurora very well. She will not interfere with your live, nor would she want to harm you."

It took some debate, a lot of time and, of course, assurances that she would be the boss of the house before she eventually settled, but I knew, in her heart, she did not want the second marriage to go ahead. She was probably banking on the law, which she thought would not permit a double marriage in the first place.

Comely and I met with a Family Law solicitor. He was aware of my law suit vs. Public Engagement and had heard about my complex make-up.

Despite his knowhow and zeal, it took a good sometime before he could grasp the picture. Once he got over the information, he quickly moved into innovative mode off thinking, just like mayonnaise suddenly gelling on hard whisking. Though, Comely was hesitant in giving a forthright consent, but frankly, this was kind of expected. She asked the solicitor, "how can you move a case for a double marriage when there is no provision in the law for it?"

He said, "this is not a case of double marriage - in the first place. We need to cook a new term, say, for example, a parallel marriage, for it."

"But there would be no such example of such marriage before."

"Yes, that is right" he said. "But again, there is no other example like your husband in his constitution."

She responded, "then, why do you have to ask for my consent for it anyway? What if I say, no?"

He said, "your consent will not be required if the court buys the concept of parallelism in your husband's constitution. But for the sake of argument, may I ask if you please, are you married with Oxymoron?"

"No, no way" she was annoyed. "My husband is Nahaar."

The solicitor said, "then, it is Oxymoron for whose marriage we are seeking court's permission."

Comely was bent on fighting tooth and nail, "if it is a marriage of yet another person besides my Nahaar, why bother seeking court's permission for it?'

"It is not a marriage of course though, because Oxymoron is gelled with Nahaar. And, just because Nahaar is your husband, we need your consent for Oxymoron."

She kept quiet, unhappy, unsettled, but she signed the paper. I blinked my eyes full of gratitude and trust at her.

***

The term 'parallel marriage' was a new coinage, which on hearing it from my council the first time the judge was thrilled. The lawyer elaborated this meant marrying someone for the body of the person, and someone else for the mind. He said, "since it is evident that the person in question comprised two parts, the body and the mind, coming from different people, the concept of parallel marriage is rather inevitable - compelling, too."

The judge said, "the provision is not in the statue, as you know, nor is there any precedent for it that you have quoted."

"I can quote the recent decision of the High Court on 'Oxymoron vs the Public Intelligence' where the honorable court accepted the plaintiff's plea based on the unique example of its kind, whereas the law remained quiet on it and the precedents lacking."

But the judge would not buy the plea straight away. The court was advised that a *prima facie* case for permission for this marriage would not stand, for, as opposed to the decision quoted, a marriage was not something easily reversible. Further, when asked, Comely fumbled over her statement such that the court became doubtful and did not issue an injunction in favor of the parallel marriage. The process thus drew out for some time, also attracting media attention. So, Aurora and I felt left in the limbo.

How amazing then was the afternoon when the court reached the verdict that the concept of 'parallel marriage' within my context was to be treated as an exemption in the law. The next day a news headline read:

"The Oxymoron gets two wives, one for each of his parts"

With this news, I found rest. I was pleasantly surprised when Comely, ahead me, welcomed Aurora in the family. We asked Aurora what kind of wedding she would like. "Very private," she said. "In fact, I don't want anyone from workplace to attend."

All the way to home, Comley and I talked about Aurora, on how to make her comfortable. I said to myself, 'tomorrow, my heart, my eyes and my house, all will be jazzed up with her presence – with my love, the love that I had forsaken for long.'

We, the three of us, plus some of Aurora's friends had a private wedding ceremony. Aurora shifted with us in the Comely House on the Rose Gardens. She chose for herself the bedroom in the attic.

# WHO IS THE FATHER?

L IFE STARTED AGAIN; THIS time, it was really great. Everyone was happy and pleased, Comely as well. Aurora was right in guessing Comely would be pleased with the change. Whereas before Comely had no one in the house to speak to except me, whose speech she did not like, now she had Aurora around. They spent hours in girlie chatting, even though their tastes and issues belonged to different age groups. More importantly, Comely had found in Aurora someone who had expunged Oxymoron out of the relationship between her and her lover. My own frustration with Comely's attitude had resolved, too. They very quickly developed an unwritten agreement for the tripartite relationship. In this federation thus there was a boss, Comely, a guardian, Aurora, and, to fill the place for masses, I was appointed.

The days merged seamlessly into the nights and the nights into the days. With Comely, in her presence, I would mostly do reading or writing, while she would be busy in various chores, us crossing our eyes off and on, without speaking much. With Aurora, I enjoyed her company, debating on subjects dear to us: philosophy, history, religion, you name it.

On that sunny day, I spent much of the morning in the rear garden. Aurora had bought some Gladioli needing planting. Around the time I finished the planting, Aurora returned from her friends. She liked the planting arrangement. It was indeed a nice afternoon with slight breeze, mostly sunny, with clouds in patches, in passing, shedding their casts, trying to censor warmth and light. Not keen to go in, we settled on the garden chairs. I asked Aurora about her friends. She rather liked to talk about their kids. "They were lovely, very cuddly," said she. "Shall we not have some of our own?" The next few minutes I spent in sorting out what she actually meant. It was revealed that she had planned in her head for Comely to have kids; in this she sounded like a mother-in-law. "This joke shared with Comely would be dangerous," I smiled.

"How about if I had already spoken to her," said she.

"And!!!"

"She promised to consider it."

I was excited about the idea of having kids one more time in my life; two around twenty years ago and now suddenly a couple more.

I asked, "Aurora, you have chosen the mum for the newborn - fine; who will be her father?"

She said, "how do you mean? The baby will bear your name, of course." But her voice quietened on the way.

I said, "think of her genetic make-up! The baby would inherit this from Nahaar."

Aurora was shocked. I continued, "in that sense, the baby would have nothing to do with me. In fact, the progeny from that lineage bearing the genetic prints of Nahaar would have nothing to do with me in any sense."

She had recovered from the shock, "Is Nahar alive? Bearing a child is a quality of only a living person. In that case, Nahaar lives despite he is dead."

I added, "and, me, for that matter, I am dead, because I cannot procreate. Not because of a medical condition but I simply don't have my genes in the form available for procreation. So, I am dead despite I am alive."

Hearing this, she said, "for God's sake, don't say you are dead." Probably, the traditional love of wives for husbands had perked up.

"You have married a mere thought, Aurora," I laughed. "I am indeed nothing more than a thought. I show presence because I can use a mouth piece, and that I use because I can think. I have no existence beyond my thoughts. Nahaar is dead despite he can procreate because he is no more there to think."

She was intently listening, "compare thought with the body. Thought is a mere fleeting figment. It is just an illusion; what else is it? Now take the body. It is a solid tangible reality." I continued, "but in my personal example, it is opposite, completely other way round. The illusion of thought in me claims ownership and existence, while reality of body in me is dumb."

"It is incredible, pretty anti-intuitive, too," she spoke. "But then, is it not something sizing up to what Descartes had said in his famous aphorism."

"Yes, yes, that one: 'I think therefore I am'!! Do you think Descartes was aware of the possibility of my example?"

"He reached this conclusion with logic, and you with an example, a real example," said she.

I said, "my example has indeed confirmed Descartes' aphorism, though in an ironic way. Philosophically I am alive, but biologically I am dead – you know Oxymoron!" We both enjoyed the conclusion.

"My urge of knowing the self is troubling me. By the way, do you remember suggesting me to see a Sufi master. I have found one... going to see them soon."

"Sounds great," she rose from the chair, raised her arms above her head and stifled a yawn. I got up too. We had a stroll around the garden. Then, she went inside.

Walking in the lawn barefooted, my eyes were on the plants but my mind was on the question who was alive between the two of us, Oxymoron or Nahaar. I noticed shrubs needing soft pruning. I brought secateurs and a pair of gloves from the shed. The safety catch had got a little rusty but I could still unhatch it. I started with the dead-head roses. My mind wandered around the verdict from the court; in 'Oxymoron vs Public Engagement, they held Oxymoron alive and Nahaar dead. I scanned the lavender for dead branches. In the verdict in the case of my marriage with Aurora, they found both Nahaar and Oxymoron alive in parallel, one having married Comely, the other allowed to marry Aurora. My eyes shifted at the cluster of hydrangeas. Today Aurora and I agreed that, biologically, Oxymoron did not exist, while Nahaar was thriving. With secateurs in my hand, in my thought, I asked Descartes about the two. In keeping with his aphorism 'I think therefore I am', he took Oxymoron its proof and Nahaar merely an illusion. I put the tools near the ornament of frogs and walked back to the chairs. I thought about Comely and Aurora, how different they were but on one thing they were rather similar in a way. The former did not want to see Oxymoron around at all, while later ignored Nahaar altogether. By the time I rested on the chair, I had reached the final length of reflection, 'and the person reflecting right now, the "I", believes he is Oxymoron.'

I turned my chair away from facing the sun. Through the glass, I could see Comely busy in the kitchen. I got up, knocked the glass and waved my hand, inviting her to join me in the garden. She came out and strolled with me, but as expected did not talk. This was her special way of spending time with me, I had learnt after all. Then, she went to the shed to return with the lawn mower dragging behind her. She unwound its cable from the safety cord-wrap and plugged the cable in the safety socket near the kitchen door. Then she pulled the mower in front of me and grasped my hands to place on its steering bar. Obviously, according to her standard, the lawn needed mowing, a decision which I would not try contesting. I started mowing. She went back to the kitchen and brought a bottle of water that she put on the table beside the chair. She stopped me with a nod of her finger and shifted her finger at my garden shoes besides the chair. I was enjoying the cool grass barefooted, but obviously, she thought of me risking electrocution from the lawn mover. She sat on the chair staring at me doing the lawn, smiling. Making circular designs on the grass, I was pushing the mower, thinking about Comely and her care, and with this thought I felt in me a wave of gratitude.

In the meantime, Aurora popped her head from the window on the upper floor and rumbled something, which I could not make out in the noise. I switched off the mower. She repeated, "the contradiction in your case actually lingers on, Oxymoron." Evidently, like I, after our discussion, she had continued to reflect. "Besides carrying your name as her father, the child would also inherit your property. That is even though you would not be her real father." I was not sure if she realized that Comely was out in the garden as well. But I was not surprised that her mind was still hovering around the issue. With this joy, I laughed, "I suspect it would then have to be a court again, deliberating on the rights of this child."

Still in the window, she nodded her head in affirmation. Then she noticed Comely present too, "I am coming down to join." It was indeed a great relationship in which to live and enjoy, I thought. Although, no sooner had Aurora said this than Comely had returned to the kitchen. Was she vying for attention with Aurora? I noticed her eyes rolling briefly and her feet stamping, which left a streak of worry on my mind. I feared the line of peace she had drawn between Nahaar and Oxymoron was under attack.

Aurora arrived, "we need to finish the subject. Where is Comely?"

"Gone. Comely does not stay for discussion, as you know," I replied. "But I agree that I would not be the father of this child. But if I am not her father, who am I to Comely? Now, if not her husband, I must be the agent of Comely's lover, or his proxy."

She said, "absurd - you acted as an agent for someone who never appointed you for this job."

"Appointed!! I had never met this guy," I laughed, cuddling my chest and belly with my hands. "Until I had him with me."

She said, "without the contract carrying his consent, you did not have any right to marry this girl." She giggled, "poor Comely – seems her marriage is annulled – in fact it didn't even begin."

Ignoring her giggles, I stared at her.

"It therefore follows that Comely's baby would be of Nahaar - meaning Nahaar is in fact Comely's husband. Then what are you doing in this marriage?

Your pretending as his agent is illegal, to say the least," she reiterated the argument, giggling, "In that utter truth, you are only my husband - purely and absolutely - only mine."

I teased her, "imagine if this marriage bore you a child, too."

Surprised, she stared at me. She seemed really bothered with my words. Her face was plastered with an alchemical mixture of infuriation and pity, as if she had heard something completely inappropriate, yet she had to tolerate it. I realized we never had talked on this subject, or in this manner, in the past - but, still. She noticed my consternation.

And then quickly her grimness got tranquilized into a smile, "you did not have any right to marry me either."

I felt shocked yet another time, "why?"

"The answer can rather be long," she replied. "Consistency demands rules applied across the board. If the marriage with Comely was on behalf of Nahaar, the constituents of the groom have not changed when marrying me, hence this marriage also had to be on Nahaar's behalf. Again, a contract and a consent were missing at this instance. Also, on a personal note, if this was the case, I would not have agreed to enter a marriage with a man already dead, in other words, a ghost."

I deciphered the points in her statement, "so, definitely, the young man's consent was needed before either of these marriages.

She laughed, "yes, that would have been a logical requirement. I guess, then, you must realize that you are a self-appointed bogus agent. You consenting the marriages was invalid. This raises profound legal implications."

We pursued the debate for some time, with each line of the argument ending in absurdity. Each time we laughed harder and harder. I controlled myself lest the horrible noise of my laughter would scare her to death, but then she continued to giggle hysterically. I noticed Comely staring through the glass, again rolling her eyes; then she disappeared briskly. I thought she must have thought of us crazy, perhaps drunk, too. Deep down, I was seeking an ultimate settlement of the nature of my self. The time had come for me to see the Sufi master.

# SEEKING THE SELF

A MAN OF MY AGE, WITH salt-colored short beard, scarcely peppered near the chin, the Sufi master stood up from his floor cushion for me. He had wrapped himself loosely in a brilliant white attire, his head with a turban of the same color, burying the upper half of his ears underneath it. The eyes so overtly smiling that in likeness I had not seen a pair before. His face bore few age-lines but no droopy wrinkles or angry frowns. With a cozy and firm handshake, he greeted me, drawing my hand slightly on his side of the midpoint. Standing face to face, I gazed at him intensely, but he wasn't particularly bothered with it. He spoke with a smile, which italicized his cheek-balls. Stepping aside from his floor cushion, he asked me to take his place and turned around to pour some juice for me. He put the glass on a slab next to me and drew a cushion for himself to face me. There was silence but it did not feel awkward to me. He nodded his head few times and opened the conversation, "it is the time of unrest."

"My unrest is not rooted in time but in myself," I said. A light appeared in his eyes. After all, I wasn't here merely seeking peace of mind; I was pursuing the question of my identity. Looking at me intently, he waited for me to tell my story. My account encompassed my struggle and search. With his head down, he let me finish at my speed. But when he raised it, the light in his eyes had dimmed, "your search is waiting to ripen. The real thirsty only see water. Water is bound to come your way but not yet."

I stared at the far corner of the room in slight disappointment. I realized what I had done. Boisterous, in the flow, I had perhaps spoken far too much. No idea, why I had dropped hints of pomposity, if not showing it frankly, even in citing my name, Oxymoron, and in narrating my cataclysmic life style.

"How to work it up - this search – sir," I asked humbly but couldn't hide affection.

He reassuringly giggled, "by emptying the cup…, before you can refill it. There has to be space in your cup, beside your self, lot more space, for your question to fit in … and there is not … much at present. Today is the day for you to make an intention and to agree a resolution. One day, you will like to sit with yourself – just with your … self alone - to purge it – purge this self; then you would start on a journey … on a celestial journey, and find the meanings right there, scribed on the horizon that only you can read."

Hearing the word 'intention', I could not resist showing off again, "I intend therefore I am." Though, in my heart, I knew I had jumped the gun - with a sentence that I had stolen from one of the twins, I think it was Logge.

The master replied, "you cannot even intend without the power to intend, a power conferred. My intention is frequently defeated, showing another intent in action, the superior intent, that of the Creator."

With this the master got up.

I walked out feeling little disappointed with myself, though the meeting with the master wasn't completely futile. I had asked about my identity; instead, I was promised with the meaning of my life. I had found out that, in chasing my question, I did not particularly need looking beyond - at the courts, colleagues, friends or the family - but looking within. For that to happen, I would need to distill my self free from pollutants, to shed extra load breaking my back. At the time, this message was blatantly clear to me; but, as always happens, in the later times, it gathered its share from the dust arising from the life rolling on a muddy path.

# THE SELF IS SITED

LIFE WAS ROLLING - on the muddy but even turf - a turf of bliss and peace. The two ladies had the roles naturally divided between themselves. Comely would go out with me for shopping, for walks, on social events, anything outside the house, but she would not speak to me accept when someone was about to die needing her to speak for their survival. Aurora will mainly hold the house and its economics. Her debating and philosophizing were a treat for me and a bonus. On the other hand, though, she would make any number of excuses to avoid going out with me, even for shopping. The two ladies, despite the age gap between them, were at good terms, chatting on things and households. Indeed, they were very friendly with each other.

I thought, in this mode, the life was running alright. Although aware of the reasons, I was not completely comfortable with Comely avoiding to speak to me and Aurora avoiding to go out with me. I hoped one day they got over these impediments.

This pattern continued until we reached the pleasant autumn evening of that Saturday. It was refreshingly cool after the pouring almost all day. It was a bit darker than usual though, with heavy clouds still looming on the horizon, teaming up to decant again. The sky would be lit off and on, with a sheet of light ornamented with red sprites from the clouds flashing. The room was imbued with rather chilled moist air filtering through the window slits, melding with the steam arising from food, hot from the oven and with its engaging aroma. Aroura had cooked, for the entrée, a casserole of chunks of meat with lots of onion, cooked with pasta sauce and, for main course, a platter of delectable biryani, layered with masala fish, which was her specialty. A scrumptious brand of tiramisu, deliciously overdosed with cream, came from Comely. She served the food, with a tray in her hands and the water bottle between her elbow and her side. The bottle was too heavy to keep it there. I expected Aurora, normally methodical, to frown on this, but instead she just smiled. She adored Comely, buying her gifts, always giving her priority, showing love and respect for her. I thought had Aurora been Comely's mother-in-law, she would rank high in mothers-in-law in decency and in winning hearts of the foes.

After the dinner, came the tea, brewed from a blend of Darjeeling young tea leaves, spiced with ginger and herbs and it was from me. Refreshed with the lip-smacking meal and with the gratifying ambiance, we would not leave the table soon, absorbed in a relaxed stroll of chitchat and laughing around things.

I would not remember when we moved from chattering into philosophy, and when Comely had left.

"Want something?" Aroura paused. She could always sense a distraction in my manners, however slight.

"How about having another round of tea! I guess it is getting a bit cold. Shall I close the window as well!"

She nodded. I returned to my chair after closing the window, while she, half-bent on the table, was putting the tea together. From that closeness, I could see her hair, lush and shining with slight curls, with occasional whites streaking amidst the jet-black locks, combed backward collecting into an updo. While pouring tea, she raised her face seeking approval for the tan in the brew. Looking at her face this way was an experience intriguingly extraordinaire; her face-cut at this angle with arching eyebrows, dancing eyelashes, button nose, a touch of rosy linings of the cheeks and healthy lips, defined with a tapered chin, all felt different. That she was actually very pretty suddenly dawned at me. Her garment looked nifty, her fragrance alluring. She settled down on her chair but I could not take my eyes off her, and I would not. I thought it was rather unfortunate that I did not have these feelings for her before. Was this gap because of the familiarity with her achieved over the decades? I asked myself. I thought of the familiarity as a bizarre thing, for while it feeds the bond between people, it can kill the attraction in it.

My ecstasy ripened into my desire of Aroura, which, I was sure, she must have noticed as well, for she blinked a couple of times, then she stole her eyes the other way. This only increased my desire. I always felt there was something of special, a special attraction or a message, in the white of the feminine eyes, of which the they are well aware as well. But then, she suddenly stiffened in both her posture and attitude and looked at me the way a headmistress would look at the boy in her school trying to woo her and, with a nod of her index finger, instruct him to come in size.

Strangely, however, I too felt disquiet, superficially initially, but which swiftly deepened into agony, as if something 'within' me was being wrenched. It was wrenched like an arm twisted in full, leaving pain behind, lot of pain. I had suddenly felt the presence of Nahaar between me and Aurora, my wife, and protested against his lewd looks at my wife. I was not at all pleased with his presence besides the two of us during these private moments, his eyes gazing at my wife. The feeling devastated me. But, then, I found its parallel in my own presence in the relationship between Comely and her lover. In either way the intrusions were unfortunate but inevitable. My anguish acquired insight and calmed. Probably oblivious of these of my internal wrangles, Aurora was still stiff in her mood. But she also won over her tussle and loosened. Likewise, I thought she must have been fed up with Nahaar ever present between us.

A couple of sips of hot tea in quiet, Aroura steered the discussion back to the topic. She cited her recent readings of Plato who professed that thought was pure only when it was in pursuits of itself but that was only possible when thought was uncorrupted from bodily sways.

She said, "the philosopher holds that the soul must be plucked from the body in order for it to achieve a pure thought, and that death is its only true plucker."

As far as a pure thought was concerned, I could probably see Plato's vision, but I wanted the notion of 'thought in pursuits of itself' to be explored further.

She seemed to have mustered in her mind a plan for this dialogue and proposed we should employ my own unique model of a person to help the question.

She said, "thought receives input and hands out outputs"

I laughed, "Aurora, is that not too obvious?"

Ignoring me, she continued, "several things underwrite thought or impact it. Of the inputs, some it receives through the body and others it receives from the body itself. If information is one of the inputs, there is information that the body receives from the external world, for example, through the eyes and ears, and then there is a type of information it creates of itself, for example, pain. Then bodily demands put their pressure on thought. Of such demands, the important one is food, which is matched with the thought of hunger, another is social acceptance, which is matched by thought of altruism."

Had she got training in biological sciences? I thought, for she seemed to show in her conversation a hint of medical parlance. I remembered her acquaintance with litigation and legal matters from her dealing with my court case. Truly a polymath.

She continued, "similarly, thought impacts body through its outputs as actions. Actions of all types, reading, walking, cooking and the rest, just follow their tallying thoughts. And then, thought is accomplished through the body, like in sexualities and sensualities of kinds."

Irked with the argument dragged circuitously, I raised my hand. She touched my shoulder and carried on, "you can see how body is kneaded with thought.

You can see why Plato holds that nothing less than death can liberate thought from the body."

The touch animated some kind of sensual feelings in me, but I pretended passing over it, hoping it to recur. I said, "indeed, quiet evidently, it is impossible to have thought without the body."

"No," she said. "Something has defied this rule, and now you would ask what is that something?" She paused, "you. You have defied it."

I became intensely interested.

Her voice gathered pitch as she spoke, "in your example, thought has neighbored the body in three different relations. In the first, to reside in the body, like every other living soul in the world."

"That done," I was a bit impatient again.

"Then, on your thought was a period outside the body when your brain was in the hands of the surgeons."

I kept quiet.

"And, in the third type, the one you have right now," saying this, she put her fists up and then turned them at each other, striking them at the knuckles few times. "Gone head-to-head in tussle – between your two parts."

I admitted it.

Of course, she was aware of the conflict between my thought and the body, even though the dust raised from this clash had mostly settled. The clash had entombed in this volcano waiting to erupt, but its wave affecting the two ladies in this house, one attracted to the body of the man of the house, objecting to the presence of 'I', the other perceiving the man merely as 'I', turning a blind eye to the body. This distinction helped appraising pure thought and deciphering the reasons of its being polluted by the body.

I said, "now! now things are different from the past, in kind and scale. The youth and his needs are driving me mad - take my word for it. You know the hormones – this youth makes me run where I find it hard to walk."

She smiled, "can you achieve thought without the influence from the body?"

I said, "not sure, really. Not really. Definitely not. Now, I can see the influence of the body more clearly and I cannot duck it. Obviously, I would still need my soul parted from the body to attain thought in a pure state. I need to meet death. On this one, Plato was spot on."

"But, then," she smiled with a thrill, "I wonder if someone were to inform Plato of parting of soul from the body actually having taken place in a person who is not dead but is alive... being here... in front of me... right now."

I couldn't be sure of what she meant. I said, "but, as I say, I only know the opposite of what you have said. In the past, my thought was under the influenced of my own body, now of this one." I softly patted the chest.

She said, "not now - but it was once the case. It was when you were in the theatre. They severed your brain from your body ... cutting all of its connections ... and took it out from your head. Then your brain must have been laid on a gauze cushion in a metal tray. They must have washed it of the clots and kept it moist to keep it going. On the operation table next to yours, another team of surgeons must be getting the head of the young man ready to receive your brain. After placing it there, they would start reconnecting it with the new body – quite a bit of welding work. And then, checking the connections before closing. A wrong connection would result in a triangle at which you look smelling sweet to you, or a melody becoming visible to you as a mosaic of shades of red colours. You know how a wrong connection could cost them going back to redo things."

"Yes, it is fairly obvious," I closed my hands and flexed my feet one by one, pretending to test the connections.

She smiled but rushed back to her point, "the question that needs asking is, what was the state of your mind at the time when your brain was not connected to a body – at the moment of switch?"

With these words, she put her hand on my shoulder again. She said, "at that moment, there would be nothing coming from the body, no data, no sensation, no pain, no indulgence, no hunger even no message from the external world – for, then, there was no body connected to your brain at all. Which means, there would be no instructions from your brain waiting to dispatch to the body, for there was no body to which to give instructions."

"I see!!!"

"So, once removed from the body – completely – also removed from the external world, what was the nature of thought with which your brain was busy?"

I pretended trying to recall, "it must be busy in some thought."

She said, "we are not looking here for the details of the contents of your thought."

I felt awkward.

She again placed her hand on my shoulder, her voice lowered, "for now, we are just looking at the possibility of a pure thought, that is, a thought without any contamination from the body or from the exterior world – a thought unhinged from any influence, corruption or contamination."

"Your suggestion must be admitted," said I, feeling her touch.

We both kept quiet for few seconds. Then, she removed her hand. I spoke as if from a dream, "at that moment, as an entity, I would have consisted of a thought, essentially pure – uncorrupted."

Night was getting deeper, and I remembered Comely who would be getting edgy. Thinking to close the subject, I lied, "I am bit sleepy, but I have one last question, you mind."

I looked at her; she was not sleepy at all. Staring at me, she said, "I did not finish yet."

In my heart, I too wanted her to continue and wouldn't mind her touching my shoulder in between. I was a real double agent.

She said, "your brain in their hands, they were actually holding your thoughts."

"Yes, you have shown that is the case. But that is not all; that is where my question falls."

"What else. Thoughts don't run on the spleen," she was cheeky the first time ever.

I remembered my dialogue with Jamie from the Humanity Department, "let me frame the question! This is about the self. Would you prefer to hold the self, like you seem to agree, which is to consider it as a cluster of thoughts, or would you rather designate it as the possessor of thoughts, in other words, their master?"

"Why do you have to invent the self as a separate entity?" she asked

"Thoughts belong – they belong to their custodian – the self," I said.

"Show my how?" she demanded.

I said, "whatever I know of a person stands as his thoughts, disposition, habits – nothing of them is as such of him, I mean instead of him." I continued, "although it may appear just a matter of how the language is used here, but it is not. I surmise self is not just emblematic of thoughts but is distinct and real."

"I mean, how?" she was looking at me.

I replied, "I can keep a thought, discard it or change it, but I remain 'I' whatsoever."

She said, "I would not object to admitting this proposition for now, except, besides body and thought, it would demand from us to assume yet another partner, the self, yet another species of artefacts."

I said, "so be it. If it is there, we have to."

"We can admit the self in this way if we can show its necessity," apparently, she had not agreed.

Suddenly I envisioned a hologram with two figures staring at me, one saying to the other, "this guy is a real slow ... does not remember what we had taught him about the self housed in the brain, schooling thoughts running around on its tracks and circuits."

"Hello, Logge and Nash!" I whispered, not being able to make who was who.

Surprised, Aurora looked at me. I said, "I am thinking of the two twin brothers I met in the past, one philosopher, the other geneticist. They taught me about the self standing as an entity, separately from the thoughts it holds. It is amazing that we have arrived at the same conclusion today, though through a different route."

"What is their different route. May I know it!" she looked keen.

"Evidence for this conclusion comes from an independent existence of intentions, indicating to the existence of the one who intends."

"Here you go!" she said. "There is the species of thought, and then the self, and now, you bring in yet another one, intention. The place is really overcrowded."

I said, "the ultimate evidence for the existence of intentions can be seen in stroke patients. In stroke, the brain is damaged and the limb that the damaged part controls is paralyzed. The paralyzed part can be rehabilitated only if the patient shows intention to move it. Amazing thing here is that the intention, if present, can be recorded. That is how they know it."

"Is that true," she said.

I said, "we can admit the self based on evidence rather than just on proof,"

She looked pleased.

I said, "would you let me try this question on my own example of transitions."

She nodded her head, patting my shoulder.

"During the three transitions that I have lived through, the one thing that did not change is me, the I in my person."

I hastened to add, "when I say person, I do not mean just the personal things, likes and dislikes, nor do I mean social relations, ownerships, liabilities. I even don't include in this category of beliefs and faith. Even though I do not find these things in any sense changed in me over time, but they might as well have. They have remained, as always, open to negotiation and to my choice."

She was listening intently, "when I say the person, I don't just mean by it the part unchangeable, non-negotiable, but the agent who negotiates and chooses. You see, I have come through all the trouble in the transition with my person intact. I am the same person livign through all the scenes of this whole theatre."

She interjected, "I cannot argue with your personal experience. Would you like to call this entity, as some people call it, the soul?"

"This term can help to make the distinction, I suppose, but we can leave it out for now."

She said, "we therefore can paraphrase your story of transition. With your brain in their hands, the surgeons would not have realized what they were holding to relocate into a new body actually constituted a person, a self."

"Then," she softly giggled. "They would not have realized what they were holding was in fact my future husband."

And, now as if her ribs were being tickled, "what if they'd relocated this brain into a girl's head?"

I smiled at the joke but suddenly realized the impact of the outcome of what she'd said. It just needed the person on the neighboring operation table to be a female, say, of Olive, or a similar name, instead of Nahaar. Since they did not ask for my permission for the switch that they'd made, they would not have asked for a permission for the transfer in the way Aurora had joked about. With that thought, I perspired.

I thought we had reached the moot point. But then Nash and Logge reappeared in a hologram in front of me, reminding me that the self subsists in the brain, and the brain is yet an organ of the body. I was increasingly aware of

Comely waiting, still I could not resist asking the next question, "but, then, wait a minute, Aurora, these artefacts in my constitution have come along with the brain, have they not? The brain is made of material, belongings to the body? Your argument that pure thought has to be bodyless is imperfect, I am afraid."

She smiled, "that's true." She was calm, "but, in one thing the brain is different from the rest of the body. Since I am married to a brain, I should know the difference very well."

"Which is?"

"Is it not interesting that the brain does not have sensations of its own? It receives them from the body, but from itself does not have any. It is very private. It is supposed to feel pain; with brain dead, one cannot feel pain. What does anesthesia do? It knocks out the brain, stopping pain from being felt. Yet, the brain is not the place where pain is felt. It is felt in the body where it has arisen. Say, you hurt your hand. The pain message is sent to the brain to feel, but where actually is it felt? In the hand itself. The brain does not even let you know it was in the loop."

She now stressed on every word of what she said, "of their experiences, all the organs in the body create data for the brain, seeking its help, approval and guidance. In other words, they pose their problems to the brain to solve. But the brain does not generate any data of its own experience for its consumption. It feels for others but not for itself. No doubt it is a part of the body, but this platform for thought – and now you insist this as custodian of the soul or self as well - in a sublime way, is more akin to this soul than to body, at best an intermediary."

I concurred fully with her understanding and would have liked to pursue this thought, but she got distracted. She placed her finger on her lips, "shush, Sh..." She whispered that I could just hear, "listen to the rain." I guessed she'd wanted us to break from rather dense, heavy-duty logic but then she had a great aesthetic sense and a spontaneous passion for it.

I tried to look through the glass; I could only pitch-black outside. We both put our ears to the rain. There was this quietness, enhanced by raindrops, now sprinkling, then pitter-pattering. On one side, it was water whooshing in the grooves, intermittently with occasional plip-plops. On the other was the rustle from the trees, rippling like a heart murmur. Deep into the night, it was a precious moment of a novel experience of her company. I could see a picture painted with sounds – a picture with a pitch-dark backdrop of silence.

"So, how was that," she asked. I kept my eyes closed hoping if I could continue with the sounds for longer. But, then, obviously she was looking for a response.

I said, "I agree that, using my example, it can be shown that a separation of thought from the body has come to pass, without it having to wait for the time of death." I continued, "though, in effect, my experiment unfortunately failed drastically. Only if I could have remembered any thought from the time of switch, without a body - but you cannot furnish a thought under anesthesia, can you? Unfortunately, from that moment, I cannot report anything."

She said, "anesthesia eventually wears off. Only if they had planned the operation to let it wear off. I am sure a thinking surgeon would have planned killing two birds with one stone, save my future husband and solve a philosophical problem. That would have been a treasure moment in the history of philosophy."

There was a long pause. Then she said, "so, my dear husband, you are the custodian of the unique experience of thought in pursuit of itself, uncorrupted, are you not?"

"But, thought in pursuit of itself, I cannot fathom," I asked.

She did not hear me. Deeply absorbed, looking in the void, Aurora was busy in a kind of loud-thinking, "without the body, you were constituted just within the confines of the brain: the sage custodian of all you would have at that moment, pure thought, a thought of reason."

I joined her loud thinking, "had I not been drugged, would I really have been conscious in the way you have described?"

She said, "There is no reason to think otherwise; conscious you would be, certainly, I believe; perhaps even in a more intense, but, yes, sublime way; with the awareness of the surroundings, sensations and information, all banned from entering your thought; basically, anything achieved through the body, all would be barred. The consciousness, freed from the duty of serving the awareness, would have nothing at which to focus but itself, penetrating the layers of pretence and triviality, one after the other, spiralling inward, rocking within, to reach the core of its profoundness, a notion that remains unknown, or incomprehensible, to me, perhaps, to most of us, the gentiles."

She continued, "when I think of this notion, I imagine the ordinary light turned into LASER[1]: that which initially is a feeble and faint ray of light, when its waves are spooled together, peaks with peaks, dips with dips, it gathers so much intensity as emitting from the earth to cast at the moon. Run of the mill consciousness of one of the gentiles would thus turn to be the *LASER* consciousness of the elite."

She said emphatically, "we have admitted that, in your example, intense arousal of consciousness was possible by offloading it from its duty of the awareness of the self and surroundings. In the same way, voluntary denial of such awareness, or refusal to attend the mundane affairs, should allow consciousness similarly aroused. This is how the experience from sessions of intense introspection has been reported by the people of vision, the Sufi masters. That is what probably is implied by the state of trance in which such experiences are had."

Captivated, I could not add more to what she had just said. But I had a question for her, "this would be amazing, Aurora. But, if not aware of anything, what is it to which it would attend, this LASER consciousness?"

"How would I know? People of vision say it attains the presence of a special consciousness. But I must confess I have no idea what this means. Those who have had the experience also resign, for not having the right language to describe it."

What had just been said was profound, for in its shades was enveloped silence, calming silence, different from the loud uneasy kind arising from want of an answer. From thinking deeply, being unaware, I was roused with a flash shown into my eyes. A fraction of a second later we received the thunderclap. It was a pretty loud one, and I still remembered the cozy warmth of her two hands that she placed out of fear on my shoulders. The blast was matched by a sudden tap on the window. We both looked that way: more taps, which quickly coalesced to form a sheet of noise from the gushing rain pouring from the sky.

"They did forecast in the evening bulletin heavy rain at this time!" I filled the quiet gap.

---

[1] LASER (Light Amplification by Stimulated Emission of Radiation) is produced with a ray of ordinary light made to travel perpetually between a pair of reflectors such as the peaks of the waves reflected from reflectors coincide with the peaks of the incoming ways, similarly, dips with dips, thus producing a multi-augmented wave. In this way, the resultant wave between the two reflectors would acquire such intensity and strength as to be shown on distant objects, such as moon, if strengthened appropriately.

"This noise of heavy rain fascinates me, probably from my childhood," Aurora indicated she wanted to stay longer. Conscious of Comely waiting, I said goodnight to her. About to enter the bedroom, I thought only if Nash and Logge could have been present in this discussion with Aurora. It had indeed been an awesome opportunity to ponder on the construction of the self.

# THE BIG BANG

FEELING HIGH, IMPORTANT, and accomplished, I entered Comely's bedroom. I met Comely marching in the room. She stopped on my arrival and turned her face at me. I said, "guess, I have made you wait long - sorry."

"Shut up," she screamed.

"What! What have I done now?" I said knowing that showing any hasty reaction would not help.

"Asking me what have you done? What have you not done to me, Oxymoron? I cannot take it anymore."

"What is it that you can't take?"

"I tell you what! You, the ancient soul, why don't you just divorce me – in fact it is me who is asking for a separation – for sure. And then you can have all the time for her, just enjoy your gibberish discussions with her - crap." While saying this, she closed the window and switched off the ceiling light.

I knew rage had stormed into her but hoped it had not consumed her. She was upset. I did not want to argue any further lest she would use more abrasive language. Trying to appease her, I replied, "we can discuss anything that you can suggest. Let us take things more calmly. Perhaps we need to draw some new rules between us."

"Don't even try advising me on this one. I want a divorce - right now and that is final."

"OK, let us sleep on it for tonight. We talk it through in the morning," I proposed.

"No - decision has to be made now; I cannot wait for the morning," she was still shouting.

I left the room without saying a word more. She shouted after me but did not follow me. I went back to the dining room but did not find Aurora there. I just sat there reflecting. The demand Comely was making now was something I myself had offered her some time ago. I searched my heart for her. What I found there was an alloy feeling of hurt and guilt. I wished she'd got out of this melancholic, limping relationship, but then, I thought, this rowdy person must be responsible for putting me into this turmoil while seeking her own desires. No, perhaps I was arrogant, selfish and careless.

I was making the decision about her demand but was numb. I needed to discuss it first with Aurora. The problem was that, to reach her, I needed to use the stairs, but some of its steps would creak under my feet, which meant Comely would straightway know that I had been with Aurora, something bound to inflame the situation further. I would gently place my foot on the step, keeping my weight on the other foot, while slowly shifting it between the two. I took twice as much time reaching Aurora's door but It worked.

Standing in front of her bedroom, deep down I felt hurt but also little relieved with this relation ending. Then, I dreamt Aurora and I, just the two of us, around in the house being much happier. My feelings elated with that prospect, I knocked on her door and entered.

The room was filled with a faint blue light, just enough for me to make out things. Baffled, she got up, zigzagging her feet on the floor in search of her slippers. In her blue nighty, its side towards the lamp imperceptibly glossier, on one side she merged with the atmosphere and emerged from it on the other. In the hue, the silhouette of her face-cut glowed. As always, she wore an earthy perfume. She stretched her hand towards the bedside lamp. Looking at me in the light, she just stared at me. I hastened to clarify, "I am not sleepwalking. And trust me, I am not trying to trespassing either. In fact, it is something very serious that I wanted to discuss with you." She still looked at me with a question mark. I said, "this is urgent I could not wait for the morning."

We both stood face to face for a moment, quietly, "can I sit somewhere." And, without waiting for her reply, I sat on the bed. She glided on the corner of the bed diagonally from me and, nervous, waited for me to say what I wanted to say.

I wasn't sure how to relate the story to her, nor could I predict her response to it. I said, "the line Comely had drawn between Nahaar and Oxymoron has now gone fizzled. Which has let jealousy seeped through. She has become impossible."

She said, "I am sorry, for I might have caused it."

"You had helped her in many ways - in good faith. She had been alright except for the last few days, when I have noticed her getting frustrated, but you cannot be responsible for it," said I.

"So, what does she eventually want?" she said.

"Divorce - that is what she demands."

Hearing this, Aurora stood up from the bed, took a step back too long and in confusion hit the wall. "May I advise you to do everything possible to avert Comely's demand. If she wants you not to spend time with me, so be it. But she must not leave."

"Why do you think I should take this route?" she had surprised me with her response.

She said, "our family would not be complete without Comely. Look Oxymoron, being with you I am on cloud nine, but we must have a partner in this relation for Nahaar."

I did not quite comprehend what she'd said. I said, "I thought we had liked to have all the time at hand to spend between the two of us."

"Spending time together is my dream, of course. But Comely is an essential part of the triangle, I have found out."

"Essential? I never wanted to marry her in the first place."

She took a long breath, "first time in life I am being so happy with my life. Please don't let it spoil. Please stop her from leaving."

I asked, "in that case, would you like to help us in this conflict?"

"You better keep me out of this. She will accuse me of things – will implicate me. Don't even tell her that we are conferring," she said.

Nothing more to be said, I prepared to leave. I paused for an extra second before leaving, even though I knew she would not ask me to stay. I did not dare going back to Comely. That night, I slept in the bedroom downstairs.

I had hardly slept when someone shook my arm harshly. Half-awake, I did not remember anything from earlier. Shaken hard, I sat up on the bed.

"I must leave you alone but will not until you say you agree to the divorce," she caused a rumpus.

Unbearably prickly, she would not take any suggestion against this demand. I tried everything to stop her from leaving – tried buying more time, tried some beating-about-the-bush suggestions. At the end, fed up, I went off the deep end and resigned to the demand for a divorce, totally ignoring Aurora's advice. She returned to her room. From the attic, Aurora must be hearing this conversation. After few minutes, she came down to console me, but I felt there was something peculiarly odd in her manners. A kind of pending fear shook me.

In the morning, Comely left the house with a bag. I saw her off on the door with good wishes and, to be fair on her, she bade goodbye to me with nice words, too. She said that she was sorry for our marriage not having worked out fine. She left regards for Aurora who was deliberately absent from the scene. I saw off Comely and waited for her to turn the corner.

I returned to our bedroom, to Comely's bedroom, and wept. Aurora must have ben listening to my choking and crying but did not come down. Later, we met in the kitchen for the dinner. I felt miserable but also understood the awkward position of Aurora. We sat around the table and waited for each other to say something. I briefly looked at her face as if appealing for mercy, as if I had known she would leave me too. How could be more ironic that only yesterday they were rebelliously competing for my company and today I was fearing left alone completely? Her face was blank and gaze on the table. I looked around, then on the food on the table, then at her, and said, "food is getting cold. Shall we start the dinner."

She took literally a very small portion, quietly finished it, took her plate to the sink and left, without even sharing a look. I wasn't sure what was going on. Sitting on the table, I reflected. I thought Aurora, that conscientious soul, was remorseful on the demise of my relation with Comely. Or, was she as a friend of Comely now protesting on her leaving? Or, was she just feeling sad? None of these - I thought she was in the middle of making some decision – some important decision. While I was still sitting in the kitchen, Aurora returned, "I believe the time to divulge the story I wanted to keep from you has arrived."

As usual, I waited quietly for her to complete her side of the conversation.

"The story is of a young man whom I knew from the day of his birth. His mum was my dearest friend. The family moved in my neighborhood when they did not have any children. In that house, they had their first child, a daughter and, the very next year, their son. Her husband was serving in military, mostly posted out at stations abroad, only to visit the family off and on during his vacations. Bringing up two small kids was difficult for the poor soul on her own. Out of friendship, I tried to share some of her burden. In this way, looking after the son slowly came down to my remit. I liked the role, and I did it with dedication, also for not having any child of my own. He was really a lovely child, very pretty. His mum and I chose his name. We searched different languages for a name meaning 'day', to match with the time of his birth. The word that sounded nice to us we found in Arabic - Nahaar. Nahaar was his name," her voice became full and hoarse, her eyes watery.

Shocked, I did not know how to respond to this situation.

127

She spoke in a quiet voice, "I remember the morning in the department when phones were ringing around with the sad news - the news of the accident and Oxymoron as a result taken to hospital. Everyone was concerned but I ... I wept." She paused here.

I did not dare to look at her.

She continued, "then I heard the story in the operation theatre." She sounded like suppressing hiccough. I looked at her, her eyes pouring. After a pause, she spoke again, "I heard of a birth of a new person from the remains of Oxymoron and Nahaar."

Looking at the ceiling, she said, "I wasn't sure whom to find in this new person if I met him, or even to find in him anyone I knew at all. About the surreal person, I was not just unsure; I was in fact scared of facing him fearing I had lost both. I could not find the courage to visit him."

Forgetting the looming situation, for now I was just interested in how she progressed on her side of the story.

She said, "then, that morning in the department, I saw Nahaar standing in the corridor. I saw him and, as expected, went to cuddle him but someone in him shunned me. I knew something in him gone missing. I shivered, for I had lost Nahaar."

I looked at her waiting to hear more.

She said, "then I hear the sweet word from the mouth of this person. The sound of 'Aaroo' takes over my mind. I find my love, my passion, Oxymoron in front of me. I forgot the appearance. If my love for Oxymoron was like a needle, I would have found out that needle in a haystack - easy."

After a quiet moment, she spoke huskily, "once I had found Oxymoron, I did not just ignore Nahaar; in fact, I did not find him since - until later."

"When Oxymoron was around, I would forget the whole world, let alone Nahaar, let alone even how Oxymoron actually looked. You were all Oxymoron for me – take-away nothing, add nothing. You were all around me." Then she laughed, "that is if you don't call me crazy."

"However, then the thread broke with Comely asserting her right on Nahaar. I sacrificed Oxymoron to release Nahaar for Comely. I wanted Nahaar to marry his love."

I kept quiet.

She said, "in the coming days, it was agonizing to deal with a person who assumed the position of Oxymoron but who in my eyes was Nahaar. But I managed it. I did - somehow. Until, of course, Oxymoron in the person suddenly woke up, proposing me."

"Oxymoron had played with me as a rag doll – brutally, kicking it around – hysterically. Or, they both, my loved ones, sliced my life. I ended up in crying many times. But now, with this proposal from Oxymoron, I forget everything. I made another compromise. I allow in my mind the two people in that figure to co-exist."

She said, "obviously, this marriage could not have been for Nahaar's body that you wear. Obviously, he was like a son to me. No, it was indeed with Oxymoron who I deeply loved, the asset of my life. It was only for him I could cross any barrier - go any length. It was because of Oxymoron that I jumped into this fire."

We kept staring at each other. Then, she blinked few times, releasing tears on her cheeks, and spoke, "you were Oxymoron for me, for Comely you were Nahaar, and I was happy for that to happen."

Things had started making sense. I got my breath back, thinking we were now about to have a knot less between us. In anticipation, I said, "you've been graciously patient, Aurora."

Her eyes wet, she ignored my words. She said, "I wanted my Nahaar to live, to have a wife. I wished he lived."

I said, "I understand how you liked Comely to stay in the marriage."

"That was not the only reason," she replied. "In this marriage, I had myself admitted Nahaar beside Oxymoron. I myself approved his presence. With this, the arrow had left the bow. Nahaar was to be found permanently beside Oxymoron, and Nahaar's wife alongside Oxymoron's wife."

"I had to accept this lest I would feel terrible with you dwelling with Comely - every night - in a room just under mine." Her voice became softer and her pace slower, "every night I felt Oxymoron around me, while who Comely had on her bed was Nahaar. So, there was no conflict in my mind - absolutely none – with which I had to cope."

I was startled with the fear of what was to come next.

She laughed, with a lot of air in her laughter, and stood up from the seat. "Comely has departed, but then I cannot assign the Nahaar in you to no one, no more, and I cannot remove from my vision him residing in you" she said in a firm flat decisive voice.

The irony had hit the fan. My anxiety skipped many steps in intensity and my heart many beats in the gallop.

She said, "I cannot have the person who I have brought up as my son as my husband."

I was speechless. She went upstairs, returned with a bag and walked out of the house. Two departures in a day. On this one, I did not go to the door to say goodbye. I even did not cry. What about her. She had to leave her beloved husband and from her cherished son, the two departures she also must make at this bent in her journey of life.

# THE UPSHOT

SOMEHOW, I PASSED THE night. I had a strange headache in the morning but preferred to leave the house. In the office, I saw a letter from Aurora on my desk indicating she had resigned from the job. There was nothing in the inbox from Comely either, not that I was expecting. I was numb, clueless, feeling directionless in life, and drive and interest evaporated. The flashing peak in the drama in my life only a few days ago was now matched with a steep dip of anticlimax. Once proudly feeling unique, I was now completely deflated, feeling annihilated. Nothing in the world could bring me back, I thought. There was nothing left for me in this story. Although, in the local press, the news hit the headlines.

'Oxymoron doubly divorced'

I would not want to see anyone, nor would I attend any paperwork. My inbox, the dumpsite of electronic rhetoric, I hated to see. At that moment of anger, I reduced the Outlook window, but just about then, a name of a particular sender flashed in front of my vision – Aliya – it was a message from my daughter Aliya. The message was brief, asking me to meet up, but would not say why. Who cared why! She had not turned up the first time she asked for a meeting; in fact, she had not contacted since. But I wouldn't care. All of sudden, on the flat canvas, with this message, there appeared a color. "I want to see you, too; in fact, this is exactly when I need you, Aliya" I wrote back. Must I be made of some kind of unbreakable alloy, I thought about my resilience.

I somehow finished the day at work. Feeling deeply wounded and exhausted, I left for home, yet had the massage from Aliya to which to look forward. I sat in the kitchen, wanting to help Comely in getting things ready for the dinner, but there was no Comely. I went to the dining room but did not find Aurora there either. I did not take any dinner – for there was nothing for the evening. I took the milk bottle out of the fridge but put it back straightway. I spent the whole evening on a chair, unattended, cold and dejected. I thought about Nahaar and simply hated him, hated his presence in me. But, then, both Comely and Aurora stared at me giving horrible looks.

By the time I went to bed, the headache had returned. Feeling nauseated, I woke up several times during the night with fever and dizziness. Like overlapping, mingled noise in a radio set at a random frequency, my brain emitted signals, plethoric in number, some intense, others weak, all meaningless, vain and futile, crisscrossing my mind. I heard myself calling for Aurora, and sometimes for Comely, but obviously I was just calling them with empty hopes, just complaining to the walls, or to whom I would not know. I belonged to no one.

Nearing the morning, I called for the ambulance. It was the morning of 17th December that I was taken to hospital, that much I remember. The attendants told me later that on the way to hospital, I passed out. The doctor who came to visit me was very calm and patient in explaining to me my condition. With an outfit of bare-below-elbow, without a tie or a jacket, he sat close to me. The strong smell of fresh alcohol gel from his hands signaled an impending procedure. He first introduced himself, then confirmed my identity, and informed me that he wanted to explain my illness to me.

After going through the list of my symptoms, he said, "the immune system in the body comprises the white cells, little warriors, circulating in the blood in billions at any time, like cops on the beat. Their job is to seek and destroy elements they detect as foreign to the body, seeing them as harmful. These foreign elements usually comprise germs dangerous to health, which is why the immune system is so important."

He paused to confirm I was listening, "in your case though, it has detected your brain as a foreign element, hence it is bent on destroying it, a condition that in medical terms is described as the immune system rejecting a transplanted organ." He said, "during rejection, the organ under attack becomes inflamed and swollen, which explains your symptoms."

He continued, "the risk of organ rejection is well known in all kinds of transplantations. To avoid it, we fine-tune the immune system to keep it at its lowest performance level so that it should not reject the transplanted organ but it should still remain active against germs. We cannot take it out completely lest the germs will attack the body being unchallenged."

I was impressed, "it seems a very nice scheme."

"Yes," he said. "This scheme in most cases is expected to work, but sometimes unfortunately the point of fine balance is difficult to find. In your case things were working OK until recently, but something must have disturbed the balance."

"What do you think has disturbed it," I asked. "Could it be some kind of stress?"

"It is quite possible. Anyway, with some new pills, we are trying to restore the balance. See how it goes."

The doctor left, leaving me to go over what he had just said. With my eyes closed, I opened a different debate, my usual internal debate: 'So,' I thought. 'After all, Nahaar has avenged my bad treatment of Comely by sending his immune system to hunt me down. I let her go; he is trying to reject me outright.'

'Or, perhaps it is not so much for Comely but for my dislike of Nahaar. Until now, I have been blaming him for imprisoning me in him; now, the prisoner will be taken through cycles of violence - what a revenge.'

'But this is not the debate to be had just now. More importantly, should it not be the worry about my house on fire?'

With the eyes closed, I start dreaming that I am leaving work very late. In a rush, I forget to stop for Zeitoun's favorite juice she has asked me in the morning. I am sure I am going to be in trouble, but feel too tired to go back, hoping the children would rescue me.

I do not want to open my eyes lest I lose this scene. But the scene changes anyway. Now I find myself in a hospital room; I find them all around me, Zeitoun, Aurora, Comely, Aliya and Ayaan, hugging me, holding my hands. The kids have the usual banter, about homework, teachers, you name it, and cracking jokes. Suddenly, the room catches fire, swiftly bathing in flames; I shout, 'let us get out of here!' and they leave. My room is on fire, with me inside it and they leave, leaving me behind. That tears my heart into shreds. I hear the flames roaring; then I see a flame bursting with rage, sprinting towards me. I hurriedly open my eyes.

With the eyes open, I see Comely in brilliant white dress, on a white chair in the corner of the room, sitting quietly but anxiously, dabbing her eyes, her innocence filling the room with compassion. Then I remember her having left the house only the other day. I rub my eyes. There isn't any Comely there no more but stern white wall facing me.

Though from the white wall emerged another figure, that of Aurora, saying, 'I have not left the house; I cannot leave you like this; I can never leave you.' My eyes well up with appreciation and love I feel for her. But she suddenly vanishes, too. I wish only if she knew, be it by Oxymoron or by Nahaar, she is loved anyway.

The doctors have come to say my condition has deteriorated while I am suffering from delirium. They explain that it owes to the immune cells of my body which have stepped up their fight to a ferocious level against the transplanted brain. Only if they would understand the right use of the language, I quietly protest. They say they will have to step up medications to calm down the immune system. Which means I risk severe infections. To prevent any disastrous infection, they want me to shift to a room supplied with ultra-clean air.

Things have been up and down in the last ten to twelve hours since my shifting to the new room. However, now, I have a new symptom of tightness in my chest. The fever has spiked again, too, and I have been in and out of consciousness. They say that an infection has hit both of my lungs. They have started me on antibiotics, but looking at their confidence, it seems that they must have seen several patients recovering from this situation.

Another night has passed, another day has arrived. I have started feeling better. I am gradually recovering from infection and from organ rejection. They have started gradually releasing my immune system in order for it to grip the infection. They keep me in the hospital for two weeks before discharging. I had come to hospital with an ambulance, now I walk from here. I have repossessed my head which was a mud puddle for butterflies when I came here.

# THE BIG CRUNCH

ONCE BACK IN THE FLOW of life, I started picking up the pieces, trying to make sense of it. Of foremost importance on my mind was to write back to Aliya explaining to her the reason of my absence. She said she was frustrated with my not responding. Now when she heard I was in fact taken in the hospital, she said she was upset. Yet, in her messages, there was no address for me, nor was there warmth. Though, after few exchanges, we agreed to a time and a place for an evening-out together.

The place had to be our joint-favourite open-air Moroccan restaurant found in the central city mall. Aliya liked the place for dining out, I too, for its layout, its live Arabic music and for the Middle Eastern chandeliers. Again, for the food, she liked harsh spicy food of the nature of dynamite to please her, me too, though she more than I, something at which this restaurant never disappointed us.

Sitting in front of the screen, I thought about the possible reasons for our meeting. I was convinced that this meeting had something to do with Zeitoun, who wanted me to return to the family after the two women having exited my life. Knowing Zeitoun, I fully understood her irritation with my irresponsible behavior. I imagined standing in front of her offering apologies and explanations. I imagined saying, "my sins are indefensible, Zeitoun, but don't abandon me, would you?"

I trusted my sensible daughter for her role in patching up. She used to patch up between Zeitoun and me and I between her and Ayaan. I mused about the other congruences between the two of us. Right from childhood, Aliya was daddy's daughter. Be it tough homework, issues at school, wrangles with friends or rows from mum, everything must be shared with dad on daily basis. With the years passing, she found liking for historical fiction and paranormal, matching with my romance with these subjects. I remembered once we both reading from the same volume of Harris' Imperium, her page marker being a peacock feather and mine a tree leaf made of toughened paper. In this way, each of us could spy on where the other was on the story, and try sprinting to take the lead. She watched topical films, again a taste pinched from me. I kept myself sort of young because of her, I had to.

She grew kind of a serious person because of me - give and take. She was good in gadgets but was not particularly fond of them. For example, she did not want Augur for herself while it was becoming a popular gadget among youngsters. I myself did not know much about Augur. On that day, in a café, we happen to see a teenager off and on laughing while focusing at a screen bound to his wrist. One would think he was reading some funny stuff on the screen, but, no, besides laughing, he was also making bodily gestures like being in a conversation, yet he did not utter a word. Aliya explained that he was using Augur. She said it provided experience of chatting of yet another nature where you don't even have to type or speak. Strapped to your wrist, Augur reads your mind and sends the readings to another Augur in in the link. Similarly, your mind can be fed with the incoming messages directly coming from other Augers.

"How else could you be more aloof than by having this technology on your wrist," said I.

"Agree, but this applies more or less to all types of screens. That is why I hate using them during family time. But I must say, at least Augur has one good thing to offer which others don't."

Looking at her coaching me like a school teacher, I just smiled and nodded my head.

She said, "using Augur, you cannot lie. You cannot think one thing and say the other. It is an anti-hypocrisy gadget."

"Thus, it would not go far in the market," we both laughed.

So many things - endless stories, between us, the father and the daughter.

*** 

On the day, I could not wait. I left home much earlier, pretending I needed time to buy a memento for Aliya. Stores on the mall were crammed with shoppers and were glowing with glitter. Impatient, I just wanted to pick something quickly and go. Thinking of her favourites from her childhood, I looked for a doll. The last thing I had brought for her was a barbie doll. She would each time laugh at my choice but a minute later would be found making a special place for the new one in the community of dolls in her glass cabinet. So, a gift of a doll was final. On the toy store, the item did not pass through the till. The girl on the till went to the shelf to check the price tag. I went with her to show the location. Walking in the isle, she asked if I bought the doll for my sister. I would not say it was for my daughter, for she would not understand my early-age marriage. She changed the topic telling me she was only a part timer here, trying to generate funds to pay for her uni. I felt she was checking me out but then I rebuked myself for being judgmental.

I still had much time left at my hand. Lurking around the mall, I crept into various stores, but my heart was at the meeting. Eventually, frustrated, I decided to wait in the rendezvous. I felt excited, but a ting nervous too. The restaurant had many entrances off the mall, two at the ground level and four stairways from its lobby on the first floor, descending as straight run, one on each side of the dining court, all together creating a geometrical visual. Whenever we dined here, the two of us or the whole family, we liked to use one of the stairways to enjoy the cool drone's view of the dining hall, and we could also plump for a nice table. I strolled in the lobby a few times, passing by the stairways, each time thinking not this but the next one. I questioned myself why I was idling. I did not want to go to this meeting, was the answer: surprise - surprise. Eventually, I settled at taking a stair leading to the restaurant but felt like entering an altar. In my thought process, hopes were struggling with despair.

A uniformed attendant ushered me to a table of my choice, though the food-court was almost deserted. It was too late for the lunch but too early for the dinner. The court was shielded overhead with an awning, which I hoped they would later in the evening roll back since it was going to be a clear night, the weather forecast had it. I looked around. As usual, in the centre of the food-court was a giant fruit trolley parked on a podium, showcasing fresh produce in kinds and colours, dispersing aroma. The music corner was quiet, but I could hear from the kitchens adjacent to the court the clatters and clangs from cutting boards, ladles playing in the kettles and whistles from the steamers. A stone oven was in full flurry in the corner. The baker, a character fascinating to watch, was busy like a bee. Once your attention is caught by his jugglery of kneading the dough, rounding, poking fire, shifting trays in and out of oven, so forth, it would be hooked. Each time the door of the oven slid open would let slip red hue from the flares to shine on the crockery on the tables and on the faces sitting around them. The aroma from oriental spices in sizzling cuisines mixed with scent of fresh bakery was enough to kick life into the dead, I thought. For once, I forgot tension.

My glances at the filmic scene in the food-court regularly got distracted by the wait. I would take my eyes off from it to scan the entry points one after the other to watch her coming. I looked at the watch; it was yet too early for her. Weary and bored, I let my inner eyes set off, to hop between visuals of her childhood. Here I am holding her in my arm against my chest, her rose petal cheeks against my neck, her breathing delicately against my chin and her arm around my neck. Her mum asks if she could feed the little one but I am not prepared to surrender her. Then, there is another string of visuals reporting her coming back from school. I see her on the door, she shouting daddy, daddy, and running straight towards me; I would kiss her forehead, take her bag off and we would walk to mum, seeking food.

She had a tough bouncing mind - try arguing with her to find out - though her heart was of mermaid-make - don't try going there or else you would break it. This fragility of her had guzzled many evenings of daddy trying to comfort her and rationalise the awful dealing she had received from others. We regularly went for cycling, though her high-tech cyclocross was of no advantage to her over my city bike to run essentially at slow steady pace. And we would pause here and there on the track, just to expand on our discussions.

Then my attention shifted to the big incident in my life, of uniting me with a new body but splitting me from my family. With the meeting today came the opportunity for reunion, perhaps. I wished it could happen urgently; even if Aliya could call the rest of the family to join us tonight. Maybe she would. Ambitious, I thought. I wished if Aliya could turn up quicker. But then, she might not turn up at all, and at this thought I was depressed, but I was relieved too, like a relief felt by students at cancellation of an exam.

I woke up from this stupor in panic. Had I missed something? I looked around: no sign of her. I looked at the watch, then at my hands. They looked foreign to me more than usual, jarring and incongruous. I would not like these hands touch my daughter. I needed to decide how I was going to receive her. I could not kiss her on the forehead, not anymore, nor could I allow her to rest her face on my shoulder, not anymore. OK, I shall ask her from across the table to take her seat. 'Oh, she always prefers the chair facing towards the baker's oven' I remembered. I changed my own side around the table.

These things settled, I floated back into ocean of my dreams, imaginations, hopes and anxieties. In this scurry, I felt a pair of eyes staring at me. I woke up to find a young lady standing on the other side of the table. 'O my, are you here, Aliya!'. I spread my arms towards her but quickly retracted them. She remained frozen, her eyes on my face. I asked her about her brother and mum, about her studies, but then I realised she had not even taken her seat yet.

Once settled, I looked at her closely. She came across poised but not particularly in her familiar way. She looked anxious but also behaved more casual. There was a fine tremor in her hands but her posture was composed. She wore a deep coral colour dress with dense grey flora, an interesting contrast but an unusual taste for her and a bit too exotic for the occasion. She had managed her hair into a chignon with a slack knot on the hind side, again different from her usually tying them with a bobble or two, sited on the backside, or with an Alice band circling around her head clutching at the temples. She wore dangling earrings instead of her usual studs. She wore a fragrance that I could smell now, my previous nose being just waste of space. The most unusual of all was a metal band with multicolour gems that she wore on her left wrist. All these things were Intriguing, but it was not the time to mull over the fringes. Probably she wanted to tell me that she was now grown up. More important were the questions in ranks and rows awaited asking and answers. I waited for her to start the conversation.

But she kept quiet, staring at me; I too was quiet, staring at her, until the silence grew uneasy. It was broken with a gliding noise coming from overhead. We both looked up and saw the awning rolled back. A timely distraction, I thought. It let the dark night to descent on the court, but the sky above was still filled with blue. Luckily, the music corner jazzed up too, joined by a lady singer. She was humming on mild notes of Oud with muffled drum beatings, enhanced with flute, a desert-mix. The lyrics told 'his story' of remembering his childhood love:

Oh, the daughter of my city;

The city of my heart would be deserted without you;

When would enshrine it;

Oh, the daughter of my city

Open sky and desert music softened the tension between us. The diners started pouring in too, giving us a chance now and then to be distracted. Decorated platters and plush Moroccan teapots were juggling between the tables, and the whispers mingling with chinks and clacks from crockery and cutlery. Altogether, it fabricated a mesmeric mix. Like the awning withdrawn opened the sky for us, being here at this moment might unlock our hearts, I hoped. I again looked at her, my daughter, my life, hoping she would start the conversation.

She did start but without any address. I expected her to admire the place and relate this evening with our past experiences here. She did not choose this beginning but instead started, "my mum and brother don't know I'm here. You know - hope they don't find it out before me telling them." She paused, "you know how difficult it's, in fact everything between us has been kind of difficult, complicated." She spoke at a slower pace, taking time to choose words, rather ostentatiously. I knew she was putting it on, which I myself did all the time while lecturing.

"Only thankful that you came. Order some food, shall we not?" said I.

"Yes, may we, now; suppose we have to. For me, not particularly keen though. Just any food, and yes drinks."

Ordering for food eased the silence further, but then the silence returned. I would have asked why she did not keep to the previous meeting but then I thought she might take offence from my asking. I said a hundred things in my head, but each one would start with, 'you remember…' something of a cliché I wanted to avoid. Yet under unbearable pressure of silence, I broke, "you remember - your first day in school, when we were walking down the Foyle." My words indeed sounded clumsy.

She too was looking for an opening, "you remember - our plan to meet. Wanted to apologise for breaking the promise – not promise really – what is the word for it. Anyway, I could not turn up. In fact, I felt terrible; too embarrassed to meet – too embarrassed even to contact. I am so sorry."

"Don't apologise; it is Ok. Was just worried. But then I thought your mum must have stopped you."

She kept quiet.

I said, "what was so embarrassing anyway?"

She hesitated.

I changed the topic, "it is over now, but I just wanted to ask you about the lady I was about to marry because she was someone from your university. I believed Comely was your classmate, was she not?"

"Yes, she was. Knew Comely very well; in fact, too well. I therefore bade you best of luck when I heard of you wedding her, but of course, I would not say so. Did she say she was a Facebook Official with you, did she not?"

I did not understand this part of her response. Try to sweep the subject under the carpet, I said, "it is over now, anyway."

Ignoring my attempt, she said, "I knew Comely had a crush on you but also knew that she would play a trick on you."

I was shocked.

She paused, "I was hoping the drama was over; but my time hadn't come yet."

"But, why, which drama, I mean, what time?"

She again ignored my intrusion, "because, then, you wedded another lady, your secretary. What was her name, Aroura!!" she said with rising intonation. "Heard you liked her a lot."

I looked away shying and smiled, "you - keeping a close eye on me!!"

"You smile the way my dad used to do. The more I see you in real the more I wonder in disbelief," she said in a different tone. She paused, then raised her hand, which was shaking, "in fact, I need your advice." She stole a glance at me. I bet she was getting close to her point. I was really attentive – but getting nervous as well.

She smiled again, "o my. Cannot stop noticing. The way you cup your palm around your ear – my dad used to do while focusing. It is like when one is hard of hearing."

She drew her chair backward, saying, "let me see if you have crossed your legs as well." She bent forward and lifted the table cloth to see under the table. She said, "there you go, the right leg over the left, and you must be wiggling your left foot too, like my dad, always, while sitting and relaxing."

She paused and then gently waved her hand at me, "you are Nahaar, but I could see in you my dad, right here."

This was the first time she made a direct reference to Nahaar. I wouldn't believe my ears for once. For the implications of what she had meant, I needed to hear it again, perhaps not to believe even then. I waited for her to return to her seat and to her questions, "so, which is the advice that you are seeking from me?"

She said, "I have a lot to ask and a lot to say. I liked my dad the bit; I loved him, his thoughts, his gestures - everything. I miss our discussions, you know. I miss my dad every moment. Fascinating to see you doing my dad, really. Loving every bit. Double role, double helping."

She sipped from her cup; her eyes mist and her voice changed, "surely, my dad would have found a way out from this mess. He was a clever man."

She took another sip. Yet again, I did not get which mess she meant here. But I held myself from interrupting her. She whispered, "but now when he is not around - it is only on me. I have to sort it out. I cannot bear it anymore."

I could not wait now, "what is that you cannot bear, Aliya? Which is the mess you wanted your dad had sorted out for you? You didn't have to suffer. Why did you not come earlier? What stopped you?"

"Your marriage - and then another one on the top of the first. That is what stopped me."

Still pretending not to have understood a thing, in fact believing Aliya had not actually meant the way she had had meant, I felt miserable on the missed opportunity, "Aliya, when did I know my marriage would stop you coming to me for help?"

"To answer this, I need to show you a couple of snaps an' a short clip, you mind?" In the meantime, they brought food, the waiter carrying the plater, the waitress arranging the food on the table. It looked nice. They advised us to have it when it was still hot, but I preferred Aliya had rather continued with her story, which she did. Aliya came around the table to take the chair beside me, which confused the waiting staff about the arrangement of the crockery on the table, but I nodded an OK to them. She punched a password on the screen, really a long one.

'These young people,' I whispered.

She mistyped the password few times before getting through, while my patience was waning. And then she clicked the gallery. The picture on the screen was a selfie showing her and me standing next to each other, both smiling in unison, lovingly.

"Is this a café behind us? But, wait a minute, I have never known this place," looking at the picture I said. "In fact, in this guise, I have never met you."

She ignored my comments and swiped the screen to bring the next picture, again with both of us on another place, and then another, and yet another, none of which I had any memory. "Have I lost my mind, Aliya?" But of course, in my head, I was getting the story, albeit I wouldn't let myself believe it - yet.

She clicked on a clip on the screen. It showed the two of us sitting on a garden bench, obliquely facing each other, my arm extended, seeming to hold the camera, we talking and laughing on everything, seemingly needlessly. Then, I say, 'wait,' and the scene goes blank. Then enter into the frame a small box of glazed burgundy colour; I unclip it clumsily, lift its lid and show it to Aliya. For a moment, the frame and focus start dancing, but then it settles. It zooms on Aliya looking into the box, her face amused. She thanks for the gift, returns the box to me, and spreads her hand towards me. With some effort, I take out the thing from the box, which comes to be a bangle with multicolour gems set all around it. Then it shows that I put it on to her wrist, carefully, and modestly.

Taking my eyes off the clip, I stole a glance at her wrist. The bangle she wore for tonight was the same as the one in the clip. The clip continued to play.

The next thing it had me asking her, "so when am I coming to meet with your Dad, your family, Aliya?" The clip ended at a click. The whole story divulged itself at that click, the kind of story never told before.

I could not speak a word. I could not think a thing. She returned to her seat across the table and spoke as if reminding to herself, "Nahaar was in the final year in medical school when I started my clinical years. They appointed him as my buddy. I thought I fell in love with him first, but he thought he was the first. The feelings soared in spiral. We worked out numerous plans, sharing hopes and dreams. But one day, he did not turn up, his phone not answering either. Found out that he was taken to hospital in emergency, unconscious, gravely ill." Frozen in chair, I watched my daughter telling this tale.

"Life without him - didn't think that way – couldn't - after where we'd reached. I cried but would not tell anyone in the family; in fact, nothing was left to tell, was there? And then, I heard my dad taken to the casualty following a roadside accident, and from there to the theatre." With these words, she sobbed in the softly voice, tears on her cheeks, her hands on the table with palms open, restless, helplessly fidgeting, praying.

I grieved with her. The chandeliers in the dining court urgently got hazier and shadowy. I wiped my eyes. People in the music corner fired up a new song. The ethereal shrill of the flute ruled its notes. It said:

> The wailing flute says: do you know why I grieve;
>
> Because you have plucked me from my mother tree

My heart sank with her hurt. I held her hands, but then withdrew - abruptly. The story had started to reveal itself but I was in denial. I said, "Aliya, your classmate sadly died on the operation table. Although, they took his body to give it to your dad to live. Your dad owes Nahaar ..."

Restless, she intervened with her piercing gaze at me. Then, she tossed in her seat, mellowed visibly, her eyes still focused, though showering tears. She said, "even though, you are not my dad…"

That was it; for me, she had crossed the limit. Completely infuriated, with open palm of my hand raised, I demanded restraint.

In response, she returned to the attacking mode and reviled, "does it make any sense that you are my dad but you don't look like him. Give me a break. If you were my dad, whose remains have we buried? If you were my dad, when in the past did you not kiss my forehead on my greeting you? Why did you withdraw from hugging me today? Why did you retract your hands from mine?

143

I can tell you why? Because you are not my dad, for sure, and because you know that as well. If you still insist, ask anybody here -staff, guests, anyone - tell them that you are my dad and see what they think of you." With these words, she had demolished my castle into tatters.

In the meantime, the waiter returned with a man in chef's clothes. She said, "is food OK? You are not eating! The chef assures me his fish on your menu he has specially cooked."

The Chef asked, "please try it or else you would break my heart. But if you don't like it, tell us how would you like it."

I forged a smile. They left seemingly confused. I mopped the perspiration on my forehead. "What have I done to deserve these insinuations from you Aliya?" I said.

She said, "I was there in courtroom when your lawyers convinced the judge that although you did not look like the Director but you were him. A show of eloquence – elegant but fake."

I kept quiet.

"Wanted to see you. But then, noticed the compassion you enjoyed from them, from all of them, starting from the judge right down to the defendants. They forgot – conveniently - I would say - to ask you some important questions, for example, when would you be retiring, in two-year time or after 35 years - that is when people retire at 60. I suspect this kind of questions would have unsettled you and rubbished your case, don't you think?"

I kept quiet.

She said, "indeed, I was deeply upset at your winning the case, because, with this winning, do you know who actually lost it?"

"Who?"

"Me. It was I who lost. Hoping to recover from it, I sent you a message to meet – a meeting which did not go ahead, sadly." She continued, "it didn't do go ahead because you got married to my friend." She stared at me, "and I couldn't contact you because, as a result, I ended up in hospital."

I had so far been struck with surprises so many times that I had been left numb. That is until I had heard the word suicide from her lips. Becoming all ears, I looked at her, waiting to know the reasons of hospital admission.

"Suicidal – I was acutely suicidal," said she.

She left me to absorb the implications of the news and changed the cue, "you were accepted back in the job - but, then, you were not accepted back in the family, were you?"

By then, in the music corner, they changed the tune, replacing the mild desert notes with louder city music. Aliya raised her voice in the noise, "and yet again, while marrying my friend, you yourself accepted you were Nahaar, not the director." I heard a big thud from the kitchen, probably arising from an accident of some sort, but it did not bother me; my own commotion was louder.

She seemed to be gathering force in her argument, "I see you as Nahaar, a complete person, plus a lot of things in you inherited – no - in fact, not inherited, but taken from my Dad. I loved you before, Nahaar, but now also for the learnings of my dad, his leanings as well that you have acquired from him. Your thought gripped me from the heart, Nahaar; now it is disabling, literally. What can I do?"

Startled with the implications, I tried to play it down, "a funny situation."

"A funny situation! It is ironic. But it is only so until you remove the idea of the blood relations between us two. Get your blood group checked, or your gene profile done, and decide your blood relations with me. The answer is: you have no blood relation with me, for sure. That somehow you are my dad is a mere thought, and you know thoughts come and go, remembered and forgotten. Thoughts are just thoughts."

The iron door on the furnace slid, with the red hue leaked from it to shine on her face. She looked relaxed, like someone who had just finished with giving out the most difficult news. She said, "I don't pretend that you are the same Nahaar; you are more than Nahaar. But if you say you are my dad, for God's sake, no, you are not."

She looked the other way and took a deep breath and said, "Nahaar, please don't discard me this way, would you?"

With these words, she started sobbing in the softest of the voice, her tears on her cheeks, her hands on the table with palms open, restless and helpless. Between the sobs, she said, "let us agree to get married."

"Marriage between whom?" not believing my ears, I raised my voice.

"Nahaar and Aliya, of course."

It was time for reaction, "Aliya, I require you to leave right now. Return home straight. Disclose all this to your mum. Seek her help that you indeed need and her advice, too."

In tears, Aliya stood up. She hesitated and then left. I watched her going.

My mind was numb, having no idea where to go from this point. No sooner had I stepped in the house than I broke and wept. My head was split with a vicious throb, my mouth dry like towel. Importantly, I was worried about Aliya reaching home safely. I regretted why I let her go on her own. She had a point to which I should have listened.

'Am I Nahaar? Maybe I am not Oxymoron.'

'Had I so far been wasting time in an unnecessary debate? How if I have accepted that I am Nahaar?'

The more convinced I became with being Nahaar, the easier I felt.

'Therefore, the source of tension in my life is the Oxymoron. Instead, I keep on blaming Nahaar. I should have accepted this truth.'

I picked up the phone and started typing a message: "Perhaps, you are right. Aliya. I am Nahaar. I am sorry for you leaving upset. I am Nahaar. Would you make sure your family accepts me this way? Could you ask your mum?"

And I clicked 'Send'.

In the next few seconds, reason overtook me differently. I quickly opened the outbox. The message was still parking there, waiting to despatch during the lag-time. I held it. I asked myself in what capacity I'd found it so hurtful to bear Aliya's pain were it not as her father? I deleted the message.

'Enough of this.'

Embarrassed and ashamed, I believe the time to end this mosaic creature has come. The choice is between killing Oxymoron with a handful of sleeping pills or bleeding Nahaar to death by cutting his wrists. It depends on who I want to go first and who to get the blame? On the question blame, I try to envisage the headlines in the morning papers:

'The Ungracious Beneficiary Betrays His Benefactor'

Or, would it read:

'The Ungrateful Beneficiary Kills His Benefactor'

It is obviously all about Nahaar, the benefactor, isn't it? I am soaked in bitterness. In either case, no one will speak of the pains of Oxymoron, not even

Zeitoun. She thinks she has already buried her husband. Now, she will bury him in reality, ironically thinking it is Nahaar. All of them, Aurora, Comely and Aliya, would mourn the death of Nahaar, and none of Oxymoron.

Then there was a flicker of light that I see. I see the courtroom and strolling in it the attorney representing Zeitoun. 'Wait a minute. Some say I am this, others say I am that; sometimes I am this, other times I am that. Why don't I settle with what this attorney says? I am a new person, am I not?'

'If I were a brand-new person,' I ask myself yet another question, 'why have I to engage with the characters from the past?'

'Not only my own, with my perpetual conflict, I have also destroyed the lives of all those close to me. This process should be terminated.'

'Where should this end? A brand-new person does not have a past, nor should he know anyone from that period. It should therefore end at a brand-new person, not born but made, having no father, no mother, no real relations with anyone who ever have lived.'

However, this statement cannot possibly be true. Not-borne-but-made a person I am, yet my mum and dad I know; in fact, I remember every fine detail about them.

The question of who I am therefore remains outstanding. In lumpsum, everyone known to me has mistaken me for someone else. Not only this, whosoever has tried addressing this burning question has got burnt from it. So much so, I am standing in the middle of this dark room, in the middle of the night, arguing who am I to Aliya, with my heart on flames.

There must be a way out. As a brand-new person, I must leave my memory aside, at least for now. Then I'll belong to no one. As a brand-new person, I must walk a brand-new pathway and find a new niche.

As soon as I reach this moot point, decidedly, a voice emerges from the corner of the room, "no, you cannot leave. You owe us…" It is joined by another voice and then by yet another, on and on. The faces of Zeitoun, Aurora, Comely, Ayaan, Nahaar, Aliya, Ayaan, Nahaar's parents, people from my team, even people distantly known to me, my lawyers, the judges, the doctors, all are here as their scary caricatures. Some of them have clambered down along the walls, others have tumbled down directly from the ceiling. One or two have grown from the floor. They start revolving around me defiantly, making a non-sensical roar, like cannable tribe members in a Sub-Saharan dance around a bonfire, shouting slogans in foreign languages, seeking blood and flesh. The uproar gets louder and louder till it solidly fills the room. The words that transpire make a confused acoustic mass.

> "What dead husband Zeitoun I sorry to this beg hand daughter but no should speak Nahaar who here Comely grant encephalitis upset application but death Public Aurora because alone miserable Aliya not marry no why future daughter" In a corner of the room, the noise is being printed on a ribbon which they try to shove into my ears like a gauze band pushed into a wound. I perceive this pandemonium as a trial of mayhem on the identity of the 'I'. Amidst this, I decide I must find the true 'I'.

Waving my hand at them, I yell: stop; the noise gets flatter. I utter: stop, stop; the noise gets fainter. I whisper: stop, stop - stop; and, there is silence. Then, I pull the ribbon out from my ear. I facepalm, my eyes closed, pretending thinking, as if I am trying to get my memory disc burnt with what is going on here. The noise slips out of control again; then, it gains volume, reaching an unbearable level. I shout, "are you mine, or are you those turned on destroying me? Leave, for I am trying to find something important. I am trying to find the 'I'." This time, seemingly scared, the caricatures fizzle out one by one, like light bulbs in a series blowing in turn. Before vanishing though, they jumble around me snatching something from my hand, I can't say what, and picking something from the room, I can't see what. My heart burns on this confiscation but I say that is fine: I have reached the decision anyway. I am leaving; I am leaving to find my *self*.

# PART TWO: THE CROSSROAD

## WHERE TO GO

HAVING MADE THE DECISION to move from here, I tried to regain control on my senses. I moved from room to room in the house. The bedrooms were seized by serpents, the house felt their burrow and the silence in it hissed. I returned to the kitchen. Sitting there, frightened, I tried to work out, how I could silently leave this place and where to go next. This place? I felt I needed to leave this street, this city.

I considered various options: retiring- I cannot survive without income; taking another job- who will appoint me with scandalous credentials; starting a business- no capital or experience. The only resource, the income from the farm that I inherited from my father, would be inadequate for living.

'Why don't I take over the farm to work there for myself? My father had taught me some farming skills in my adolescence. My reluctance to help him or my procrastination were generic symptoms of adolescence; basically, I used to be a durable worker on the farm, my memory assured me. Plus, now, I was stronger as well. In this new life, there would be no hassle from people around, no stress from courts, no quibbles with the employers. It was a perfect way to stay away from all those whom I knew, in fact, from people of all kinds. My father, too, was mostly on his own, yet he was happy, cheerful, easygoing, so would I be, I hoped, if I'd chosen to be aloof. There would be ample time for thinking. None of the ploughing, sowing, weeding, reaping particularly interferes with thinking, that is, if you want to. Farming checked most of the boxes. Done. This new hope killed the serpents in the house and restored the poise in me. With this new enthusiasm, I got up; I should dwell on my own farm then, I thought.

I wrote to Sul, the current in charge of the farm, about my plan asking his consent. I also mailed my resignation from the job.

Packing was not much of a hassle, really. I would just throw things into the lone suitcase, though, while packing books, I paused on each. I glanced inside the titles, making a mental note of the future reading list. Between the pages, I frequently checked my mind for the to-do list. Something kept irritating me, bothering deep down. Like a drifter lurching on flood waves, the thought wandered on brainwaves but likewise quickly sank before I could realize it. This time, it surfaced for a little longer but still was too short to read, though the implications unnerved me. I murmured to myself, 'what is going on, now, please, mercy!' But I was watching it closely in apprehension. Rising from the depth with an impetus, this time it rocketed through the surface. I seized it; it read: 'it is noble to pay a parting visit to the grave of the loved ones.' 'No way; why would I want to do this?' I protested but could not shake off the thought.

'Listen, you owe a visit to your closest chum whom you have left to rot in the grave. And who could be closer to you than your own body!'

'But then, is it not that my chum has actually left me to loiter in the boots of others.'

'Listen.'

'No, you listen.'

'Wait, betrayal is not the case here; wouldn't you agree it is the one of triumph?'

'I am already up to here with this triumph; doing life as well as having died is not a laughing matter.'

'Why complicate things; it simply is a case of the two eternal friends departing.'

I was getting closer to deciding, although I was curious about how I should feel beside my grave. 'OK, then, what should I say to the resident of the grave?' I asked. 'No idea; let us see,' came the reply.

# WHERE IS MY GRAVE

WALKING IN THE CEMETERY, I felt like a criminal walking in shackles to face his victim. 'How would I look into the eyes of my victim?' The cemetery was still, wearing poignant earthly ambiance of a meadow, peppered with all kinds of greenery. Trees in rows marked its main pathways, slim circumference of their trunks spying on their young age and the age of the cemetery. The place lacked life, except a couple of people, upright, spotted at the distant left corner. After an overdose of humanity in the city, I seemed to have liked the quiet in the place.

I looked out for my grave, expecting it to be on the flank of the populated district, since I had only recently died. Graves, paraded on both sides of the pathway, were mostly barren, some partly covered with grassroots, others wrapped in flowers, daisies, roses, and whatnot. The occupants of the flowery residences must have left their heirs pleased, now to get repaid in flowers; or else, was it guilt of some kind driving some souls restless to pay homage? Thinking of guilt reminded me to buy some flowers for my chum. But for this, I realized, I needed to go all the way back to the cemetery gate. I walked few yards, then fumbled, 'who cares - who would complain?' 'OK, let's not bother then.' However, I turned around one more time, 'how embarrassing it would be if Zeitoun or Ayaan spotted me empty-handed around the grave of their loved one?' I smiled on the thought, but panicked too, 'meeting them here wouldn't be the best of ideas – what will I say to them standing beside my grave?' I decided to buy flowers and felt relieved. Out of the gate, I first passed in front of the florist shop, just in case if my family members were also there. In particular I would not like to face Aliya. In my peripheral vision, I looked into the shop. I entered the shop, pretending to be looking around. Eventually, I bought a bunch of daisies - they had them in abundance, selling cheap. I returned to the cemetery. 'What was that which worked me up so much at the florist?' my mind was now counter-arguing. Indeed, the self is an indomitable horse.

I was reading the headstones. This one looked more like a placard of the size of numberplate, nailed on a wooden post. It had my name on it. The handwriting was of Aliya, for sure. 'Why couldn't they order a proper one made of marble? Shall I organize one? Afterall it is my grave.' The grave looked one of the ordinary, roughly in the middle of the second last row. Its soil had hardened but was not yet brittle or ruined. A cairn of stones had been gathered on the top of the mound.

153

I felt empathetic towards the resident of the grave. But this way did not work well: it was time to say something, an apology, an excuse, or a simple honest farewell. I opened the bunch and arranged the flowers around the slopes. 'They look not bad, really; but, say something!' Sweating, I looked away, reading the headstones of my neighbors. Oops, they got this epitaph messed up; spellings were wrong, too. 'Is it the fault of etcher or the engraver – anyway, a sore in the eye.' Once my critical survey of the surrounding graves completed, I looked up in the sky, in case it was going to rain, in case I needed rushing to take shelter. Of course, there was not even a shred of a cloud there. I looked at the gate across the cemetery, scanning for an acquaintance walking in. None of the distractions came to help, no excuse; it was time to say something. I was drenched in shame. I sat down, my hand on the soil. The first time I met my cadaver was when it was laid on that cold metal tray in the hospital mortuary. It was a creepy get-together of the two parts, the self and the body, in that chilling environment. Then I bumped into my body caged in a coffin, but then I did not dare getting close. 'Was it not enough of meeting; why did I come here?' I rebuked myself. Despite, I patted the shoulder of the grave. I patted it gently lest a pair of hands would snap through it, grapple me at the throat and drag me into it, like a star into a blackhole. I raised my hands to offer prayers in favor of the resident of the grave but urgently got confused about what to say. I dropped my hands and uttered, "do you realize the wreckage you have caused behind you?"

The one from inside the grave spoke, "do you know who jumped the ship, you or me?" With these words, I heard soft weeping. Of course, I had touched a wrong cord? I squatted a step away. I heard a woodpecker pecking at a distance. Fine breeze meddling in surges with tree leaves sounded like someone speaking to the silence. Then, a sudden flutter thrilled through this silence. For a second, I thought the grave had exploded, with the two hands cracking through it. The sound was followed by a series of flaps, which soon muffled out. A goose circled above, lazed around for a moment, then cut through the air straight to another destination.

In the disquieting silence that followed, I heard footsteps of someone approaching from behind me. The sound was uneven, with steps in between shuffling. 'Was this someone injured or lame?' but I would not dare to look taht way. The noise approached rather speedily, mixed with noise of dragging of something. I hurriedly dismissed my duty to say something to the resident of the grave and turned a blind eye to its headstone and slipped away quietly, pretending to read the headstones around. From the safety of a long distance,

I looked back at the scene. There was no one there. I sweat, my gate imperceptibly gaining speed, while I was rushing towards the gate.

# FAREWELL PARTY

I reached the house, had a final look around and sat down exhausted. Ignoring the recent grapple with Aliya, I decided to write a final note to her and to Ayaan:

> "I know you do not see the real me from my look or from my voice, for none of these artefacts are mine, and that is the reason I better not see you, but the syntax and phrases in this message are mine that you will recognize, I hope. Aliya! you remember complaining, 'Dad, you write in really long sentences.' Here we are then; this is your Daddy, talking to you, in sentences that are never ending. You know what! I have planned that I will be leaving your world – now; and my only wish at this departing moment is to be surrounded by you people seeing me off, bidding a farewell– but I know that is not possible; in fact, if it were possible, I would not have to leave anyway.
>
> Remember the lateral thinking that I taught you when you were small. You can take it that whatever happened to your dad in the accident or afterward was not of his doing. You sure know I would prefer you over everything else, but that choice during this story was not been available to me. Now, I cannot wait anymore. You would agree that I am a new person, then I need to find out this new person myself, and a new niche for this person, too. On my journey of search, out from your life I am forever from now on. But if you think I will forget you people and your mum, that is not possible; however, I draw a blanket on the memories, so should you."

Regards

Your Daddy

I dragged the luggage case out and locked the door behind me. I lifted the flap of the mail-slot to drop the keys inside; instead, I glanced through it. Cutting ties hurts. Standing on the footpath, I looked at the Comely House. It was one of the houses in the street, of the same design, windows, eaves, everything. There was no one left after me to leave this place. Though the window of Comely's bedroom was slightly open. She liked fresh air in the room. The curtains in Aurora's bedroom were partly drawn. I could see through it the flush ceiling light; she liked it cool white, I remembered. Now, all was history anyway; a home had morphed into a building of bricks. Only the last night, I had the final act of the nightmare played. Why should I stay here anymore, surrounded in bricks? I took out my phone and wiped the contacts, all of them, and blocked them for good.

***

There was still an hour left before the train departure. I decided to walk to the railway station. I switched on the motor on the hand-hauler. My shadow on the footpath, longer than my height, walked ahead of me. The rhythm of the wheels wrapping over the cracks on the footpath absorbed my attention. 'When would these shadows shrink and my life eased?' feeling tired, I yearned. But then, did the journey ahead not promise to take these shadows away? Yes, but who knows? Such pains are not there to vanish.

A thud from the wheels passing over a large crack on the footpath woke me up. I looked at the watch and increased my speed. I tapped my back-pocket to feel the printout of my rail ticket. I tapped the other pocket for the phone. The traffic on the road was ripe, with dozens of vehicles passing by every minute. Suddenly, I saw this one, coming this way, the same make, the same color, the lorry that had hit me. I shivered; the hauler slipped from my hand. I squeezed away from the road, hitting in panic the hedge on the pavement. I looked back at the lorry. The scene locked on me - my breathing, too - from which the lorry phased out gradually, its smoke fizzling in the air; eventually it went out of sight. I started breathing again, slowly, and then was gasping. I got hold of the hauler and was back on the footpath.

But soon I returned to the stream of imagination. Whole world went mad at my reformation. Everyone wrangled about my identity. My family deserted me; I abandoned Nahaar's parents; my employers dismissed me; the court wrangled, too. Another tussle clasped me between Comely and Aurora, all time competing, first, in marrying me, and then, in divorcing. Though, these casualties were nothing compared with the tragedy of my own daughter mistaking her daddy for someone else. One by one, these scenes came to relive in my mind, plus, of course, the horrible scenes of my frequent meetings with my dead body.

# RAIL CASUAL

I TURNED THE CORNER AND there it was, the grand edifice of the railway station. From here, I would start my new lease. I shoved my luggage into the front compartment of the train, held the door-pull handle and looked around at the platform and beyond. History was in the making here but none paid any attention to it, the fellow passengers, the vendors or the train despatchers, even the train driver, who popped his head out from the front compartment, giving a careful look around, except he was not bothered to look into my way. None of my three wives went to the trouble of seeing me off on this important journey. 'Silly you, as if you don't know,' I rebuked myself. On this irony, I smiled, though I feared with this sarcastic smile might ooze out the agony, the anger, the void with which my mind was satiated. I controlled myself, lest the people around, who wouldn't give me any attention, would quickly spot my tears, although they might still pretend to be oblivious.

I entered the train and took a forward-facing seat. I checked my cell for the time. 'Why time? nothing awaiting me.' 'Excellent,' I tried but could not remember the time when time did not bother me. The train-despatchers whistled at each other; its driver must have pulled his head in from the window. The wheels eased with a metallic screech and set into a grumble.

Greif returned but I quickly shifted focus from the frivolity to substance. Anger and worries were important, but mow was the turn to explore my self - this beast, the self. The endless thoughts and the hum of superfast train, interrupted with the clickety-clack toots from wheels passing over rail joints put my eyes to droop. But with the eyes closed, I feared loneliness. I tried to see outside: it was a nice scenery but was repetitive. I glanced over the people in the coach. They were scattered around - not too many of them - some dozing, others busy with the screens, one or two reading and a few chatting between themselves or nibbling. A young lady sitting around a table not many rows away from me caught my eyes. She was alone. She was extremely attractive. She got her cell from her handbag but quickly tossed it on the table. Now, she reached the book on her table but closed it instantly. She looked out in the window, but then pulled down the blind. To my eyes, she looked frustrated but she could be merely bored. I would not take my eyes off from her stunning beauty. I forgot the presence of other people around in couch. I forgot my age, the objectives of this journey; I had lost my mind. She noticed me staring at her. She reached for her holdall lying on the overhead rack, struggled with it a little but did not take anything out of it. In the twirling of her body, she looked tall and agile. She was simply gorgeous. In my head, I debated whether she would be interested in befriending me, but then probably she might not be. I wanted to speak to her, but my mouth went dry, my eyes burning. Then she looked the other way but only to return her gaze at me. I knew that she knew of my staring at her. I tried looking the other way but was soon back at her. 'I must try to speak to her.' 'No,' I rebuked myself. 'The train romance has to progress with the speed of the train: Shall I or shall I not!!!' 'Coward!!!' I then tried to put a break on myself again 'what has gone wrong with you?' What will happen to your plans?' 'Are you that weak to give in so easily?'

'Listen! for how long would you put up being alone around that secluded farm? With the new life, you would need a new partner – sooner or later. Go and speak to her! Maybe! Maybe only for contact-exchange!'

She got up once more to reach her luggage, with her eyes glancing at me. That gave me a chance to try this petty opener; with my hand on my chest, I mouthed, "need my help?" She did not fall to this ploy and brought it down herself. I, Oxymoron, had indeed let myself down. After a minute or two, she left the couch. That helped me to return to my senses, even though I kept hoping she would return.

It was only while waiting for a taxi on the taxi-stand when I actually regained sanity to realize this lycanthropic spur in my character. I could not come up with a proper excuse except to settle with the petty one, 'surely, it wasn't me; it was the youth in me.' Deeply embarrassed, I was on the next limb of my journey.

# ACUTE BEND

THE TAXI HAD TO MAKE rather an acute turn from the main road to get on to the country lane. It was getting darker but still enough life was left in the dusk. It was a single track, uneven throughout, often broken on the edges, sometimes running over steep hills, meeting with bends here and there, some double. It was lined on both sides with trees and bushes, their branches intruding the road, occasionally rubbing against the car. Through the gaps in the tree-line, I could see the crop fields and grazing pastures, sporadically punctuated with farmhouses but I did not see any human around by this time.

"Are you sure there isn't another route to your place?" the driver broke the silence. "Can't believe I am driving on this trash. The tyres would go rotten; I'm sure the body paint would also need touching."

I was embarrassed, "sorry, don't know the area much. Some forty years since I lived around here. Have never used this road before."

Suddenly, a van emerged from the bend ahead, running speedily towards us. Both the vehicles somehow managed to stop nose to nose. My heart stopped with the vivid memory of my fatal accident. The other driver lowered his window and asked the taxi driver to reverse the car to the pullout behind us. The taxi driver hesitated but did not know any better. Fuming, he put the car in reverse gear, with his arm stretched on the back of my seat, embarrassing me with his looks. 'Not a good start of my new career,' I thought.

Once the path was cleared, we started again. There were signs scattered all along of cattle and wildlife crossing the road, even one of 'Overtaking Prohibited', a hardly relevant sign in the given conditions, but the one we were looking for, but so far could not find, was of the Parrot Farm. It used to be the workplace of my father which I regularly visited but things had changed over the decades. I was told of a hump-bridge on the way, followed a furlong later by the sign for the farm and an exit for it on the left.

"It has been quite some time after the hump-bridge. I fear we might have missed the exit?" I was scared to ask the driver, but I did.

The driver kept quiet but made a U-turn on the next pullout. Back at the hump-bridge, we made a U-turn and started again, this time just at a creeping speed, with the eyes on the left for the sign and on the exit for the farm. Even at this slow speed, each time the tyres passing over a big bump created a thud exceptionally heavy on the ears and a jolt hefty on the heart. I kept on thinking any moment the driver would refuse to go any further. Eventually I noticed a sign which I thought could be the one we were looking for. The driver noticed that, too, and stopped the car past it. I got out of the car and walked back towards the sign. I saw on the other side of the road a barn. A horse was poking its head out from over the top of the wired hedge. At noticing me, it snorted and flipped its tail and head, when its halter chain rattled. Then it rotated his ears forward in unison as if they were mounted on some conjoint cogs, its eyes staring at me. The odor of horse manure filled the atmosphere and my nose, completely. Strangely, it did not bother me; instead, it captivated my mind with the nostalgia from my childhood.

The signboard displayed 'P'….T FAR.' with few letters missing. Adjacent to the board was the exit. It was really a small exit, camouflaged with bushes. I went back to the taxi. His left arm on the back of the passenger seat, his head turned 180 degrees, his face furious, he gassed the taxi in the reverse gear to approach the exit. He took the turn into the exit, although my heart was filled with fear in case this was not the right exit. There was a chuckling noise of the gravel on the drive flying from under the tyres. The car headlights were sometimes shining on the gravel, other times dancing on the tree trunks, lining the drive on its both sides. We soon entered a cluster of big Oak trees, at the center of which was the farmhouse, my next dwelling. It was dark by now, but I could recognize the building. What if I did not find the key? As I was told, I found the passage to the door lined on both sides with a series of massive rocks. I counted on the right the third stone from the door, and under it there it was, the key, shining in the twilight. It worked in the lock, too. "Hurray," relieved, I murmured. I pulled my luggage and hurriedly entered the building, not to look back lest the driver might say something unpleasant. Completely drained out, I went upstairs for the bedroom and straight fell on the bed.

Feeling hungry, I woke up at the middle of night but did not feel like leaving the bed. I could have finished the leftover sandwich I bought in the train but felt its distaste. However, I would not go back to sleep either. Shining on the wall was a beam of yellow light sifting through the leaves of the climber, kissing the window glass. Its halo, trembling on the wall, suggested a mild wind blowing outside. Occasionally, there would be screeching sound of twigs rubbing against the glass. The ambiance made me sad from the past and frighten of the future. 'Why had I to come here? Why did I come here? Where else should have I gone? I belonged to nowhere. Would I be able to survive? Farming was not my cup of tea. Seeking solitude, did I not want to discover myself? Finding no one around, I would have no one to talk to, but me.' Thoughts tiptoed in my mind till the morning light broke.

Exhausted and excited, I got up. I looked around in the property. It was the same two-bedroom double-storey country house which I used to visit with my dad. With minimalistic décor, distressed paint, hefty doors, and empty rooms, it felt a pretty dull and dreary place. Musty odor from the dusty dank carpets was unmistakable. The stairs, with stout wooden handrail and bulky newel, climbed down to the living room, which had scanty basic furniture. Though, the kitchen was newer and modern. There were even some cans of food carefully arranged in a cabinet and some eggs, a bread and a bottle of milk in the fridge – all within expiry dates - sufficient supply for few days - seemingly left by Sul – a nice gesture. A frame with a picture was hung on the wall behind the dining-table. In the picture were two very lovely teenagers, an older girl, and a boy, probably sister and brother, standing side by side. I, too, had their pictures, from their childhood to the fore, hung on the walls all around my house, and had them serially printed in a photo-book too. Whenever I and Zeitoun would want to sample the past, these pictures would be our tour guide. How sad that it had to be Aliya to demolish all the possibilities of my returning to the family, just with one stroke. My disaffected memory of my family owed to her insinuation that evening that a daughter could marry her father, although she argued her father had died and I was not the person who died. With these bizarre thoughts, I was again torn in the middle. Who was I? Had I died? I must find out my identity. 'Not just the identity; remember, you wanted to know who you are, you nature' I reminded myself.

I went outside. Enveloped in the soft morning light and light mist, the house looked even prettier than its picture. There was this figure of parrot embossed on its name-plaque, not from my father's time. The facade was extensive, and the grass lawns streaked with rhizomes spread around it. The barn beside the house, now dilapidated I would say, was empty. I wouldn't be populating it, considering my medical condition and the drugs that I was on, downsizing my immunity. I had been alerted to the risks of zoonotic infections from the livestock and from their manor. I went out to have flying tour of the farm around, though alone but feeling happy.

# FRANK FROLIC

SUL CAME LATER IN THE day. An XX-large guy, with a broken nose, turban ears, spiky scant hair, and a tattoo of tiger across one side of his muscular neck, he was hell of a man. He was the youngest son of my father's friend whom my father gave the charge of the farm on his death. Surely, he must have a name longer than Sul, but that was what he asked me to call him. On the first sight, he examined me and trained his eyes on my disposition. I had tried to explain to him in my earlier correspondence about my special composition, but he did not seem to have registered it or wasn't bothered. He did not mention it at all.

During the next few weeks, I worked with Sul, mainly helping him in securing his produce. Judging from my naïve farming skills, it would not have taken him long to find out what kind of newborn I was to the vocation. I looked young, and had urbane mannerism, which made me look unsuitable to horticulture. Off and on in the middle of work, he would poke his toughened big hand into his back pocket for a sugar packet, tear its corner and pour its content on the other hand to transfer the heap with a jolt into his mouth. What bothered me was his taking raw sugar but more teasingly not washing his hands before this operation. For me, during work, I would often wash my hands or tap them many times when soiled, to dust them off the dirt. Looking at me and my behavior, Sul would ask about my background. In return, I would laugh and say my background was as meagre as his name. He suspected my motivations of coming to work in the farm and, like a genuine villager, was not shy of saying it, "O' you, city-boy, what'a you doin here? Ya'say you sharecropper. Must be joking, young man. You surely sinked your money here."

I hated him for his open cynicism and, like him, was not shy of saying it, "you don't know my motivation, Sul, because you can't understand it." And we both would giggle. He was good at work, and I at talking, as long as it was not about me. I wouldn't think he learnt anything from me, but, of course, I learnt from him the farming skills, which he was not miserly in showing or talking through. But he was always short at words, mostly trying to find the right ones, when I would jump in, to help him, 'oh, Sul, do you want to say this…? oh, I see you mean that….' He would take words from me but with no thanks, giving me a strange look instead. I suspected his mind would still be working on me and my background.

On the final day of our teamwork, I invited Sul to come to my house. He entered the house ahead of me and reached the family room before me. More,

163

he chose a chair for himself without my asking or even waiting for me; and, yes, he sat heavily on it, yet, spreading out his legs by far. After a minute, he went to the kitchen, saying he wanted to fetch a cup of tea for himself. Irritated, I was about to go berserk on his brusque manners when I heard him yelling from the kitchen. He wanted to show me behind the boiler a covert cabinet, which he recommended I should use for keeping valuables. Silly me; I had forgot this house was actually his dwelling before I came here. It was he who had left the ration for me, enough for several days, though he would not mention this favor at all.

Standing beside the dining table, he wanted me to look at the frame hung on the wall behind it with the two teenagers. With his hand at my shoulder and his other palm spread towards the frame, he told me these were his kids – a proud dad. Placing his mug on the table, he delicately touched their faces and carefully removed the frame off the wall. I could not tell him that I, too, had a set of them, two equally handsome youngsters, belonging to me. I did not want to; he had already cultivated his mind with doubts about me.

First with his concern about my comfort and security of my belongings, and now with the care shown in his manners, he changed my mind about him. I felt embarrassed for having him misplaced as rough guy. Rough, he was, no doubt, yet he was a 24-karat pure person. At the end, he allowed me to contact him for advice, though, in his manners, I could see his contempt for my skills – but was it for my skills or for my age? In either case, I did not mind it, for the sincerity in his offer was as visible and, anyway, I needed his advice.

*** 

It was the crop of Barley with which I started my horticultural career. Sul listed its agronomic attributes, its merits in controlling weed and its suitability in crop-rotation. (He just had finished with Soybean at this land.) "Would be easy on you. Soil an' moisture is good, you see", he said. "Do the fallows, as well – those on the west part - enough rest for them now and good moisture they take. Get them - they're ready for cropping."

"OK – I will. What will I be doing with straw, Sul? I couldn't possibly feed it to the livestock - I have no plan to breed livestock," I asked.

He laughed, "straw! I shall buy it from you, OK young man!" I quickly realized why he laughed. Sarcastically - on my silly question. But, in fact, in my mind, I was trying to show off my knowledge about the crop, my foresight and upbeat for it.

After Sul had finished, I was left with only a small window of a couple of weeks to till the land and sow, expecting an early rain afterwards. They were the pretty harsh, lengthy two-weeks for me of arduous work and learning on the job. During the evenings, I would google things for PDFs and YouTube clips, place orders for fertilizers, have a word with Sul and draw plans for the next day. The days I would spend in shorts and a P-cap, with lot of water to drink and with energy bars now and then. I noticed I could now unwrap a bar sometimes without washing hands.

On that evening, after finishing sowing, I returned home, tanned, rejoiced, soaked with accomplishment. The feeling was like I had felt after winning a massive research grant, but this time it was raw, original. Though not making a way to the national gazette or being talked about in committees, it was something that owed purely to me and was for me. I was happy with my decision of taking this vocation. I gave Sul a call, thanking him for all the help, had my dinner and went to sleep, tired but not fatigued.

***

Beside few routine chores at the farm, now was the time to discover the place. Once settled, walking on uneven paths, sweating in the field, living tough, all seemed velvety to me. Days came and went, one after the other in an un-telling way, like pages turned in a textbook, boring, just run of the mill. As much keen I was in working at the farm, so reluctant was I in meeting with people. I just did not want to speak to anyone. Had I become misanthropic? I just wanted to buy some time for myself, to heal from inside. For this reason, I would always come up with excuses to avoid going to town. If I had to, I would try finishing everything in one go, kitchen supplies, equipment repair, fuel, my medical prescription, and the rest. My usual frugality paid off in running a simple life.

But then I had grown very alone. I would get up at dawn and go straight to the field. I would go out even on days when I did not have much to do. On these free days, usually I would get to the road, walk to the hump-bridge, and then turn right to the riverbank. The first bit of the walk was on unformed paths through bushes, but then I would find a track of reasonable width under the shade of thick mature trees overarching it. In a couple of miles, the path would enter a dense jungle. I noticed a lot of birds there. I just loved these little things and thought I should give a serious go to birdwatching as a pastime. In my trip to the town center this time included buying a gear for this purpose.

***

165

This morning, it was first time I planned to go to the woods for birdwatching. I got the rucksack and binocular, filled the water-bottle with lime soda. I wanted to wear my favorite P-cap. Searching for it, I unpacked the remaining stuff in the suitcase. Instead of the cap, I found in the contents the globe with the sleeping rose.

With the globe in my hand and my eyes on the rose, I was jammed in that posture. Then, I slowly melted, feeling the warmth of a solitary tear on my cheek. I felt rush of some kind, and from this rush, someone shouted, 'you want to enter your past, don't you? You in fact love it and the characters who played in it, don't you?'

'Leave me alone; let me cry - after all I am not made of stone – even stones split,' replied I, in a hoarse voice.

The globe in my hands, I waited for Aurora any moment sashaying around the house and tiptoeing from the kitchen with two mugs, one in each hand, the red one for her, the blue one for me. Refreshed with tea, we would go for a walk around in the vibrant zesty air in the farm. 'No,' I then thought, 'no way, she couldn't be here. I had come too far from her; I had crossed the point-of-no-return. In fact, they, all my associates, had crossed it, too.' The manner in which they deserted me, one by one, recklessly, callously, haunted me. I felt in me the heat from fuming of anger and riot from rebelling from my loved ones. They had in fact made me redundant, I thought. On the idea of redundancy, I smiled, for, in a similar manner, I had abandoned Public Engagement. I put the globe on the shelf in the kitchen. 'Bravo!' I whispered to myself. By then, the tear on my cheek had gone dry. Standing beside the shelf, I thought how one could be more inconsistent than me: from being happy to becoming sad, then to being angry, then sarcastic. Within few moments, the peace that I initially felt got swapped with agitation, then with resignation. Nothing outside had changed. Feelings were being traded within. What was within; who was its resident? Who was I?

***

With the rucksack on the shoulder, I headed towards the hump-bridge and then from the bridge turned right into the wood. It was a winterish sun, yet under it, my skin tickled and prickled, soothed with puffs of cool breeze. I would slow down to rush down few sips from the bottle of soda, tasting pleasantly sharp on my tongue. Comely loved soda, too; in fact, it was from her that I had acquired the taste. I loved Comely; I acquired several of her likings, trying to win her over. With the ting of soda on my tongue and a gush of love in my heart, I badly missed her. Only if she were here with me, sharing soda

166

and the experience. 'Can people share experiences? Is it not utterly personal? You seeing an object as green is supposed to be the same as I seeing that object as green. But it could be different, for there is no guarantee that our 'greens' are the same. In experiencing things, each one of us stands utterly alone. Who is each one of us? Who am I? Am I sure I know the answer to this question? Would I ever meet 'me'?'

Absorbed in these profound questions, with my eyes set on the void, I was wobbling on the narrow ridge between two fields. The ridge joined a broad way, bordered with bushes, adorned here and there with a blossom of honeysuckle and wild jasmine. I could smell in the air their subtle sweetish, delicate fragrance. I suddenly felt the presence of an inner eye, twinkling, with which I could now and then catch glimpses of me.

I threw a look at the sky, this time catching a sight of a couple of hawks hovering high in the space. I heard fluttering of a bird nearby. My eyes trailed up to the sound to find a nightingale swinging with a green twig on a large tree. It was quiet – wrong time of the day for singing - but I did hear some hoots and caws in the background. I guessed there must be a whole watch of nightingales around. They must have migrated long flyway to this location in search of insects and for breeding, I thought.

Then, again, my inner eye blinked. It focused on the artefacts of seeing, feeling, tasting, smelling walking, thinking – the slaves, the executive pawns. It looked for the puppeteer, master, the chief executive, the royal highness, the self. It returned barren. It could not find me, really. Maybe one day, my inner eye would meet this agent. Looking up at the sky again, I noticed this time the clouds building up on the western horizon. With the hope of rain, good for my Barley, I decided to return home.

On the way back, I was again hit by the feeling of aloneness. One of the ways out of this was through visiting the past. The urge in me to revamp my memories of the past was on the rise, yet the idea made my heart sink. I just did not dare to enter that valley.

\*\*\*

The clouds that evening grouped but did not pour. I felt thirsty, which increased with each day passing without rain. The thirst would urge for soda, water, tea, but of the farmer, could not to be quenched by these things. Only rain could quench it, I knew for sure. Looking at the sunshine, I detested it every minute stealing moisture from my land. I wanted to hold the sun away from my Barley. I hated the weed and grass scattered among Barley shoots, gulping moisture, but they were too many to uproot.

Sul came with a word of advice. The crop looked unwell except in the fallows. All in all, it was not a very good scene. Indeed, we both knew the crop needed rain, but he came despite, this nice person, to support me, offering consolation. After the stroll, he came to my house for a cup of tea. "It is too late for a thank, but thank you, Sul, for leaving ration for me to begin with," I said.

"Why mention it, young man, it is indeed late now," he laughed. "No, but you think I would bother packing a little bottle of milk and few cans to take them away?" Then his eye shifted at the shelf, and on it the globe, with the rose sleeping in it. He stood up, "where did ya buy it – nice piece - eh? My daughter is in art in school. You know the parrot embossment outside! She made it. Would love a look of the globe- where did ya buy it?"

"You can borrow it; in fact, why don't you take it for her, a gift from her uncle, or brother, or whatever." I had said it, but while he spread his hand towards the globe, my heart came to my mouth. It was the drop scene of a life-story finishing at a blast, but here I was, with my wet eyes closed, and I quietly feeling the salt down my throat.

Saul had left. Aurora came and, as usual, sat on my left side, sipping from her red mug. I knew she must have noticed the rucksack carelessly thrown near the door. Looking through the window at the dancing trees swayed by the high wind, I said, "I know I leave things here and there, promise I would find a place for the rucksack." She took my promise quietly. "Oh' by the way, I've given the sleeping rose to my best friend lest I break it. His daughter is an artist. They would value it, I am sure." She kept quiet. "Good man, Sul; he helped me in work." She kept quiet. Perhaps she was in a bad mood; perhaps I had disturbed her. She was certainly not happy for the sleeping rose given away. I changed the topic, "you know I was new on the job, but Sul says it is the draught that has failed the crop." Did she say, 'never mind'? I wasn't sure. Perhaps she did not want to talk about the crops. "Planning to go to city in the morning to get some fuel." She did not reply; perhaps it was not a question needing to reply. "This place is little cold?" I meant to ask her if she minded putting the heating on. She did not respond.

I got concerned and looked at her sitting on my left, but my eyes caught just the empty chair. She wasn't there. Had she already left? Did I see her today? No, I was just talking to her, but she did not say anything. The last time she talked to me was that evening, at her leaving the house on the Rose Gardens

168

with her luggage. I did not bother to get up to put the heating on. Feeling cold in my chair, I just squatted my knees to my chest and folded my elbows between them, with my hands cuddling my face, the fingers covering the eyes. Soon I noticed my hands getting moist and I feeling pain. The pain was not in the hands, or in the face … in fact it was nowhere in the body - I had carefully scanned whole body looking for it. It was an ache roaming around the throat, drifting in the chest, suffocating, faint in intensity yet slaying in effect, slowly, playfully. It felt like a blend mildly amiable on the tongue which once down the throat turned malevolent. I knew this was the ache in the self, the puppeteer, the subject which Aurora named as the soul. Aurora had left my life and left me on the path to meet the soul, my soul. It is mostly through pain that you meet your soul.

# MISTY SPUR

THERE WAS NO RAIN for the crop, and it was getting too late for it. The crop failed. I had a lot of time before the next turn. Days passed without any particular chore or plan, although I would frequently visit the riverbank. That day, the day put on pale-yellow sunshine, lightly baked in hushed haze. As usual, I reached the hump-bridge for the riverbank, but my heart was cooking another story. I could not resist the thought of visiting the place of my upbringing, only a stone's throw away or maybe twice as long. My dad used to cycle to the farm or even, on a nice day, would walk to this place and I with him. Instead of heading towards the riverbank, I went straight ahead after the bridge. I looked on my right for the scurvy track that I knew leading to the state where I had lived with my mum and dad. I could not find it. I went along the road passing between grazing meadows on its both sides. They were mostly empty, except this one, which had many cows, all clustering in its far corner. They were busy with their heads down on the grass, except one or two staring in the void. I paused at the scene thinking what a leisurely lifestyle they had, with the simplest of the schedules, comprising eating, sleeping and occasionally breeding – that is all. Look at me; how sophistications with which I had woven my life.

I was about to leave when I noticed a solitary cow heading this way. I wanted to see her from close. She walked straight towards me with an intent and oomph. From the close, she leveled a glare on me. A fawn-colored beast, she had dark brown speckles all around the body, with a bigger patch like continental map between her eyes, extending outward to line the eyes. Although she had walked leisurely, with a tardy gate, and had only petite horns if at all, while nearby me, the way she snorted, her throwing out air in big boluses, her tail stiff with an archly attitude and contempt in her eyes left me in no doubt that she was up to something not good. Trying to tell me off, she lowed a few times in deep bass. But then, side by side, she launched a standing toilet, though seemingly unaware of the events at that end of her. Feeling ridiculed, I was about to leave when she took half a step closer to me, the hedge between us being the only defense I had in case she decided to tackle me. Not knowing what she meant, I quickly stepped back and drifted away, keeping my eyes on her. But of course, I was reassured that she was not of the predators, and probably knew her limits. Unlike true predators, cows don't attack for usurping or dominating. Some humans play by these rules, sometimes even more effectively than regular predators by adding the spices of conspiracy, plot, incitement and ostentation. But then, none other than humans can engage in good things, such as asking questions, doing mathematics and giving charity.

Counting these of our distinctions, I moved on, leaving the cow snorting behind me. I was sure on my back she must be basking on her victory.

Only at a furlong along the road, I noticed the road forking. According to the plan, I took the right prong. It straightway entered into a built-up area, but I could not recognize it. After a couple of blocks, a massive building on the left of the street winked at me with familiar wipes. It was indeed my school building. Despite many decades had passed on me and on it, I recognized it. I compulsorily gravitated towards it. Passed the gate, though my feet on the ground, I was floating like a bird. My love of the past and of this place seized me such that my eyes kissed every brick, every tree and each of its paths. There was no one there, not even the janitor in his room, nor the maple tree beside it anymore; the brass plate hanging from a hook on its trunk had gone missing, too. At each hour, the janitor would strike the brass with a hammer in trilogy to signal the end of a period, when, according to the customs in those good old days, the teachers would switch classrooms. A longer sequence of bells marked the recess, when we would rush toward the hawkers waiting on the street; or the unrelenting sequence of the bell which would announce the end of the school day when pupils from all the classrooms would rapidly pour into the main courtyard besides the headmaster's office, cramming it jampack. From there, they would slowly ease out, leaving home for the day.

I spotted the headmaster's office at the same place as in the past, an annex alienated from the main bloc, connected with it through a short corridor, invaginating into the courtyard. I used to pass by this corridor rather timidly, feeling a bad taste of some past disciplinary experience, but today it was different. Today, having grown out of fear, I was no more that little child. I hoped my portrait holding the best-student trophy was still hanging on its wall. Its door was open. I fancied any moment someone would emerge and greet me. Someone did emerge, rather a biggish younger man, in near-forty range, who did not particularly greet me, but straightway charged me with a question about my presence there. He said he was the headmaster. 'So,' I thought, 'the things had not changed much in the school, really,' though I pitied him at his ignorance about me. Unperturbed, looking at him, I reminded him, "son, I used to be a student here some fifty years ago. There must by my trophy of the student-of-the-year still there in - in your office." Extending my arm towards the office door, I said, "I mean my picture with the trophy. ...." Then I changed the direction of my arm, "see that room – the third door down the row, that used to be my classroom."

He looked at the door, but quickly returned his gaze at me as if he'd forgotten something, "are you in the right mind?" His shaking the head and squeezing the eyes was not a good sign at all.

Before claiming any respect from this young employee, it was clear that I had some obstacles to overcome. "Why? … I mean, can't I be an alumnus of this place?"

"Not from fifty years ago," stressing at the word 'fifty', he continued searching at my face. "Also, did I hear it right that you have called me, son?"

I had undoubtedly messed up the script. No explanation could repair it now. Ironically, walking away from the scene now was not an option either. He would call the police for my trespassing. How easily had I created this impossible situation for myself? I would only be lucky to set free from here. I dodged his question with a smile, "O, I know, it is my look; you know the pricey plastic surgery these days; I like it that way: looking young." I briefly showcased my face at him, still trying not to pose too cheekily. I gently drifted away from his range, saying, "but never mind; you must be busy; maybe another time." He must indeed be busy in resolving in his head the riddle that I had posed, for he remained paused at the spot, while I successfully slipped away.  Once off the scene, I literally sprinted, only to calm gradually.

My next stop would be the place where I spent my childhood with my parents. I walked in the streets in the state like I had walked fifty years ago, inattentive to the surrounding, thinking of homework, friends, mum and dad. From this trance, I suddenly woke to the reality of my house standing at my face. It had changed only a little. The external light, the bell, the number plate, letterbox, all were more or less on the same place. The newly painted door on the side of the house was open, with a waterpipe appearing from its cleft. A couple of children were romping around the front lawn with a tennis ball. That's where I used to play with the boys from our neighbors. I wanted to absorb the images, tallying them with my memory, but wouldn't dare gazing at the place lest someone here becoming suspicious too. I would not dare to approach the house lest facing questions like the ones the headmaster demanded from me to answer. Peripherally eyeballing at the place, I merely satiated myself from distance - the place of my upbringing where once I had no such restrictions.

I see myself in the front lawn playing with the boy from the neighbors. My mum appears on the door, calling me in for the lunch, but I am not keen. My dad appears at the corner of the street, walking with grocery bags in his hands. Watching mum and I haggling, he walks towards me and, with his right palm on my back, the thumb on my shoulder, the fingers holding the bag, he persuades me to go in.

Many years skipped, I pretend to be busy in the lawn, with a distant hope in the back of my mind that the young lady, Zeitoun, from the family visiting us joins me here. I am standing in that left corner, right there, with my back at the door and my ears on it, when she quietly joins me, "I wonder if you're into plants. I love flowers. People in the city hardly know how to mind them."

Though, with the botanical names that I precisely articulate, she is not impressed. I am disappointed, in fact, embarrassed, slightly. I drift the discussion to my new job, but no, she is not interested in my job description either. From this point on, my focus is at wooing her interest, which makes me wander from topic to topic. She remains keenly focused throughout but also intensely bored right through. She must have noticed my irking. She smiles and excuses herself. I strike my left fist on my right palm. I follow her into the house. She is not visible. In the living room, our mums are busy in a meeting. They pay me brief attention. I pop out in the back garden, to see our dads laughing their head-off. They pay me no attention whatsoever. I return to the front lawn. I think of her. Several decades have skipped. The irony has been that I have since been trying to woo her interest without success, a game she, as my wife, has relentlessly played on me.

***

A bird cawed, busting my trance. I returned to the bitter present. I noticed a man around 60 mark emerged from the neighbors. I approached him, "are you Rosh?"

He hesitated, then halted, focusing his eyes at me, "I am Roshan; but no one here calls me Rosh."

"You were the only child in this house. We all, your mum and dad, I called you by this name by then. You had lots of art toys, though you always liked to play with the wooden blocks, completing with them the picture of a boy on a horse, the one of brown color."

"Sorry! who are you?" he appeared completely taken aback.

"We started the school together. … But it is not fair on you. Can we sit somewhere and talk?"

He stared in the void for a second, returned to his door and invited me in. He showed me to the sitting room and pointed to a chair in the corner. He drew a couch near me, "who are you?"

I looked around. The room looked arty, though slightly overwhelmed with artefacts. I praised the place.

The next thing we knew was the darkness seizing outside, but talking for hours had not done us in. Curious of our voluble banter, his wife and their son popped in, checking if we were OK. Rosh imitated rolling his eyes while introducing me to them. The wife was staggered with the explanation, the son stunned. The joy of sharing the memories with him was only rivalled by the delight of home-cooked food that she cooked for us. Rosh would not let me leave but we parted with a promise to meet again. On the way back, I was walking but my feet were not on the ground, nor was my head in the air. In another world, I tasted this pleasure of meeting my chum on my palate, savory, zesty, aromatic, significant. How urgently I needed this recipe, I had just realized.

# ACCOUNT BALANCE

I HAD NOTHING MUCH to do till the next crop. To fill the time, I persuaded myself to pen down the events that had paved my paths and the debates that had carved my thoughts. I did fumble over where to start, though I was able to start the same night. Assigning the story to paper changed its shades from what I had in mind in the beginning. The characters that in life I took as brutal emerged in the story as neatly uptight. The wounds of the past got over time less sore and looked from distance less awful. I frequently found myself pleaded guilty for being intolerant to them. I discovered the only appropriate way to fit with other characters in life was to appropriate my own size. I cried, I laughed, I conversed with the characters in ways that if you were to watch me, you would consider me mad. I purged myself.

***

I am on my way to finishing this project. I have sought every opportunity to write; the best of them have been availed at my favorite spot on the riverbank. Ironically, the closer I have got to the finish line, the more nervous I feel, as if I am about to say goodbye to my best friends. Fortunately, the time for the next crop is approaching. It is late in the evening that I am about to place the last leaf of the story on top of the pile. Now I smooth the pile as if patting the shoulder of a friend, 'so, Oxymoron, what are you going to do with the script?'

I am preparing it to send to a publishing house. With it, I write a personal letter to the editor, a friend of mine from the past:

> "We have not met since long, and in case you do not already know about me from the papers, in this pile is my story. That is about it. However, if you'd asked me if I'd like it to be published, I am not sure. Not that I am that kind of person, uncertain, vacillating – no, that I am certainly not, but it is just because of the type of the life material that has come my way is weirdly odd, though some of its bits beautifully weird; and, of course, the characters in the story are real, mostly alive, too – I pray they may live long. Happy to wait to know what you think of the script. If you felt it should be published, be my guest."

# PART THREE: THE VOYAGE

## EFFORTLESS EXODUS

I STARTED YET ANOTHER TIME for the next crop. Tillage was perfect. I scattered soybeans seeds on the land and waited for the rain. Sul was a friend now and would in passing drop in now and then. He saw it for himself and praised my skills. Patting my back, he said, "you proved me wrong, ya city boy. Bet, I couldn't do that good."

"It all depends on rain, doesn't it, Sul?" pleased with his approval, I said.

For now, cultivation was accomplished. At dusk, feeling nervous, I went for a stroll on the riverbank. My eyes frequented the sky, seeking clouds. Instead, I caught the glimpse of the conical crown of a solitary tree, proudly spreading its arms like spokes of a wheel all around its shaft. To me the picture painted a symbol of ego, reminding me of my self. Then I remembered Logge and Nash who revealed my self to me, I would say, from distance. And then, came in my life my dear wife Aurora, who introduced my self to me from flush closeness. I returned home, yearning for a handshake with this thing, my self, and to ask it the questions waiting on my lips for long.

I would look up in the sky all the time, waiting for the grey clouds laden with water and hope. This morning too, there was no sign of them. Though in the letterbox, there was letter waiting for me. My editor friend had written back:

"I seriously empathize with your position. I must emphasize that we must get this piece published. However, presently, it is incomplete. I would like to help in completing it but for that you must trust me; as, for now, I cannot divulge my plans for it."

I was kind of happy with the response, although I had no idea why he thought the story was incomplete or how he was thinking to complete it. I briefly replied to him saying I would be looking forward to his contribution. For now, my attention was on the crop.

A few days passed when the moment came. Only a farmer could know how elated and thrilled I was on that day at returning from my farms, this day of raining after the long drought. For the budding young crops, the rain on that day could not have been better timed. And, it was gentle and leisurely; bathing the soil; nourishing the roots; neither torrential nor in buckets such as to sweep away the delicate roots in the soft bed; and, it had been on for hours. I felt as if it were not the crops but me who was being nursed, with some delicacy; it was my thirst, not than that of the plants, which was quenched, not with water

179

but with nectar. Ecstatic, I returned home with all tension gone. Now, I would want to make a nice cup of tea, put my feet up and unwind.

I put the kettle on and, in the rumblings from its simmering, I was absorbed - that much I remember for sure. This sound always fascinates me, for it arises from vigour and dynamism of something boiling, yet it is calming. On that day, it was exceptional, as if, muffling near the boiling point, it had folded me in, swallowed me. And then, something out of ordinary happened. Something gently eased me into another world. From there, like the alleviating chimes from a camel line fading deep into the desert, my life that I'd known departed from my body. I was lost, but kind of aware of being lost.

From the void, I emerged in a new place, in a strange valley, filled with a vast labyrinth of alleys. As far as you could see, there were alleys, of all kinds, short and long, with joints and bends between them, some arthritic and other smooth and slinky. I was floating inside the alleys, but also outside of them, as if I could transcend their confines; in fact, I could witness several of the alleys in one going. So, there I was, hovering in the valley of alleys; where I could see as never so sharp before, except without the eyes, and I could hear a feather drop, except without the ears, for I did not seem to have these artefacts with me. I did not even have my body with me, yet the feeling of its existence was so real that the body I had left behind felt as its mere shadow. I was captivated by this fascinating world, new to me, at the same time in a strange way known to me. I knew this territory as if I owned it.

Like a child trying out a new toy, in excitement, I was randomly sailing around, at times soaring, other times diving. Once my curiosity was noshed and I tired, I tumbled down, slackening amidst the alleys. While at recess, I calmed down a little, only to be thrilled with yet another display of wonder – a kind of traffic but without trekking. You must have seen in a relay-race a racer with a baton in hand to surrender it to his partner-racer waiting on the next beat. On receiving it, the partner sets off on sprinting to reach the next partner, so forth. Or even a better example is of bricks stuck up in a row, where one brick falling over the next one knocks it down, so forth, thus setting off a domino effect in the whole row of bricks. The glimpses of such advances I witnessed all around me.

I eyeballed the place more closely. Each alley was lined with hedges, each comprising somethings looking like tulip shoots arranged in rows. Just like tulips, these shoots were stiff but sufficiently supple to twirl to all comers, except the tulips in this scene would dance only in a particular order. For a start, only one of the shoots bows to the wind-force. But when it recoils, its bloom strikes head-to-head the bloom next to it, making the shoot bearing it to bow as well. The sequence of the shoots bowing and recoiling one after the other in an incredibly rapid succession thus continues along the whole length of the hedge, creating a shimmy, a dance – the 'tulip-dance' – which gives the impression of something streaming along the hedge, along the endlessly long hedge. And, then, there are other hedges in this tightly packed avenue, some on the right and more on the left; some lying above the others and some below; some diverging, others merging, like spaghetti rail tracks around a rail shed, or like a junction on a motorway, if it could be infinitely multiplied in complexity and enormity, except not as stern as rail sheds or motorways, but furnished and beautified with the tulip-dance, occurring here and there, sometimes here and sometimes there, sometimes speedily and other times leisurely, emerging and vanishing, like tides in the ocean waxing and waning, in cadence without sound, in harmony superseding mayhem. You may, in your imagination, brush the tulips in rainbow colours, some hedges in blue, others in pink, and the rest, some even trilling in different colour-combinations. Surreal this scene might seem, its reality was unsurpassable, just an otherworldly relic.

# NEW-FOUND CONFIDANTE

THE SCENE WAS FANTASTIC, true; but was scary, too. I wished only if I had a companion here with me, who could join me in the fun, streaming around, turning, and tossing – a real jubilation. I looked around but could not spot anyone. Then, I hear a voice from distance, "sanity" it says," … this place is for the sane, not for the intoxicated." And then, a figure gradually emerged. He was a silhouette of a man, looking relaxed, confident and elegant. He introduced himself with his hamlet name, Sage, which he said was adapted from the role he was assigned. He said he his role was to confer and share, helping to articulate the meanings of what was going on around here. He said he had been doing this role from the ancient times, having been with all kinds of people, philosophers, teachers, merchants, more recently also with lawyers, doctors, and mechanics, you name it, those of the mankind interested in meeting their selves.

As for the terms of business between us, he hailed, "you are welcome to ask questions anytime, but you don't need to, really, as I will be able to pick your questions straight from your thoughts." I was nervously attentive to him, of which he made fun of me, "just relax - you don't need to fawn." I pretended relaxed. After a pause, he said, "may I try at guessing?" I instantly reverted to the same obsequious posture. He just smiled, "do you realize that this city of alleys is in fact your own territory, the harbour of your consciousness and thoughts? You could call it your thought city if you'd like." Surely, he already had started reading my mind.

After a quite pause, Sage chipped in again, "every act of the tulip-dance on display here, slight or sizeable, in different colours, carries a thought, be it a thought fetched from your memory, the one arising from your feelings, the one made of information you have received, the one generated of the logic or be it the one carrying your instructions of some kind for the body to discharge."

"O' I see, these are the tracks and circuits in the brain on which thoughts run," I instantly remembered Nash and Logge explaining the layout of the brain., "I must be trespassing the territory of my brain, am I not?"

He continued, "no, not trespassing at all. All these thoughts lugged on to this tulip dance, transpiring along the alleys here, all of them, belong to you."

"To me! All of them!!" overwhelmed, I said. "Something most elegant – what I see now I could never have conceived."

No sooner did I have this thought than the tulips had freaked out, flocks after flocks, red, blue, yellow, shimmying, which set me into panicking, and made me dizzy such that I had to hold the hand of Sage. The storm was swishing, a kind of gust but without the wind, a sort of flood but without the water, coming over me as if it would sweep me away, or it would bury me underneath, or it would suffocate me, ending at my demise and nothing I could do to avoid it. But, when it actually came over, it turned out to be none of these, as I found out. It was the most mild, subtle, sublime, delicate thing that I ever had come by, embracing me, like when pure silk or an ethereal leaf cuddle the face.

*They sicken of the calm who know [this] storm.*[1]

Surely, therefore, it was not the tulip-dance in that valley that set me off into panicking, for this scenic dance was simply delightful. My panic must have pinched off from something else that I did not exactly know. I looked up to Sage with searching eyes, to which he responded, "the storm that has just passed was in fact of your thought – your feelings - that overwhelmed you – you remember when I explained to you your thought city, you got really excited about it."

"Is that what happens here when you get excited?" asked I.

He continued, "such storms can take over the whole of your thinking apparatus. But normally, it is not that dramatic. In mature people, it would not happen easily."

I was embarrassed but was overwhelmed again; just about then, another big storm ran past me, followed by storms after storms. But, by now, I had learnt not to panic; they quietened down, too.

Once calm prevailed, I shook my head in disbelief, "I can't piece these together, the dance in the alleys and my thoughts."

Sage nodded randomly at an alley, "see that one, for example, see that alley in the orange, busy in the dance. With it is running are the signals of a flicker of your thoughts, a thought in the making. If you go a little further along that alley, you will see a pasture containing many alleys, some red, other blue, converging into one, a grand alley. In this way, the thoughts from various sources are being intertwined. Many grand alleys run cheek by jowl in tracks; these tracks reach various stations, for example, the station of vision, anger or of pain, you name it. It is here, in these stations, that the consolidated signals are corroborated as thoughts." Sage paused.

---

[1] Dorothy Parker in the Poem, '*Fair Weather*'

Awestruck, I was speechless. Nash had told me about the stations, but now I was able to witness them as well.

Sage said, "thoughts from different stations are despatched to a *Thought Hub* to create an overall sense."

# THOUGHT CITY

TRYING TO SHAKE OFF MY awe, I exclaimed. "Let me try in this place with few things." Sage waited. "May I see how my thoughts are worked out in this thought city. Let me see."

The first thought that I played on the system was of my farm dowsed with rain. Several alleys on my left staged the tulip dance in a mixture of colour, dominated by white. They quickly merged just before vanishing into a station. There was a second heat and a third, on and on, of this dance. "Yippee, aah," shouted I out mawkishly, with tears in my eyes.

Sage pointed at a station, "there it is! your Happy Post."

On the high, the next thought I wanted to try was of screaming with rage at Sage… for no reason. (Sage was a friend by now, at least that's what I thought of him.) A new tulip dance, mostly in red, engulfed a cluster of alleys close by and whooshed past me. But then, right in the middle of this operation, activity changed both its direction and in colour. In a moment of chaos, it made a figure-of-eight excursion, disappearing into another locale. What happened to my screaming? Instead, from the angry words that I was trying to put in my mouth, a giggle oozed. Sage laughed, "*Thrill Hub* – that is where the signals this time have reached, even though you have wanted them to go to the *Axis of Insolence*, but you were merely pretending an insult, not meaning it." Quite obviously, my plan was not followed through exactly, for pretentions by the novice are destined to fail.

This time, for a change, I wanted to try an ugly thought – I tried the memory of the time of Aurora's departing. Then again, several alleys were overtaken with a new dance, this time on the far side, disappearing into a series of stations further down. I felt shaky, weak, and insulted. Sage pointed, "*the Hurt Centres* – there they are. That is where you feel regrets and sorrows." Though the dance did not cease at that station; beyond my control, it ensued from here and, taking a hairpin turn, ended up in another station. I noticed my memory had skipped several years to recreate a scene of my wedding with Zeitoun. I guessed it was the Happy Post that ultimately received the signal.

Sage said, "you must by now be utterly exhausted. Why don't you take some rest?"

We glided for some more distance before landing on a high turf, overlooking a large canvas of dynamism. From the top, it looked like a city, a great city, with an array of monuments and landmarks regularly punctuating it, with crisscross constellations of enlightened streets and pathways connecting them, buoyant with whizzing traffic. The multitude of vehicles trading around in the city reminded me the busy bees operating in a beehive. Information trading replaced the honey.

***

FROM our observation post, the tulip dance staged below in the city looked stunning but seemed meaningless. Without taking my eyes off the city, I asked, "Sage, you claim knowledge of my thoughts. How, if I may ask, do you discern it just by skimming over the Tulip-dance? Or, is it that you perceive it from the station at which a particular dance terminates?"

*Sage* gave me a snubbing look, "can you make such guesses in that way. If you can't, how am I supposed to? Remember what I told you in the start - I only know what you already have in your system and as much. On this point we are not two, but one. My job is only to dig out for you the answer that you already have in stock, sometimes buried somewhere deep down."

"Then, obviously, I must confess, I definitely cannot make out from the look of a storm which thought it is carting. That let alone, before this visiting, I even did not know these storms or the stations that house them." My voice softened a bit, "so, then, what it is by which I myself come to know my thought."

"You know it only once it has been decoded – and I know it from you," *Sage* said. "Now, please do not ask me how your thoughts are synthesised, encrypted and infused into storms? How these storms are framed in tulip-dances? And, how they are decoded back into thoughts that you could discern them, as of that I myself am completely ignorant."

With eyes closed, I pondered, 'a *de novo* thought, a kind of top-down thought, arising from deliberation must spontaneously trigger a new tulip-dance. And then, there is the other kind, a kind comprising bottom-up thoughts - arising from, for example, fear, from memory or from received information - must also find right alleys to display their drama. But how would I know to which of the alleys to allocate which particular thought, even when I have no prior knowledge of these alleys?'

Sage was closely reading into my reflections, "you must have realised the precision in allocating thoughts? It must be perfect. Handling a logical thought constructed, such as if A then B, is different from holding an information thought, such as there is A and there is B'. So on and so forth."

186

I returned to reflection mode.

This regalia, thus managing thoughts, humbled me. I had come a long distance to look at this graceful wonder. If ability to think was important to me, setting it up was not my business, nor was it my responsibility. I felt deeply grateful. I felt grateful that this headache was not left for me; I was relieved of this duty in favour of merely enjoying its fruit, the luxury of thinking. So intense was my gratitude that the tulip-dance and the storm it raised in the alleys would not cease.

Sage giggled, "if thought management fascinates you, you must visit the Thought Hub, the place where thoughts are segregated, kneaded and mellowed; where they are tagged with executive codes and issued for action."

These words induced a flashback, zooming at Aurora, in her hand a list of artefacts to be found in the intellect, the item, the agent, underlined in red. I said, "Sage, are we going to meet with the agent?"

Sage replied, "the agent, whose only function is to intend. The agent intends and it is."

"Is it that simple?"

"You get only that you can chew; and you can chew at any one time only one notion. Which one depends on your choice." "At every corner and roundabout here, there lies a choice to be made. Choice is nothing other than an intention minded. And an intention waits for the agent to make it."

He continued, "a lot happens between making an intention and that which is intended, but the two overlap in such a way that they seem indistinct from each other."

"Sage, would you not agree?" I paused.

"To what?"

"In that case, it must be the intention that the self is entrusted to make? All of the relics in the city are geared up to hand over the intended to the intention."

"Yes," said Sage. "The self, the agent, is only liable for intention."[1]

---

[1] Ethics of Pure Intention seems to be operational here, with a mitigation that the self has a chance to examine the consequent thought before releasing it in words or actions

I did not attend much to what he just said. Excitement of meeting with the agent gripped me. "Sage" I retorted. "Do you think I would be able to meet with the agent?"

"*Realself* - Realself is his name. If you are a self, he is your Realself," Sage said.

I waited for Sage complete his answer.

"Surely you would have questions kept for the meeting."

"Yes, for example, who is he? Is he yet another thought?" said I, remembering the argument from Aurora.

Sage was irritated, "on that one, take my word for it. Responsible for intending or perceiving, in itself, *self* cannot be yet another thought, loitering around here. Your self is not joy or sorrow, nor can it be logic or pretention, no, none of these. These artefacts just belong to the self, your Realself."

Sage was contemplating, "if you ask me who Realself is, what I know of him is only through you. If you don't know your Realself, I don't him either."

What Sage said just now was too profound for me to digest. Right now, my issue was anticipation of my meeting with Realself. The whole valley blew up in tulip-dance, waves after waves, glowing in shades of reds, blues, and greens.

"Why don't you get ready for the next length of your journey? In fact, get up; let us go."

"Where should we expect to see him?" I yelled while taking off.

"In his lodge - that is where he resides, this Realself – in the Thought Hub in Downtown, among other lodges and servant-quarters, with their occupants, a small community of them," Sage shouted from distant.

---

[2] A hamlet name of Realself is given to the self

# THOUGHT HUB

THE NEXT STRIDE WAS NOT to the left, nor was it to the right; it was rather like a frame in a camera converging from all sides on to a particular point. We spotted a creek and alighted beside it. Within its rough embankments flowed idly murky blue, molten, gooey stuff.

Sage said, "Blue Ropey Lake[1] is its name - a pretty important landmark, situated close to the Lodge. I always look for it in my visits to this place."

This was a scene to watch, but my heart was set at my meeting with Realself. Sage noticed it and gave another move-order. We crossed an expanse which, from helicopter's view, looked a spectacular colossal network of millions of roads[2], arranged such that they looked like the ribs across the human chest.[3]

"Wow, can we pause here? I have not seen a motorway wider than its length, and that busy."

"Two million lane motorway!!! but for now, let's continue," commanded Sage.

Soon we were hovering over a spread-out edifice of the shape of the human chest. Sage got excited, "your final destination." Amidst this edifice were two buildings face to face that I could configure, one with a flag on its top waving gently. On getting closer, the rest of the buildings zoomed in, too. Going lower, I could also figure out a plethora of criss-cross roads and streets, some jammed, others idle.

Sage said, "this is the Thought Hub - the central sorting. Thoughts are shuffled here for deduction or induction, to be granted with meanings or subjected to moral judgement."

He mumbled, "the idle roads are recruited when you learn new skills or acquire new knowledge. They can also be recruited to ease the pressure in the busy districts."

It reminded me the rail-yard; watching disjointed coaches shuttled to assemble into trains always fascinated me."

---

[1] The anatomical name: Superior Sagittal Sinus
[2] The anatomical name: Corpus Callosum
[3] Raza, M. W. (2022). Anatomy of the Intellect in the Quran: A Fresh Perspective, Al-Bayan: Journal of Qur'an and Hadith Studies, 20(2), 182-216. doi: https://doi.org/10.1163/22321969-12340113

We alit near the flag house. It was set on the busiest of the junctions here. "What is about this house, Sage, it looked splendid from the top. It looks even more spectacular from the front."

"O' this one! of course, the *Palace*."

"Whose palace!!!"

Sage announced, as if reading from a sheet, "this is truly your abode and of your thoughts, of which you are conscious; a post that you inhabit and command, to the exclusion of all others; here you perceive information, cradle ideas, cuddle fantasies, make decisions and issue instructions; the home-office of Realself. You reign from here," said Sage. "All the roads in this city eventually merge into its basement.

I was already impressed with the awe emanating from the place. Now, I wrestled with the idea that I kept repeating, "Is that where I actually live?" A long way -really a long way – had I walked to reach here. What I was seeing in front of me was not some special breathing exercise fruited or some meditation culminated. It was not a pretended fantasy, nor was it an illusory dream. It was a real structure in which to live; unique though, in which for the self to live.[4] Afterall, I had made it. What if they don't recognise me, or even banish me as an outsider or an intruder? I was consumed with trepidation, as if it was a ghostly castle that I was about to visit, expecting to meet the unexpected. Sage kept smiling, enjoying my fluster.

When I got my breath back, I could hear a faint hum coming from above. It sounded of some liquid gushing. Sage noticed my distraction and reminded me of the Blue Ropey Lake.

"Could we actually go into the building now - please?"

"Not me - I can't enter this place; from this point on, you are on your own," said Sage.

"Traitor!" I joking said, trying to appease my hesitation, bloating by the minute.

***

He smiled, but his smile hastily wore solemnity, "while being there, you must remember few rules."

"Here comes the usual training course," I looked at him.

---

[4] The Quran identifies a particular place for the self in the brain near the Ropy Blue Lake. Q50: 16

He smiled, "first, without getting too excited, give yourself time to understand the system. Try picking some serious thoughts to observe - not the mediocre run of the mill kinds you previously chose - and run them through the system."

He continued, "thoughts either arrive here, or they arise here, so go for one of each class."

Sage said, "De novo thinking is the primary modus operandi in the Palace. So, be creative. All ingredients are shelved in your thought machine, waiting to be recalled by your attention, to be used in creating new thoughts."

"Just by the way: there is one more kind, which take yet another route, bypassing the normal routes. When petty and trivial, classed as distractions, they are dumped in the junkyard of the memory; when aggressive hardliner, they are imposed on Realself as dogma."

I browsed the premises for Realself. Sage noticed me, "he is not here, but you would meet him inside."

"When is this training going to finish?"

Sage said, "that was just first item… Don't forget the occupants of the building around in this valley. It is only in the palace of yours you can meet with them; therefore, don't miss the chance."

By now, I had learnt that a pause in his speech was to ensure my undivided attention. I waited for the next thing to come out.

He continued, "the edifice on the other side of the Palace!" He paused.

"What about it?"

"Prudence; that's the name with which it is acclaimed, and entitled too, this edifice."

I waited for Sage to say more.

"It is only visible from the well-lit palace. You will soon find out how to increase the light in there."

"You are only making me anxious about Prudence."

"So must you be; you must not miss it."

"Why do you think I can forget it?" I asked.

"Many people do. It is a place reserved for wisdom accoladed, the kind that rise above the procedural or customary understanding of things. It is a gift that only some avail – or else it remains covert, with shutters down."

"A place for wisdom remaining estranged, does not make sense, Sage."

He said, "Not everybody asks the questions for which Prudence has the answers."

"So, what should I do? I mean how do I connect with it? Is there someone to whom I can speak?"

"No, No. just try despatching your questions to it for evaluation and see for yourself what happens next."

If he was trying to incite my curiosity, I couldn't wait anymore to go in. But, with a wave of his hand, he stopped me once more, "the space interceding the between the Palace and Prudence!!!"

"Yes, what about it?"

First becoming reticent, then overwhelmed, he whispered in awe, "highly restricted, this place. This is an observatory from where to watch Realself's making intensions, applying his will."

This said, Sage had in fact deflated the juvenile excitement in my curiosity. Mellowed at the full tilt, I suddenly became. I was about to enter the zone where I must show, at least pretend, abstemious mannerism.

# OPERATIONS MANAGER

I MOVED CLOSER TO THE building, looking for a doorbell, or was there an ID-check at the entry? But the gate was unfastened for me just at the right moment. 'Did they know me? Were they expecting me?'

It was dusky and quiet inside, but was it that because I could not as such see or hear? Yet, I knew – I just knew. From here, I tried my senses; I could see my farm, my house, the kitchen- but this was not by way of seeing but through knowing. I could hear the hum from the boiling water in the kettle, but again this was not by way of hearing but through knowing. In this place, I could only know things but also knew if they were to be seen or be heard. I still knew what seeing and hearing separately encompassed. I knew that very well but I only knew. Meanings of the objects arriving here had thus transcended the usual precincts of how they were sensed.

Unlike an ordinary room with four walls and a ceiling, this foyer comprised condensed atmosphere, a definition without definite borders. And, I knew a light in the room of such captivating shades as to seize your attention, but nothing at which to attend or to look. To me, the atmosphere here felt consciousness personified.

Nothing much to report from the foyer, as the things there were merely seeming, perfunctory, understated. I knew a console in the centre of the foyer set on which were an array of knobs lined up and a couple of joysticks, very minimalistic furnishing, really. If anything, the most significant presence was of myself. There was a wide, cushioned backrest beside the console - thank God - from which I knew this place was not for sitting and resting but for working. Looking at the arrangement, and experience of life, I shouldn't have been surprised if the cushion were to be replaced with a lattice of thorns of some kind.

Like glimmers in a dark night from a contingent of fireflies drilling in a lawn, lurking around the foyer were faintly knowable sparks from the chords, several of them, all connected to the switches. The most peculiar with this network was that not all the messages reached the switches – most of them did not make for the switches - just blanked on the way or seized prematurely.

Then I noticed mirrors installed in the foyer in every direction that I faced. I thought about the point of installing mirrors when you cannot even see. However, I realised this place was about virtual seeing through knowing. Of course, then, I must have wanted to see how I actually looked, as the original

Oxymoron or as the young Nahaar. Not that it was important now after how the issue of my identity had so far been battered, but this was a good chance to get the longwinded debates on this subject concluded. However, every time I tried looking into a mirror, my image vanished before I could register its glimpse. Facing a mirror, I closed my eyes, then opened them on the double: no use, there was an image, for sure, but was gone as quickly. I tried to pretend closing my eyes while seeing from a slit: no, this way did not work either. 'The first disappointment!' which reminded me the frustration at the lack of information on the wave-particle duality in the double-slit experiment in Quantum. But there it was consciousness which was at play; so was here as well; here the consciousness seemed to work against itself.

Busy in trying to know the place, I forgot its owner, Realself. I noticed someone parting from the backrest. When got closer, I realised this thing in fact wearing my silhouette. I suspected it was him. Smiles exchanged; I inadvertently grabbed the thing and embraced it, a uniquely soothing experience. I knew that the feelings were mutual – in fact perpetual. Considering of the hugging been prolonged adequately, we wanted to let each other go. But we were separable no more; we had merged. Now, there was no one outside the silhouette of my torso. So, I was Realself, at least for now, and Realself me.

The drama continued on the hype, as the next thing in the list was even more vivid. Just as I took the place against the backrest, suddenly I felt having spread across the whole of it, not multiplied, nor divided, but just spread – spread in three – like bubbles on a balloon … or pouches on an organiser, oh, as parts of a sandwich that had been incompletely cut by its dividers. Although separated in that sense, we knew the mind of each other because, not just connected, we were parts of the one self. There were thus now three genuine participants of the self, also to have three separate voices, something to be learnt soon.

On my left flank was part of my self, with an eye for things - bubbly and chatty – Bubbly was his name. He looked fresh, with his facial features heaving as if gravity had not plunged them at all. He was incarnation of cheekiness. His job plan was to keep me informed about, in fact, attracted to, interesting things. As artful as he was, he would surely sell me anything in the name of joy and pleasure, and I would surely buy it – ever-ready and never complaining.

Flanked on my right was also a part of my self, scornful, rational and nit-picking. Frowner was his proper name. His facade bore a million creases, which if you ever had happened to see, everyone one of them would look like a frown, and scary too; mostly would be like paw-prints of several dozen crows strolling on the mud. You could guess from this façade that he would not need to become angry afresh, or critical, for he was so, anyway - permanently. His wrath was visible all the time, his face outpouring lava, streaming in the facial creases. His role was to throw looks at his target, like a warden casts suspicion at a thief. He would send sniffers around every item of thought, like custom crew unleash sniffing-dogs on every item of baggage. A caricature of a daunting warrior, he would thus avail every opportunity to jump into any ongoing tussle in my self.

And, of course, there was the I in the centre – playing as the authority - the chieftain – hence, perhaps, you would appreciate why I was stern and direct: I was in charge here, incessant and dogged. It would be peace if I were at peace, and it would be trouble if I were in trouble. It was up to me to decide; taking sides in the game played here would not fail equity or justice; in fact, that was my main role. In nutshell, therefore, I had a friend and a foe, both within me. I, thus, constituted the three of us.

No sooner had I settled than Bubbly whinged, "may I know what is the point of putting the mirrors all around the foyer when you can't even see yourself in them. I was not going to steel anything by just looking at my own image. Have they put a ticket on mirrors? It would be ridiculous to expect people to pay for looking their image in a mirror." He then laughed, "they do ask in public places these days to pay for using hair-dryers, but for mirrors, it is indeed unheard of. Plus, of course, I hear this place is belonging to me – in fact my ears have started to ache hearing this rhetoric."

I said, "images are of the bodies, and the bodies do not matter in this place."

Bubbly was quick to return, "what is the point of putting mirrors, then, if I may ask? I have come long distance. One may like to see how they look before meeting others. I cannot understand this place."

I responded, "the point is to show that the body does not matter here."

Bubbly retorted, "why then put the mirror on, in the first place? Afterall they are not the cheapest things in the world to buy these days or the easiest to install."

"To show the body exists but is fleeting, and chasing it futile," said I, trying to keep my nerve.

Bubbly seemed to concede at this point.

I said, "would you like to know something even more insightful than this if you were capable of understanding it at all."

Bubbly was embarrassed.

I said, "of its substance not much knowledge that a self can have, except its elusive glimpse."

I noticed a cleft on centre of the console. A monitor hoisted from the cleft, reminding me my arising from slumber. It straightway gripped my focus as if on it were compressed my consciousness. If the rest of the city and the alleys in it represented the production lines of thoughts, it would soon be evident that this monitor was their business hub.

The monitor had multiple screens, each showing different contents, but at any one time, I could focus at only one screen. There were knobs to control the screens, some blinking, a joystick and a wheel. I ran my finger over the knobs one after the other. The blinking screens would display their contents live, text or picture. When I scanned the contents cagily, a set of screens glowed; [1] when sloppily a different set glowed. [2]

In the meantime, I noticed Frowner on my right flank nodding towards the top left screen, showing the gridded map of this city gone live; pretty boring – I ignored it. But the one Bubbly went for exposed a beautiful girl in boldly erotic clothes and alluring gestures. Had I mentioned earlier that Bubbly had an eye for things? Here was one example. I gave in; Bubbly prevailed. The girl was so beautiful, indeed - the girl on the screen, that I had completely been done with. Did I mention the rule that if I had agreed to go with Bubbly, Frowner would slip into sleep? Frowner thus dozed.

"It is a private place; surely no one could see us," assured Bubbly, while he twisted the knob underneath the screen. It started the girl making seducing gestures one after the other. "Goodness me, the link is live!!" Bubbly tried on the joystick. Seduction had worked me up, when a chord in the far end of the foyer sparked, releasing a surge of radiation, at which point I wobbled, then agitated, which was followed by a wave of dry heat in which I floated, at the end, leaving me soothed and listless. I momentarily lost the orientation. Another gesture from her and a current gripped the chord, emitting continuous sparks, releasing radiation of manifold more Rads and, of course, heat, plus a fume of rainbow colour – giving me a holistic experience, leaving me oblivion of the surroundings. She blinked and parted; the screen went blank. With these proceedings, the light in the palace grew noticeably dimmed.

---

[1] Default Mode Network
[2] Executive Network

Bubbly looked around: no one else was there. Bubbly wanted to try something different, something more powerful. "Are we forgetting something?" came a feeble protest from me. Bubbly was agitated, a sign of disappointment, "is this the time to be fussy?"

"OK, OK - everything else can wait," I resigned. Bubbly smiled.

# BIG ENTRY

THIS TIME BUBBLY APPROACHED the wheel lying at the bottom of the multiscreen. He looked around – no one else was watching. He turned the wheel. And, from the door there entered Charmer, whom I could recognise even before he announced his name, for I knew him well, just naturally, as an associate and a comrade. For now, he was dressed up in a guise of youth, bouncing, animated, with cheeky smiles and with manners in politeness and courtesy unsurpassable. His charisma was such that, looking at him, I forget to blink. And he spoke; and, when he spoke, nothing else could distract me, for his rhetoric was capturing, his expressions jovial. His speech was enticingly polite, uniquely eloquent and convincingly powerful, such as to envy a London barrister. He promised me eternal pleasure, but also between the lines warned me of the sadists around campaigning against him and his ideas.

He eventually came to the point. With his eyes rolling between Bubbly and me, first, this cheeky little devil boldly told me off. Why? For having stuck just to the same girl so far. He showed how to get the complete drop-down menu of attractions and allures, and gave instructions how I could get everything I wanted, all real, all in real-time. Bubbly was through and through a yes-man to Charmer.

He then brought a series of pictures on the screen. I could spot his pausing deliberately a little longer on this particular one. This girl waved her hand at me; she was exceptionally beautiful, her looks enthralling – no doubt about it; but if Charmer was boasting on his find, this show-off was, so to speak, extortionate. Bubbly prompted me to project side by side the image of the girl from the train-romance. I recalled that picture and put it up. She literally jazzed up the things around, except Charmer's choice, which, instead, appeared dimmed in comparison. Absorbed in her charms, I even neglected Charmer.

Charmer was not embarrassed, "I know this girl from the train. Yes, of course, she is beautiful. I made you go for her. Don't you remember?"

"You made me go to her!!!"

"I wanted to help her - you know" said Charmer.

"Help her!!!"

"Yeh. The guy loved her – her husband - a bit too much, I would like to add. A small mistake this 'husbandy thing' made on that day – from then on, it was easy for me, I must say. I just instilled in her head the idea of her being suffocated by her husband - you know!" Charmer giggled, "she really fell for it… started feeling uneasy in his presence. The poor soul, eventually, decided to leave. That is when you met her … in the train. I thought it wasn't a bad idea to connect you two, hoping to firm up their separation. But she wasn't ready yet, this poor soul."

"O' I see, it was you, then, who pumped me" said I, feeling exonerated.

"Don't shift the blame. In fact, there isn't any blame to shift. You wanted to propose her, didn't you? for a long-term relationship. It is legal and morally apt, you know. Quibbles aside, she is still around – still undecided. Shall I arrange things for you!!" said Charmer.

Bubbly said, "is that possible? I bet her husband would be sending her text messages, constantly apologising? What a bad thing this husband of her must be! For not leaving her alone. Charmer, can you not sort him out!!!"

Charmer snubbed Bubbly, "I know my job." He continued, "in the meantime, why don't you take some alternatives. Merely by looking at a beauty on a screen, or in the street, what harm can you cause to any one? To yourself, you must only bring the bliss; would you deny it? If someone looks good, and spending time with them innocuous, why would you not like to spend few moments together, nice moments. Just help yourself, should I say. I promise you more fun. Remember, life is for pleasure. Give yourself a chance. Just give me a shout, whenever. In fact, why don't I pay you regular visits." Then he wagged his head towards the wheel near the screen, "there it is – more you turn this wheel the faster my service you get."

Having an eye on things, Bubbly smiled. I was impressed, too, with Charmer's altruism and promise - and with his argument of 'meaning no harm to anyone' - amazing. He noticed my appreciation. He said, "remember, it is you who started this show. It is your show, your idea. I don't start things; I only help them running. Remember, my help is tending without trespassing; persuasive without pressing. Take it or leave it."

I suddenly became fed up with his verbosity, boasting, his word-gymnastic and playing with sentiments. Frustrated, I said, "enough, Charmer, you may leave now."

Though, what Charmer said in response was shocking, "I did not come here with your permission. In fact, I can stroll around most of this valley, and, for that, I don't seek your permission, nor do I need one from you. I can give you a hand in the operations taking place here; just watch the space. But there is no need to be scared of me, you know me; we are friends." He wickedly smiled and winked, nodding at the particular screen in the foyer.

Suddenly a thought hit me, and I pretended to be friendly, too, "Charmer, I sympathise with you, for your job is philanthropical – no doubt – but it is pretty bumpy, too, isn't it? Some people even curse you, regularly. Can't you just give it up?"

"You must be joking. I have seen many heroes… like you, who have given up their heroism right in front of me," he said, breathing out a lot of air.

Now I wanted to pursue the course, "I hope you don't mind asking what made you take this role?"

He snorted, "What are you, by the way? You are too small a fish to ask this type of questions. I have looked after billions of cockroaches like you, don't you realise? I have even played on your greatest grandfather. Go and check the records"

I got the point.

And, he left, but just on the door, he turned his face and threw a smile.

# MORE CHARACTERS

H E LEFT BUT HAD LEFT me numb, my sentiments messed up. 'A Chameleon would not change its colours as many times, and as quickly, as this guy changed his demeanour,' I thought. But the guy had such a pull that, after having cursed him and asked him to leave, I wanted to go with him. Even before Charmer had closed the door behind him, Bubbly was back at the screens.[1]

"Where would this show end, then?" Fed up and feeling frustrated, I looked helplessly at Bubbly.

Hearing these words from me, Frowner with a scornful eye, the nit-picking Frowner found an opportunity to wake up. He woke up with a twitch; I felt it as a shudder. My recently acquired intoxication feigned sobriety. In that apparently haughty demeanour, Frowner would fill the whole place. Bubbly wished if Frowner could immediately return to sleep, or at least, could announce the purpose of his waking up and how to accomplish it quickly, but he would not dare to ask. In fact, he would not dare muddling with this thing on my right flank ever. Bubbly could sneak through with his plans but would not even whisper when he heard the sharp squeak of Frowner.

Frowner said, "do you realise whom you have just met?"

We both kept quiet hoping Frowner didn't know the contents of the meeting.

"Charmer has been your nemesis from the word go," Frowner continued.

Frowner had clearly spied on our meeting with Charmer. Drenched in shame, I attended his annoying discourse even without blinking the eyes. Though, the more vigilantly I heeded to him the more frowns he bore. His discourse ended on the advice:

*"Unexamined life is not worthy of living."*[2]

The light in the Palace intensified. His discourse helped the things return to order; girls on the screen now looked like ghosts. "Is that why you took all the pains to reach this place; to put this soot on the screens?" disappointed, Frowner rebuked.

---

[1] "I don't do the good that I want. I don't want the bad that I do." St. Paul
[2] Aristotle: Apology

With these words uttered entered the scene two new characters, reaching one on each side of the console. With his elbow digging into the console, the hand supporting the head, the fingers fanning out, their terminal phalanges bent, probing deep into the hair, this one, on the right, stared at me. From that close, the silhouette of his intense facial expressions, framed in a hoop of annoyance, lined with shame and guilt kneaded together, looked ethereal. My heart sank. I wished I did not have to witness the ghosting in the image of his hand he waved across my face. I looked the other way, but could easily make out him hiss his name, 'Regretter'. Was I surprised?

I could not help smiling at the next announcement, 'I am Resenter' from the other side of the console. But, of course, my smile was short-lived, for no sooner had I looked at her than I felt nauseating. A truly sad figure that she was, she fired her gaze at me from close range from her swollen dim red eyes, fixed in her head, which she held between her hands, her long fingers fanning into her long dull black hair. With her hair fanning over her shoulders, she looked like a widow in mourning, which, mixed with her gaze at me, made me believe as if I was her killer. Disgusted at her look, I thought this loser of some class was rightly called as 'Resenter'.

I was thinking what next to happen when Frowner nudged me. I said to these intruders, "my apology, guys, for troubling you. I don't need your services. You may leave – immediately, please." This place had so far been like a magic carpet, if anything, needing little calm.

# A BUZZING PLACE IN THE HUMMING CITY

THE MAYHEM HAD ELAPSED, replaced with peace. It was time to achieve some understanding of this place. While in the valley seeing thoughts in the making running around, I wanted to see them integrating with each other. Here, in the Palace, I had the opportunity of seeing that happening. My eyes were on the screens. There was this particular screen showing the live map of the city. Around many of its districts could be witnessed electrical arcs, like those caused by a pantograph of electric trains brushing against the overhead catenary, more visible in dark nights.

I wanted to see how thoughts arrive in the city, and how they arise in it. I cherry-picked an item of childhood quibbles. Several districts blew up with the arcs, arising from transactions in the districts which I believed would be branches of the memory bank. They all coalesced before proceeding towards here. I picked different thoughts, with each were sparking different areas of the city. The sensory contents were fetched into a quarter in the city marked as the Heeding Centre before their despatching to here. A separate quarter of the city was reserved for the de novo thoughts, where they built up like mini cyclones, slowly gathering momentum before the storm shifted to here.

Some thoughts were wordless, appearing as fog, others roaring with words, descending as stone storm. Some were luminous, with rainbow colours, others dark and dense or in shades of grey. Some thoughts would come rolling in straight lines, others would zigzag like a ball passed among players in a football match. All were herded towards here.

From the closeness of my position in the foyer, I could see thoughts of various kinds arriving like boluses of fluid, soon to change into curd with my examining and comparing them. Thoughts would mature with further questioning until ultimately hardening like bone. Of these, I could see some set as concrete questions; others congeal as firm affirmations.

I wanted to sample specific demonstrations. A screen displayed this one from the memory bank: "a struggle within the self is harder than the one outside." A blob morphed into words: "personal growth is sought in pain, not in pleasure, except when pleasure, too, is endured as pain." A cyclone uncovered these words: "after the game, the king and pawn go into the same box."

I chose a wordless thought floating as a blob of fog. Suddenly the blob shifted its direction to enter a building labelled as 'Word-House'. Words there were available from huge inventories running on rotors; some from the data arranged on drape-down split-flap displays, as you find them dangling in railway-station lobbies. The choosing of the words for thoughts was so fast as not to let me witness it in any detail.

I soon ended up in feeling jaded with these difficult densely packed thoughts. Skipping the next few screens, I stopped on the one which ran a tiktok of a marvellous underwater waterfall, appearing as a pit, continuously sucking water and sand; yet, on its surface, there was calm. Was it for real? I got close, even closer, and then, without warning, I myself was sucked into it. I did not resist. I was in a wormhole, which delivered me on the other side into a new world. I reached a fantastic place, with colourful lights shining on the walls, sometimes whirling, other times curling. Multicolour georgette drapes glided in a mellow wind, sometimes necking the face, other times snaking around the neck and arms. With each step taken, the thick soft rugs at some places would cuddle my feet, fiddle with them at others. With each step, I sensed a new scent in the air. However, what straightway caught my attention were the picture-frames hung in rows on the wall on my right.

I glanced over the pictures. All showed familiar people and places from the past. On the top was a panel with an instruction: 'Touch a frame to interact with the person and tour the place'.

'Is this stuff from the memory bank?' I wondered.

Suddenly I felt a presence. Oh, it was Charmer, with a bottle in his right hand and a measure in the left. I ignored this unsolicited presence, my mind being more on the frames. The one on the far left showed a girl whom I recognised from my school. I remembered the frustrating school years when I longed for her attention, a craving that ended in vain. After school, I lost her track, and now I could see her here. I decided to go for it. I straightway touched the frame. There she was. This time, she even accepted my offer to walk her around school corridors and lawns. Then we found a quiet corner and she reluctantly agreed to share with me its solitude.

This fantasy spiralled up. At the completion of the spell, my hand was still on the frame but the girl disappeared, though Charmer stepped in. He poured a small measure from the bottle for me. The liquor seemed like a nectar wrung from voluptuous thoughts. It landed on my tongue with a spicy tinge, out of which raged blizzards of mingled tastes in a succession, sweeping the palate, soaking the tongue.

I tried another picture, it resulted in another erotic drama, all live. I looked at Charmer hoping for another measure offered to me, which he granted. Each time I got a measure, each time I felt wanting more, oftener, too.

Exhausted eventually, I stepped back from the wall. Feeling the nectar on my tongue, I regretted why I had denied myself of the pleasure of the fascinating company for lack of making a little more effort. Appreciating my sincere regret, Charmer this time took out a different bottle and poured a bigger measure, filling up to the lip of the vessel. I gulped the liquor. It swapped my exhaustion with trance, the serene trance. I soon got light, seeking another portion.

'What is it which I am ultimately trying to get?' I asked myself.

Something pleasant and ultimate; be it pleasure, or is it peace? With each sip, the liquor promised me so but did not deliver. I felt I could grasp it by taking just one more sip, just one more time, just one more chance. The goalposts constantly shifted away, being always ahead of me. Of this chasing, I became leery. My trance worn out to give way to exhaustion. That it was a trap by Charmer, I now had begun to realise.

"Enough of this," I asserted, calling Charmer a deceiver and with other glaring bad names. "I wish you never return."

He laughed, "I don't have to, but you will return to me, for sure. You are nothing; I have seen warriors bowing at the door of this fantastic place."

I laughed, too, "no way, Charmer, not me." But I knew my laughter was empty.

I got the air from here to return to my real world in the foyer, landing besides it. I lamented why I had let Charmer trick me one more time.

Going through these sentiments, I heard familiar stamping of the two walking this way. 'Must be Regretter and Resenter,' I dreaded. They literally plunged me for returning from the fancy place too early. I hesitated. Frowner woke up, "you fool, you don't have to visit every dungeon around here." In my heart, I knew I would return to that place anyway. For now, to calm down Frowner and get rid of the pair, I stopped whinging. Goodness me, this city and this lodging was some difficult place, with hazards waiting on every corner, at every screen, at every second.

# FIRE IN FREEWILL

WHILE PLAYFULLY EXPERIMENTING with thoughts in this place, I soon realised that it wasn't merely a game; it was in fact life, all about life. Each screen on the panel projected a life scenario, presenting options in each of the categories of knowing, accepting and executing, from which to choose. There were boring and dull, so-called green choices to make and there were other electrifying and sensational, so-called red choices available too. Every choice had a meaning and a consequence. The show simply comprised choosing, erring, learning and correcting.

Physics of choosing was fascinating: there was this weak force, for example meek goodness intrinsic of things, which drove the dull type, green choices. Afterall, what is so exciting about charity: you contribute what you have, only to return home empty handed. But how about the bright red choices coming by flying horses; mawkish and cool, of which the world is of full of examples, most driven by desires. Who wouldn't want to take a red choice, provided they are a dare devil - you know - not possibly put off by Frowner, the law or the society? On this thought of mine, Charmer winked at me from a screen and we exchanged smiles.

Thus, sitting in front of the panel, I take red choices one after the other. I suddenly feel tickling on my feet. I notice a legion of insects, amphibians and reptiles of different sizes and shapes creeping around them. They nip my skin, releasing their venom; though I wouldn't withdraw my feet, finding it amusing. With each sting, I site on the central screen my ego bloating like a rubber balloon inflating with each stroke of air-pump.

How wonderful it is that, with the ego inflating, I feel sovereign, superior, supercilious and snobbish – because I am better. I notice on the periphery of my presence some dwarf egos. How nice it is to know others being meek, minor, minion and menial – because they deserve it. It feels so nice. My ego is so tall that it has to bend to attend to the prayers of the dwarf. They - these fools - venerate my bowing in front of them as humility; some like this so much as even ending up in worshipping me – how nice.

Besides making it tall, the venom makes my ego desire more. I just realise what I own is less than I deserve. Let me paraphrase this: 'what I own is less than what I need' sounds better. How stimulating this idea is for personal development. It is absolutely apt to seek more. Charmer winks from the side screen and incites, "the wish to acquire is in truth very natural and common, and men always do so when they can, and, for this, they will be praised, not blamed." He continues, "a man must be ready to pay for the timidity from not acquiring that which he otherwise can." [1]

Babied with this approval, I look time and again at the population of dwarfs around me. I notice that not only my ego keeps on swelling by the minute but also the surrounding egos, in parallel, keep on shrinking. How is this possible? This trick cannot go far. This must be an illusion. I am upset, for it is not real; I must end this deception; I stop taking red choices, at least for now. On sensing my anxiety, Charmer intervenes, "keep enjoying, you stupid. If you didn't, Regretter and Resenter would thrash you for the lost opportunity."

I become double-minded. I hesitate. People, know that hesitation unsettles Frowner. He shouts at me, "Wake up, oh you narcissist! Walk out of this wilderness or else you will come apart at the seam, your self shattered into shreds."

I complain, 'do I have to walk on a tight rope all the time? Give me a break.' 'My disc burnt with the idea that I am better than others is fake'. Showing approval, Frowner speak politely, for once, "Charmer does not just go for your assets, friend; he goes for your legs. He first makes you feel tall so that when he pulls you down, you get real hurt - watch."

For now, I thus renounce the red choices, withdraw my feet from the floor and dust the insects off them. My intoxication quickly wanes, which feels really bad; however, with it, my perspective has been restored. Now, all egos look equal, almost. I can now see why, for vanity, an ego must need the company of dwarfs. I can even appreciate the remedy of this problem. I can see why my solitude being on the Parrot Farm has purged me. The room is flooded with light now.

With this reminder, my focus shifts at my meeting with the Sufi master in the past. In the process, I take off my eyes from the screens - from the world – to be lost in the void through the window in the wall in front of me. From the void suddenly descends a light, a mosaic of gold and white lights, mingled as if reflecting from alternating gold and silver plates, rushing through the window like *Aurora borealis*. The light freezes at a premise in the void. How come I have not noticed this premise?

'Perhaps because I have not looked for it.'

'But what is this, anyway?'

---

[1] *The Prince*, by Nicolo Machiavelli

'Oh my God, I have completely forgotten Prudence.' I now remember Sage talking about it, explaining it would be visible once the light in the foyer is at full.

# THE WISE PRUDENCE

IN THE FOG WAS THIS edifice of a unique architect, of the shape of a mini monocular movie cabin. On its nameplate was written in the most profound font: PRUDENCE – in the middle line, the Mighty Commissioner of Meanings. In small letter, the bottom line read, "For Ontological Questions".

As soon as I attended it, the blinds from the monocular rolled up. What I saw inside was simply stunning: a room extraordinaire, looking much larger than expected, filled with light of varying colours imperceptibly mingling such that you wouldn't be able to tell the colour; or, even the source, for there was none - everything in it was lit as if they were made of light, muffled and gentle light. And, everything there was standstill, in peace, as if peace oozed out from every grain of its confine. I could report to you only that on which I could spy, as my view of its interior was although clear but not complete. I witnessed in the centre of the room a uniquely glaring structure, something like a pair of pincers.

I remembered Sage's advice that I must try Prudence on some clarifications.

"What are you?" I asked.

"Well, because of me, there would never be a post-religious era on humanity."

"Why is that?"

"I proclaim the core sacred question, which I do irrespective of the self liking it or not. The self cannot escape from this question, and I do not from posing it."

"which question?"

"if God exists? The most favourite of all the questions philosophers have constantly asked over time. Plus, of course, the rest of the ontological questions."

"OK, then!" I did not know what next to ask.

Prudence continued, "these questions need demonstrative proof to test them; this place being the only workshop to carry out such tests."

I got the hook, now wanting to try what I thought were sample demonstrative proofs. On the spot, I could only think one of 'magnetism'. I tossed the question, "could I know what causes magnetism?"

Prudence held my question between the pincer's heads like a gem-cutter, turning and tossing the uncut gem in full-circle, "yours is a 'how' question. Its answer you must find out there, in city, in the thought city." The pincer moved one more cycle, "the values entertained here must belong to the realm of wisdom. You can ask, why magnetism?"

I got the point.

"What is in the goodness which differentiate it from the evil?" I posted the next question, thinking this question Prudence must find appropriate.

"Again, resolve this question in where you are sitting. Rational means in the thought city can tease out the merits of these categories. Reason is regularly received in this place; but, mind you, the only commodity despatched from here is of the wisdom. You can ask 'who determines things as good or evil?'"

I got the point.

I decided to test Prudence with a question about the supplies: "what could be the wisdom in one year depriving crops of water and people of supplies and in the next in their access."

This time, it jazzed up like a zealous teacher on receiving an immaculate question: "through this duress, you are tested both in deficit and in excess, in fear and in hope."

I styled the next question, although I realized I was scatter-gunning with the questions, perhaps for being too excited.

"They say my GIVER is universal and claim my existence essentially depends on HIS gifts. Then what place my gratitude for the gifts is supposed to have?"

"He who looks away from the Giver to the gift accepts it with his soul, his grief vanishing. He who looks away from the gift to its Giver seeks satisfaction from his own effort; and the effort is necessarily painful."

I noted these profound exchanges for future reflection.

I placed the next question: "why to allow Charmer and the rest of evil characters to work in this city? These intruders unrelentingly stew fiery tussles."

"The tussles fought in the city are for a purpose. Every asset of your self - intuition, learnings, knowledge, instincts – must be tossed into this fire, ignited by your desires, and you must stand the fire or quench it. That is the game and that is the battle, but it is not the easiest of the battles – it is not supposed to be."

In awe, I kept silent, expecting more to come. "What appears to be a tug-of-war between virtue and vice is in fact a game of partisans. While your job is to choose noble things parading before you, Charmer seeks to hunt your self down, which you must endure. The conditions of a fair test are thus created."

"Charmer has got such massive powers!! He is impossible," I insisted.

"People are fierce and poised or they are fragile and floppy, some being more vulnerable to Charmer's pulls than others. Your benchmark is your own competence against which you would be judged."

I noted this statement, too. This all was pretty serious stuff. I had planned to use these scholarly contents dexterously to impress my associates on my return to the world out there. But, for now, I did not find myself accepting the reason of giving Charmer a freehand. I pressed on with questions in order to get the response that I wanted.

Poised and sovereign Prudence did not stand as buoyant in haggling. It soon gave in to my wishes but in the process the pincers-head got crooked.

I felt triumphant even though I knew the approval from Prudence that I finally got was skewed. I felt a hint of distaste as well. Had I inculcated Prudence? I had messed it up.

The hearts are pure, not for corruption,

For the worst of corruptions is that of heart;

Avoid at all costs to be taken to task

for that which

Your corrupted heart would then garner

Taken by remorse, in a trance, I imperceptibly lost my focus, leaving it to wander in the void. At one point, I woke up from the trance by a fleeting seam. I skimmed the neighbourhood in the void. Yet again, while spanning, my vision fleetingly befell acuter. However, no sooner did I try focusing at the locale than I would be proscribed from perceiving it.

This was marvellous place. Its intrigue seized me literally, its awe toppled me overtly. I did not know when I had vacated the backrest in the foyer. I was standing in attention, with my head bowing in humility, that much I know, but what I don't remember at all is how I managed to keep myself. I wanted to say something but was not sure if speaking at that moment was even possible. I vaguely remember my self trembling but I was not scared, nor was I poignant or weak. My eyes were wet, but not due to pain. The experience was so profound that I could no longer remain bolt upright; and, in the awe, I fell. I did not feel rising. I was not expecting Charmer to pop up at this moment and to hiss into my ears, hassling me to rise, but he did return, "you know, you are here to complete a mission."

Standing against the backrest, my eyes on the foyer, I couldn't believe what I had gone through. I even questioned if I was in trance but knew for sure the life before I could have spent in trance but not this. I decided to keep the rest of the questions for Sage.

# RESIDENTS OF THE THOUGHT CITY

BACK AT THE CONSOLE, my attention was drawn to a screen showing the city map, which, with a flicker, changed to its orthophoto version. Expanded in the shape of the human chest, the prairie was filled with a myriad of tracks, punctuated with buildings here and there. My location, marked with a red cross, was surrounded by a mews of quarters. I could even see the nameplates, some with some familiar names, Regretter, Resenter. 'Bad neighbourhood,' I murmured.

Beyond these quarters on the left was a premise allotted to Charmer. 'He is not far from here either, to keep an eye on me, with nothing else to do.' Looking on the other side, I found a property labelled with a name, Noble. I wanted to meet the inhabitants of all these premises. I issued an instruction to the legion to gather in the senate. It was my first chance to see them all under one roof, which might be my last as well.

Hurrying towards the senate, I took the last door off the foyer on the left. It opened for me. The characters in the senate gave me a standing ovation. Gazing slightly above their heads, I casually looked at them from my peripheral vision, slowly nodding, not particular concerned if I looked pompous. I warily took the presiding chair and brashly scrolled through the paperwork stacked in front of me. I looked around one more time, this time with piercing gaze. I signalled them to take seats. I knew such posturing was not me but thought keeping those who work for you under your thumb was important.

The meeting opened with a round of introduction. Prominence in stature was the order in which they must be listed here.

He occupied the chair in the middle of the order on my right. Within his silhouette, light was transparent in his stillness, translucent when he moved. It trailed his hand gestures, flapping here, twinkling there. In a voice as soft as moonlight, he asked, "how did you find your Prudence?"

Feeling uncomfortable, slightly embarrassed, I shifted in my chair, not saying a word.

Unassuming, this figure of nobility smiled, "Prudence is given to everyone but its access only to few – only to the auspicious." If he meant to admire me, his words did not tally with my profile or with what I had done to Prudence only a few moments ago, but they lifted the anxiety from me. His nameplate read *Nobel*.

While my exchanges with Nobel pleased some in the meeting, it made others uneasy, but to Charmer, it caused distress. He was wearing the same rank as Noble, though in the opposite camp, sitting opposite to him across the table, but, between them, they would not exchange looks. Slid forward in his chair, his elbows on the table, smile on his face, Charmer acted as important, neglectful of others around. I felt he lend me some weight only to gain more for himself. He tried bartering his attention given to me for taking me easy.

He probably had thought, I would open the meeting with a word or two to be had with him, or a joke of some kind, to show some prior acquaintance, giving him importance. But I just looked at him sternly. The ire of envy works up people making them quake and sweat or utter words which they later regret; but in Charmer, it was different: with the ire, his lips and cheeks melted away from his face, leaving bare bones and teeth, which made him a horrible sight. But, the guy was a real drama: no sooner did he show those vilest colours than he returned to his normal disposition, as if nothing had happened – smiling again for a start. Still, I did not speak to him, this cheat, even though he might be thinking that I myself was arrogant.

I shifted my attention across the table at the chair opposite to me. Present in the chair is the most attractive of all those present, *Passion* her name. Since when I am here, she has been restless, her face iridescent. Her cheeks would look blushed and mild, giving a touchy-feely impression. The very next moment, brilliance in her pink face can easily be mistaken for inflammation; but of course, now it speaks for her excitement. But then look at her and you are bound to ask, 'why! what makes you laugh? Or, is it a show of sarcasm?' And she would say, 'am I laughing!! I don't know,' and, she would still be giggling - a real cheeky lassie. But, expressions on her face may change depending on from where you look, just like colours in a lenticular image. From one angle, she would look the mildest, with her eyelids drooping half-way. From another angle, the same eyes look piercing and staring with flames of anger. Now, her glossy lips are covered with left-over juice of some scrumptious fruit, her tongue working between them to signal sheer enjoyment. Then she is grinding her teeth with anger and growling. Now, her forehead is the most visible of all features, brushed with perspiration, about to coalesce to form droplets, showcasing her embarrassment at one time, her toil at the other. One way, she had a typical baby-face, as if insisting on things, bent on agitation, without giving a clue as to what is wrong with her. In another way, it looks like that of a cheeky carefree teenager. In short, she seems to have been dolled up with contrasting dispositions of features and variations in mood such as to disable your judgment about her.

Before moving on, I must report here a small incident. Someone in the meeting threw a teasing remark at her using her nickname, '*short fuse*, something she did not obviously approve – who likes to be called with their nicknames. However, this taunt - rather trivial, I would like to think - provoked a massive response in her, with tears pouring, the cheeks bearing the burden of their streams: some stuck to the delicate curves, others having a free-fall, such as to soften the heart of a mountain. Her sobbing with muffled cries made me adjourn the meeting. So much so that I had to leave my chair, walked all the way around the table, placed my one hand on her head, my fingers combing the hair, with the other mopping her tears with a hankie. But then she acquired composure as suddenly as she had lost it. The meeting returned to order.

I must also mention that Passion was quite self-consciousness and little bit attention-seeker, too. And why not so: the distinctive fragility in her feelings and delicacy in her person made her too vulnerable to be left unattended. Beware, if by any chance you discounted her, she would create a situation with her screechy noises and shrieks impossible to ignore – no chance. In this way, she would prove her robust foil. Not that I was particularly averse to it but, from the look of it, she was in effect the chairperson of this meeting.

Let me not be carried away with Passion. There was a strip of other characters relatively less important, which you may still want to know. I should first mention the character sitting adjacent to me on my right. I turned my face to look at hers and forgot to look away, for you would want to pause on the seamless proportion and contours, trying to find a fault. Yet, it seemed so delicate and fragile that I felt I should not look at her any longer lest my gaze dent her evenness. Brilliant light, but not dazzling, breezed out from her, soaking the atmosphere and everyone present with its fragrance. If she rested her hand on the table, you would feel resting with it. When she moved it in a gesture, your head and eyes would sway with it. Simply, you would try to be on the same wavelength you found her. *Serenity* was her name.

Now on my left, there was sitting a stern and grim, fidgety man. His face was matte, absorbing all light, reflecting merely dusky shades. His eyes were particularly gloomy and lustreless, as if they were two mini-blackholes, taking in everything, nothing to give away. He would squeeze his focus at your face as if preparing to prey on you. He would look at your hands as if to snatch things - even the air from your palms, if nothing else. Such a hungry and ruthlessly ambitious figure thus he seemed. If you were there, just by looking at his face, you would notice commodity of hope escaping you, just like sand slipping out from your fist. His nameplate read *Affliction*.

The character next to Affliction turned his face towards me to cause a shiver in my backbone, which he also noticed, yet did not soften. I wondered why I was so fearful of this person: because the guy was named *Fear*, as his nameplate read. From his look, I could not make out if he was threatening or himself threatened. I looked at him and he took me on the brink of a cliff, from which I just had escaped when he took me, this time, underwater and filched the air supply from my nostrils. I did not want to even say hello to this guy, thus named *Fear*.

Moving further to the right, next to *Serenity* was *Hope*, looking up at the horizon. On the right side of Noble was sitting *Planner*, in his hands a hardback notebook and other materials with which to write and make sketches. Next to him was *Glossary* wearing heavy prescription glasses and a dress with newspaper print. On the left of the table beyond *Charmer* were the two seats taken by the twins, *Resenter* and *Regretter*, whom I had met earlier in the foyer and did not have any appetite even for sayng hello.

And, then, there were several bumping-posts installed in the empty place on one side of the table, some were with cabooses parked on them, others vacant. On one of them was present *Hearer with an* antenna on the top of his head, reporting on the outside world. On another caboose was seated *Observer*, who said she was here to report on how the outside world looked. Just arrived in the scene was a caboose with some meek character popping out from its doors, as if they were just returning from business. They introduced themselves as *Doers*. In the back rows, there were several more characters, whose names were not announced. Some were even sitting along the walls on the floor, collectively called as *Desires*.

'So', I hissed. 'There is my self, for which a whole army of characters, equipped with weaponry, has been deployed to take me to the task. Present in this senate, they looked subservient to me, but some of them would play obscure dark games on my back to trick me and topple my kingdom. 'There is a cosmos out there and here is a microcosm in my self here.' I felt I must be the most important artefact around in the cosmos.

\*\*\*

I got up from my chair and nodded my head signalling my intention to leave the meeting. They all stood up. The microcosm was departing. What an industry and what an artefact, my self was. Walking showily in the passage, I passed by a rather dilapidated part of the building, with a sign on its door reading, 'Egosphere'. I took a step back. I thought, before leaving, I must meet with this character, too. But, then, why did Ego not turn up in the senate? I felt a little irritated. I paused in front of the door, hoping it to open for me; but it didn't.

'Shall I knock? No, it is very much my own place,' I murmured and banged on the door. It was pitch dark inside.

No sooner had I entered the place than came a slap on the left side of my face. 'What,' I squeaked. I was still perplexed when my face received another blow, this time on the other side.

"Don't you know this is Egosphere?' someone shouted. 'This place is here only for me. Ego is my name; you must know Ego. How dare you enter here?" the tone left me in no doubt that more violence was to come.

I was trying to absorb the insult, still thinking maybe there was a mistake, or shall I leave, when Ego took me from the arm, shoved me into the door on the opposite side, tossing me out with a kick on my back, and shut the door behind me.

I found myself stuck in the mud outside the building. On my knees, my head between my hands, face down, I cried. Tears flew, less of pain, more of hurt. Frozen at that place, I thought now which story of this journey I was going to tell. Which story!!! Nothing left. What wrong had I done? So helpless and so vulnerable I felt - the microcosm was reduced to dust in this menial dark place. And who had hurt me? my ego - my own ego. A thought crossed my mind, 'if my ego has hurt me like this, how nasty could it have been to others?' Between the tears, I reached an important decision.

'Where is Realself?' I suddenly remembered and panicked. He had already left me. I did not know when, perhaps even before my entering the Egosphere. Though, I felt a hand on my shoulder. It was of Sage. I got up quickly to show as if nothing had happened. He smiled, which I could not interpret as of sarcasm, sympathy or just courtesy. Maybe he knew the account of my treatment that I'd received in the Egosphere. Maybe some of his previous visitors had taken the same return route; maybe not. But I dared not mention it to him.

He laughingly said, "you didn't take long in there. It was rather quick!"

I noticed he had not asked me about the trip but just the time it took. I said, "I did take quite long time, really. Are we in two different time zones?" Dusting myself all around, I said, "It was busy time in there, though I kept thinking about you, Sage. Sorry, you had to wait."

Sage said, "no mention. Previous visitors had a similar experience of time. Time in that place is probably dilated.' 'Are we ready to leave?" Sage asked.

"Yes, of course, Could not thank you more, but perhaps if you allowed me few moments to meet with some people in the Memory Quarters before closing the trip," said I, thinking about my earlier decision about being humble.

"Of course, I am in no hurry."

Facing away from Sage, I shed some more tears, trying to absorb the insult; but the words hit me time and again: 'my own ego', 'my own ego'. After all, Sage broke his pretention, "in fact. OK, fine. I had seen you thrown out from that door. I bet it must be Ego. You know, with this incident, your story has become unique. You know how much you have mustered to tell in your story, about the valley and the city, about this building and Prudence. You tell people how the characters that you had met behaved face to face; plus, you have now Ego in your story as well to show its true colours.'

I stopped sobbing and smiled. I said, "I shall tell them the story of all of my rivals. Of course, on the top would Charmer, who entices with fake promises. Providing him the fuel were my own desires, gone out of control, which injected delightful substance into my veins. No, on the top would be my Ego, which managed to throw me out from this fascinating place." With these words, I lost my voice and broke on Sage's shoulder and cried. I was released from underneath the huge weight of insult.

We slowly walked to the Memory Quarters. On the way, Charmer crossed one more time, whispering, "I was once thrown out from a place as well and it was because of you. We are equal now. Look at me: despite the insult, I have kept my person; you must keep yours."

"So, then, it must be you who pumped up Ego to do this to me!" shouted I. He smiled and vanished.

We kept on walking. Sage said, "Memory Quarters are an amazing place. Nothing goes waste; every element and every slant of your thought, experience and action is preserved - preserved here in these quarters."

I looked at him but was not interested. Despite, he continued, "the things in these Quarters are not crammed like junk in a backyard but are arrayed like items shelved in a superstore." I was not interested. Apparently, I was grieving at my insult in the hands of Ego, in reality, in the hands of Charmer, this bastard. I regretted going into his room. Everything was going so well when I bumped into this thing.

With these thoughts, I did not know when we reached the Memory Quarters. I looked for my parents' house. They were there, same as before, waiting for me. My Mum kissed my forehead, while with Dad I had a pump-fist. I kissed my Mum's hands with which she cooked for me when I was hungry and dabbed my eyes when I was in pain. I patted my Dad's hands with which he laboured for my living, my bringing-up. Thinking my dad would be happy, I shared with him the news that I had taken up farming. They prayed for me, although my Dad was ambivalent on my change of profession. I did not tell them about the accident that had changed my life or about how the world had been treating me afterward lest they felt hurt. At leaving, I said, "Mum and Dad, Dad and Mum, I miss you in my life; I really do."

From there, I strolled around, looking for another person - Comely. I found her sitting in her room, as usual with her face towards the window – she always liked light. She turned around and smiled at me. I praised her beauty. I thanked her for the nice time we had together. And, then … I said goodbye. I walked by a few yards, paused and reflected, 'as always, in this case, too, my ego has sullied me. Look at me: here I am, with Comely, but still am not prepared to give up this ego of mine.' I did not really need to go far in the past to remember how Ego had treated me.

"No," I said, and returned to Comely. I said, "Comely, I am very sorry – very sorry indeed - for my arrogance in treating you. Please forgive me." I could see tears in her eyes, some special tears that I had seen once before in the eyes of a prisoner released from jail for a crime he had not committed. This was the moment of an experience: a hefty boot pressing my chest had come off from it.

Undoubtedly, this action of mine tasted superb to me. Was it because I had recognised an injustice with which someone had suffered at my hands? It must be more for my ego which, with this apology, I had now defeated. 'An apology therefore puts the ego on its place,' I had to come so far to learn this lesson. With this, I could see even from here a light sparked from Prudence.

I had one more name on my list, of Aurora, hoping Sage wouldn't mind a little more waiting. I needed to forgive her. I needed to forgive her for hurting me for none of my faults. I trusted her to stand with me in all walks. She gave in. She was the one whom I missed at every stage, with pain. I must forgive her. I looked around searching for her. I spotted her from distance, but then stopped, 'do I want to embarrass her? When you forgive someone, you just forgive; saying this on the face is not necessary.' I found a quiet corner on a nearby bench and spoke to myself, 'you know, if I had a point, she had a point, too. She was wise and sincere, and more, she had a point. Perhaps she could have tried to find another solution. But she was sincere and wise and had given me so much pleasure in my life. She did not deserve my anger. 'I forgive you, Aurora. In fact, it must be me. Of course, it was me - and my own conflicts with which you had to cope. In fact, you don't owe me an apology, Aurora. You have your life, too. Aurora, in fact, it is OK, you know. No hard feelings. Be happy in your life.'

I thus forgave her and I smiled. The second boot of the pair offloaded from my chest; another spark arose from Prudence.

***

I met him outside the quarters "yes, Sage! I guess my time to fly back has arrived!"

"OK, yes – but would you afford some feedback on my performance."

"Only if you promise to give me a testimonial to add to my portfolio." This was the first time Sage gave a little smile.

We went back to landing pad near the build-up area. "Sage, you mind if I said goodbye to Realself."

He nodded his approval.

We had a great talk, Realself remaining inside and I standing outside. He said, "thanks for coming. How was it; was it good?"

"Of course – different though." Pretending important, I said, "I wanted to come even though I was seized up with numerous problems out there."

He said, "the toils in your world are not slight, that I must appreciate. That you labour for breadwinning and are struck with disease, poverty, war, all kinds of tribulations, in there, I know all."

I felt a pat on my back from my senior partner.

He continued, "now, after this stopover, you might also know the ordeals of my world: it is being tough here, too, if not more. See the characters in the senate. You know what! they do not finish an argument or do a scene, and go home. No, not at all. They reside here in my territory; they sleep after I go to sleep and are awake before I open my eyes. And, they do not let me rest for a minute; arguments and disputes, temptations, wiles, harassments, undermining, insults, my weak moments, all are but a few of the trials of my life, a real pain, day in, day out. Whichever side wins at the end, the arguments are held here, with my Prudence at stake and, with it, at stake is also the battle of my life – my soul, my self."

"And," his voice now breaking, "the most embarrassing of all is when I fall, for I fall knowing I shouldn't; I have promised that I will not fall – a fact I have confirmed with Prudence several times."

I replied, "my dear friend, I do value your work, without which I must lose the battle of my life out there as well." With a stooping posture, he accepted my acknowledgment and disappeared inside.

"Goodbye Realself,' I mumbled. I walked to the pad, muttering, 'undoubtedly, your achievements are not insubstantial, nor are they easy to snatch from the clutches of the characters you have to deal with.' I was not yet out of the reach of Charmer, Affliction, Regretter and Resenter, plus, of course, the cool Passion and the fuming Frowner and, yes, the menial creatures, Desires. I glanced at the building and shivered. What a great theatre it was, full of fancy characters. And, then, there was the serene Prudence, with the awe congregated around it from the special Presence. I suddenly remembered I wanted to mention to Sage, "I had some great conversations with Prudence, but without a single word uttered!"

Sage said, "the medium there is wordless; the coinage there is meanings. That was the moment for you to receive the meanings."

I suddenly realised that the narrative was sharing with Sage were words I was coining to embrace the meanings."

I said, "Sage, there was this utterly exclusive moment around Prudence, which I hoped was completely private. But it wasn't, to my surprise."

Sage nodded his head, "it must be Charmer intruding, was it not? The guy has been given full access to your self and power to trip you any time. That is the game."

Thinking I had finished with my questions, I said, "I have come so far, through so many bubbles and troubles, but would have returned empty handed had it not been for you, Sage, to help me."

Sage replied, "I have played no part in your achievement. Curiosity you can pursue or piety you can seek; but the favour of proximity you cannot seek, for it comes only as grace."

I looked at Sage saying wordless thanks and said goodbye. We both took our ways.

On my way back, I flied over the valley of tulips. They were still dancing with the same fervour. Flying from my bona fide dwelling up there, I landed in my residence with a postcode, with a click, synchronising with the one from the kettle. The water had boiled, ready to brew. Meanings had arrived, set to accomplish my earthly life.

# PART FOUR: GRAND CLOSURE

# COMMEMORATIONS

THE TRIP TO MEET REALSELF must be written up, I promised with myself. Freed from the anxiety from the crop not getting irrigated and pleased with the gift of the voyage, I wanted to start the project straightway. I wrote few scenes but got involved. To break, I took some tea and then wrote few more. I did not stop; I went for the third round of writing. Deep into the night, I felt tired, though still excited. I retired but I was not even dozy. With my head on the pillow and my eyes closed, the scenes of the tulip dance and of my dwelling arrived buzzing, and the buzz would not let me sleep. Then I heard an unusual tapping sound. 'It isn't a part of the scene!' I murmured. The tap was thumping into my ears – oh, it was of my own heartbeats. But some beats had gone missing like trots interceding a gallop. Did it result from the recent indulgence in caffeine? The play remained on for the whole night and kept me awake throughout.

Waiting for my turn in the GP surgery, I wondered. Unaware of my surrounding, I wondered on my journey. In 'From Me to US', I remained bothered with my identity. In 'the Voyage' instead I had found meanings of life. I had found that it was in fact all about meanings. Tussles on the way are created for the meanings to reveal. Conflicts have their roots here, in my dwelling, in the Thought City. All that manifests, the altercations, wrangles, the clashes, the greed, the wars, all of it is staged in the city before it is played to the fellow audience on earth.

At last, I was called in. The doctor examined my heart and looked at my ECG tracing. She knew my history. She laughed, bantering if I had fallen in love with someone. Which meant to me nothing was seriously wrong. She increased my blood thinners, but agreed the heart rhythm problem probably owed to the excessive tea and lack of sleep. I promised I would be careful, but I lied. The vision I had wouldn't let me rest, that I knew for sure.

Back at my place, I discovered in the letterbox an item from the publishers. It read: "the editors have gone through your work. We are thinking to launch this work formally. Would you mind to spare a day for the event, which we propose to hold at your place, for it can make a nice day-out for the guests. You should be expecting around 30 people, including some press representatives. We offer you a choice of the following dates: … All the arrangements and costs would be borne by the company. With this turn we hope your story will reach a proper closure."

I agreed to a date of a week later, with a note: "your guests are welcome to come to my place; however, they would dearly appreciate a warning that reaching this place could be trying." In anticipation, I got up a new signboard to place on the roadside; on it written 'PARROT FARM' in green fonts with a red backdrop.

And guess what I did with 'the Voyage'? I was worked up even more, aiming at finishing it before the event. I wrote to the editors about my plan to present this part of the story to the event to get their approval. The reply came, "we trust it would be as interesting as the first part you have sent. You have half an hour in the schedule which you could use the way you like."

I had taken this on me; however, with this, I made my heart yell into my ears many times a day. Writing up 'the Voyage' was pleasing throughout, but at some places, hard to narrate. While reporting on my meeting with Realself, I laughed. I laughed feeling the misery of the surgeons who transplanted my brain, having failed to think on the spot, letting the opportunity of thinking-without-the-body slip from my hands, the opportunity that Plato asserted one can only have when one's self is plucked from one's body. Though I was yet again gifted with another chance of meeting with my self, of having a pure thought, for which I did not have to wait for my death. I did finish the Voyage in time before my death.

# RESOLUTION

IN THE EARLY HOURS OF THE DAY, the doorbell rang. I looked through the window from the bedroom. A big van had arrived in the porch with some workers, with a marquee, lots of folding furniture and other stuff strewn beside it. I got down and opened the door. There was present a lady wearing a hat. I thought she must be Billie, the event manager, as the editor had informed me in his letter. With her hands linked at her back, she greeted me. She was wearing blue jeans and a pink polo top, with a mosaic color duffle bag dangling on her left shoulder. I returned the pleasantries. She removed her hat, squashed it flat and shoved it into the bag. She tossed her branded sunglasses got tossed into the bag, too. She looked at me curiously. Then she took a step closer to move to the shadow, and hesitated as significance grew in her eyes, "have we met before?".

"Briefly; in the train; I was on my way to here," I recognized her face right away, even though I had seen her roughly minus-five-KG ago. I had met with her again in my dwelling, when Charmer informed about her divorce from a nasty husband. But now there was a problem: I had reported in my novel the train encounter with her. Now she knew what game I was playing in the train. But then, I also mentioned the two encounters with her in the Voyage. I made a mental note to sort this out at a suitable moment.

She said, "yes, now I remember". But she completely ignored th train part. "So, it is your story that I was given to read. Oxymoron! you must be the Director." She spread her hand towards me, "my name is Billie." "I knew bits about you from the press, also, you know, from the court proceedings. Always wanted to interview you." Her hand was small and warm while her pearl white face was glowing in the morning sun.

Holding her hand, I said, "so then, you can start your interview right now!" I waited but she did not hint of taking her hand away; eventually I let it go.

While talking, she searched her bag to ship out a pack of cigarette. She smacked the pack upside down on her fingers, slid a cigarette out in the first go and installed it directly into her lips, all in one action. She faintly tweaked her head, offering me to join. I just smiled; I was still thinking at loosening the knots in the little history between us. She laughed out smoke, condensed in the morning cool, "why, then, your protagonist was so foolish. He constantly loitered among the women with whom he had shared the past. A victim of confusion he was, this poor guy, but he was its source at the same time." She looked at me intensely, "he should have tried friends with someone outside his circle, someone like me."

I was sure she had taken this much liberty from my naïve interest in her in our train journey. I said, "the past is past."

She laughed and changed the topic, "your story is absolutely unique. I thought we should inaugurate it in a unique way as well."

I waited, expecting more to come.

She said, "I have added a surprise in the plan. For you, please - if you could stay in … if you don't mind, until you are called to join the event and to meet with the guests."

I nodded a yes.

"Lot of preparations that my staff need to do. I take it that you are happy for us to use the side garden. Lot of guests have been invited. We shall be ready for the first arrival by the lunch time. By the way, hot lunch would be served."

I said, "hope you have factored in a slot for me," I said.

"Yes; of around 30 minutes; how about near the end of the program." And, with this, she left in a matter-of-fact manner.

'It probably is not without purpose that our paths have crossed one more time,' I was reflecting about meeting with Billie. That reminded me the summary report from the Voyage I had prepared for this event. I deleted the scene with Billie from the report, but kept her in my thinking.

***

Around lunchtime, I received the message to join the event and went out. The air was filled with a familiar whiff of charcoal smoke. The porch was packed with oddly parked cars. Zigzagging through the spaces between them, I was feeling as calm as the surface of looking glass. Billie was standing in the roller door of the marquee. From distance, she looked taller and slimmer. She greeted me with a smile, a naughty smile, I noticed.

I entered the marquee. I scanned the presence there. I instantly realized what actually Billie meant from the surprise factor she had planned. The only one person in this gathering to be surprised was me. From the calm surface of my mind cropped up a gigantic turbulence. In that marquee, sitting around the table in the center were all there, Zeitoun, Aurora, Comely, Aliya, Ayaan, all of them. Their eyes focused at me, mine hungrily stalking at each of them in a jumbled-up order. They raised from chairs. I walked to them with a drunken gait. They let me in the circle. I had lost power in my knees. They did not look angry.

Time had stopped. We all were quiet. Like me, they must also be filled to the brink with feelings. Of myself I knew for sure if I'd uttered a word, I would see the barrage around my tears crack. So much to say but nothing was said, except some wordless messaging, with the eyes onetime curious, other times welled up. They were all the same as I had last seen them, except Zeitoun, who bore new creases on her face, her head leaning forward and the shoulders curved as if she had since born a mammoth load on her back. Aliya was reticent but I saw in her eyes a flicker of a daughter, seeing her dad after long. Nahaar broke the lull. His arm folded around my shoulders, he related how the family had read my story and felt about my ordeals. Aurora was restless, trying to say something, but each time she looked in the direction of Zeitoun for approval. Comely looked as pretty as ever, and as carefree. I needed a whole century to glance over traffic of thoughts in my head while I had used so far only a moment of it. But I wasn't completely happy. I checked myself; my heart was torn with the trepidation of them leaving soon.

I had calmed now, or had I resigned to the rush? I looked around. Nahaar's parents were there too. Gus, the notary elite, was unassumingly sitting in one corner. Few of my colleagues and neighbors had also arrived. Nash and Logge were there with their mum. There were few other people I could not recognize. Aurora took me to meet with Nahaar's parents. They hugged me, hesitantly complaining that I did not keep my promise of seeing them regularly. Then, together we went to see Gus. He approved my skills of my transcribing in my story his long meandering debates in the court. He merrily said if by any chance I had created any more problems needing legal attention. The twins, Nash and Logge, winked at me in unison.

Someone from outside the marquee announced that buffet was ready. I could see through the window pane smoke arising from barbeque. People returned with plateful of food, with steam curling up, travelling with plates, releasing hybrid fragrance from basmati and charcoal-burnt barbeque. I took a chance to get close to Comely, wanting to say sorry. She whispered in return to say that she bore a child from our marriage. I was stunned yet one more time, my heart beats puzzled. "How is she? Does she look like you? Send me some pictures," that's all I could say to her.

"Yes, I will. Jade his name - will be six-month tomorrow; looks like his dad; even smile like Nahaar," she was brief.

In the meantime, Billie approached with a giant, obese figure, unknown to me. She introduced him as Milk and said he was the driver of the lorry involved in the accident. My heart stopped and legs stumbled. I was sure it was not a good idea to invite Milk here but did not say it. Though Milk said that he had got detoxified after the accident and had since been sober. He said he had been extremely careful in driving lately and had come here only to apologize which he would prefer announced. I quickly moved away.

Billie walked to the podium and asked everyone to take seats. She said, "which novel in the history of literature would have been completed with all its real characters actually meeting under one canopy." She continued, "now when you all have already read the story, there is no secret of one character left from the others. The story is profound. Would you not agree that you would take each other differently now after reading the story, say if you'd bump into each other in a high street or a bookfair?"

She smiled, now looking in our direction, "we don't have to go to a bookfair to test the difference. See Oxymoron sitting peacefully among three beautiful women around the table. Three wives with their husband, all in one piece - clearly that was not possible before."

She ended at inviting all to send their feedbacks and views. Finally, she announced my name and gave way to me on the podium.

# ULTIMATE TALK

I OPENED MY TALK WITH something out of order, but now on the foremost of my mind.

"From my work, it is clear that my destiny was each one of you. Also, my destiny was to meet the lorry in the morning of accident. But don't you ever think it was written because the lorry driver – sorry, what is your name again, please?" I looked at the big man.

"Milk, sir; they call me Milk…" Everyone laughed.

"Yes, thanks. Now … if you think it was written - even before my birth - that Milk and I leave for work at particular times that morning, hence meet in the collision that is not the complete version. It was written but as a living document which Milk himself wrote in real time - sitting behind the wheel. That's when he wrote it. Police record on the accident showed alcohol concentration in his blood standing on two feet and many empty lager canisters lying on the passenger seat next to him. Anyway, so it happened. He has been a changed man since. We all learn our lessons on the way, sometimes at high cost. I forgive Milk." I had a couple of deep breaths, feeling little relieved.

Delivering usual pleasantries to begin the address, I glance at the guests. Soon I had hungrily parked my eyes on my loved ones, "look at you; look at your happy faces: they clearly tell that you have forgiven me. Is it because you see me in the story with my hands tied? But I am going to show you that my hands were not altogether tied, even though by revealing this secret I risk you taking your blessings away from me. This I shall reveal with another story that I have called the Voyage, the one from a solo flight of mine - a flight flown on trying lands, trying but one thing: my freewill. Those are the lands on which we, each one of us, in our own solo flights, write our stories in real time sitting behind the wheel."

They were intensely focused. I continued, "I once promised someone sitting among you that I should one day find meanings of life. I think I have kept my promise. Would you also like to hear about my find?"

Aurora blinked with a smile. I looked for my folder, "Oh, it is there on the table; Aliyah, can you pass me …" I enjoyed asking Aliya for something like this.

I read to them the salient highlights of the Voyage. I told them about the valley, about the city in it and the Palace in the city. I felt they were flying with me, being excited at places where I was excited, curious in scenes which had incited my curiosity, being happy, hurt, confused, firm, fed-up, assertive, all with me. They laughed at the characters whom I had found funny and were scared of those whom I detested. They felt personal about Realself. The mention of Frowner dispirited us all, but that of Charmer animated the atmosphere, even though I had hoped only if the guy was taken seriously. I warned them of what I had seen of Charmer in the city. "While he tries whitewashing his own lies with his left hand, with his right, he keeps writing new ones."

I painted the picture of Desires only to notice few feet withdraw from the grassy ground underneath. Reporting the exchanges with Prudence enthralled them, while relating the intriguing experience following that, I myself was entranced. Completely unexpectedly, the treatment from Ego that I had received was taken as something hilarious. On this one, annoyed, I lowered my pitch and increased the volume, "I hope you all know this vulture. While Charmer just entices with words, this beast actually hurts with its archaic corporeal methods." All in all, reading the report was a rejoicing go. I hesitated a bit on the lines on the Memory Quarters trying to hide names of those I had met there, something that occurred to me at the eleventh hour.

Finally, I told them about the wizardly Passion. I read, "I have met there a character called Passion. She has several nicknames, like Emotion, Commotion, Short Fuse, but really gets stormy on their calling, I have witnessed the scene with my own eyes. I think there is no harm if I'd disclosed her secret. Realself is obviously not at ease without her, but neither is he at peace with her. Even more importantly, what I have found out, and am reporting here without hesitation, is that the guy is clearly in courtship with her. He has appointed her as the co-chair in the senate; in reality, she is the real chairperson there, I am telling you."

Now was the turn to share the meanings that I had received from the Voyage. I was pleased to find my audience still focused.

I sorted out my paperwork in order and started reading, "I hope you haven't noticed that I admit in my person the presence of hypocrisy by a hint, a cue of greed, lust in traces and a touch of envy, all swept with an overcoat of selfish hue. Surely, I would never like these facets of my character publicly known. Had this been the face with which to present myself to the world, my life would have been nothing less than perpetual shame. For the world outside thus, I quickly recoup my usual self, considering it must be acceptable as long as I could fake piety, at least, decency."

I continued, "however, in the world of Realself, such jugglery is not possible. In that place, there is no hideout. Hypocrisy and lies, which in the earthly life necessarily comprise secret plots, are cooked up in the city in the open. Duplicity is invented there – granted – but it is candid; though it is practiced only in our world, where it is essentially concealed. Would you then not agree that the life of Realself up there in the city is tough – tougher than ours?"

Feeling very tired, I paused here for a sip of water.

I continued, "you would like to know what is that which actually keeps Realself going? There are things of wisdom and reason in the city, continuously clashing with things opposite to them. These clashes are constantly presented to Realself in his dwelling for him to take sides. That is his main job. I was soon fed up with this tug of war played on Realself on and on, of which only some episodes I have sampled for in the Voyage. It seemed to me that the poor guy himself was the tug."

"People! mind you, this role of Realself, however simple it looks, is more difficult done. People! mind you, this of his role is mandatory in furnishing the earthly lives of ours. In my case, evidently, I use his services discursively and comprehensively, I would like to admit. Depending on the choices Realself makes for me, how many decisions I take on daily basis, what is good for health, which route to take, when to call which friend, so forth. With this service, I solve mathematics and conduct logic. However, there is another service which I use only tangentially and fortuitously, the one provided through Frowner, detailed at telling virtue from vice. Before the Voyage, I had almost flouted the tussles in this critical realm, the real taste of freewill. You may already know its worth, but for me, the subtotal of the voyage that I could extract was this realisation. The total sum would be perfected by adding the role of Prudence in the equation."

I paused here to take a chair. "You might be waiting to hear about the experience of the special moment. I simply don't have the words to relate it."

"I am almost done, just the last page. Let me present the summary. What I have seen up there, contained in that little space at the north pole of human, the head, is an unthinkable thinking apparatus. It comprises a physical world superimposed by an abstract world. In the abstract world, the city behaves as thoughts incarnate, the foyer as consciousness personified and Prudence as wisdom embodied. There is yet another world that lies on the top of the abstract world, the one of meanings. All of them - thoughts, beliefs, reason, intentions, desires, instructions, orders, wisdom, memories, you name it – are generated, transported and hoarded as meanings. The whole hierarchy in this kingdom subsists in the meanings."

At this point in the reading, I gave a deliberate pause, eyeballed around and said, "it was this quantity in the city which humbled me with its awesome simplicity. Found myself in the special moment, I thus could not hold myself in the awe and fell - that much I could tell you from that moment."

I had a couple of deep breath. "All done; now I want to speak to you from heart to heart," I folded the paperwork and put it on one side. "I must admit I was shocked at finding you here but it morphed into pleasure at the speed at which my comprehension works."

"Shall I start with my thanks to my parents for bringing me up kindly. Corporeal treatment of kids was popular in those days. But you would not believe I got smacked only once, I mean, on the face? Anatomy is important here because I don't mean to list the rest of the body involved in this process at such rarity."

"I am grateful to my family, my wife Zeitoun, my lovely daughter Aliyah and my Son Ayaan, for letting me taste the family life, I mean, with kids. In fact, I want to dedicate this work to Zeitoun. This is but a little gesture to cherish the time spent under her rule, or with her rules, depending on the day and your luck." She smiled.

"I am greatly obliged to Nahaar's parents, for it is only for their son's body which I have adopted that I am alive today and raving around. And, of course, thanks to Nahaar himself, who remains my buddy till the day I live. He is obviously right in front of you now but, unfortunately, cannot speak for himself. Exploiting this handicap, I have continuously wrangled with him, which always has been one-way - sorry man. By the way, the humility I show here and there I must admit I have learnt through the hard way. As you know, Ego has taught me this skill with his own two hands."

"My thanks to Comely and my apology to her, too. She had to bear with me in the marriage." (Goodness me, I stopped just before uttering, 'and bore our child.')

"How could I miss out Aurora if you know what I know? The iron lady. If she were not to be found in a particular scene in the story, she must be just around, not far away. That was how much she had tangled my life with hers. She has continued to make appearances in the Voyage as well. Such a tenacious character."

"I wish to say few words about Gus, my attorney; few words, because he himself is a man of few words. His speeches in the court were a piece of art, shaping the debate like drawing a face.

I mustn't forget the twins, Logge and Nash, whom I set against each other, I am sorry, so that I could extract knowledge from them."

"Good, people, thanks for listening. May you live long!"

# ENDINGS

BILLIE STOOD UP AND HASTENED to remind me to send her the script of the Voyage to add to the rest of the story. I returned to the table with my family. Accomplished, though I was completely exhausted. I felt even more so, having the opportunity to resign my care in the hands of my loved ones now around me. Was I thinking the things as usual from now? 'Was it just wishful thinking? Would the tangles in the relations allow reversal in the situation in some form?' With this realization, my heart floated onetime, the other time sank. Zeitoun was the first to notice something wrong with me. She suggested I should go back to the house and take some rest. The two hastened to help me from the chair, Ayaan on the right and Aliya on the left. I apologized from the rest of the guests.

The two walked me back into the building. Ayaan supported me from the arm, while Aliya impatiently walked in front of us in an oblique posture, keeping an eye on me, the other ahead. She held the door for us, made the way to the solitary easy-chair in the living room, eased me into it, draw the footrest close to me and went straight to the kitchen to make a cup of tea. Ayaan gave me a shoulder massage. I wasn't sure if I was indeed feeling frail or merely feigning fragility to enjoy the exceptional care, something that I was used to and granted routinely, now forgotten somewhere in the dark, behind the doors of the past. Or, was all this drama just a mere phantom, too good to be true?

Soon, the ladies arrived, too. They were frankly bantering between themselves, frequently glancing at me in between. I thought we were indeed a strange bunch of people, each of us hurt from others but none to blame. However, for now, it seemed the sting and anguish of the past had worn glee and giggle. Only if I were feeling better. Only if I were able to cook for them some of my own recipes. How nice if I gave Zeitoun a scare by stir-frying on high flame. She never trusted me in the kitchen. I would have taken them on a visit of the crops I had seeded. I would have taken them to the riverbank where I did my reflections. I would have taken Zeitoun to see my parent's house where we met the first time.

Aliyah brought tea for everyone. I just took water. I was calmly resting, my heartbeat calming.

*****

239

I woke up around two hours ago. The night is still some way to go. The silence in the room is broken by occasional creaking and popping from the roof. The mood-light from the corner lamp has underlined the room fixtures in pale dark. I don't remember exactly when I had fallen asleep and they had left. They had left me carefully covered in blanket, with my head resting against cushions on each side. I remember how their presence in the house slackened me into a trance. I have just found freshly cooked food in the kitchen. Surely, perhaps, I could invite them again. Will I ask them to stay for few days and they would agree.

This is the final draft, ready for Billie. I hope she will like it, particularly the part in the train, or in fact, she might find it too personal, asking for its exclusion. I think I am fine either way. I am fine anyway now when I have discovered my family, thanks to Billie. I have done my journey. I had tussled with my identity; in its place, I have found meanings of life, plus, of course, my family have returned to me. I have done my journey. What a day! I am going to bed now.

Tomorrow would be another day.

# OBITUARY

The person, the author of this piece, has been reported to have died quietly in his bed in his house on Parrot Farm on the night of 23 October 2027. A fellow farmer, called Sul, discovered his body. Doctors believe a clot arising from his heart had shut his brain.

As a person fabricated, not born, he met this destiny at the age of two. He claimed himself to be Director Oxymoron, a retired officer of the Public Engagement, who, according to another version, had actually died before him. The body of the person was claimed by the parents of a young man, called Nahaar, who had died before him as well.

The person was occupied with horticulture during the latter of his two years on earth, on a land which he claimed to be his inheritance, but the original family of the Director, a wife and two kids, have now filed a lawsuit claiming it, declaring its possession by this person resulting from a slight misunderstanding. He has left a grand total of three wives and two children, and a manuscript - this piece - named after him, which he completed in the last night of his life.

As the editor of this piece, I have met him a couple of times. His work is for the readers to judge, but I know that, in himself, he had felt like a fallen leaf, all-time tumbling in mid-air. Knowing him what he actually was - a fabricated man - he did not as such have to die or be buried, but he did live, for sure: this is his work.

**Billie**

www.ingramcontent.com/pod-product-compliance
Lightning Source LLC
Chambersburg PA
CBHW050340030726
47503CB00008B/2545